BOOKS BY PAUL W. RICHARD

Exploring the Galapagos Islands

Colorado's North Park, History, Wildlife, and Ranching

Growing up Wild: A Mountain Ranch Childhood

Smokey: A Dog of My Own

Departure of the Cliff Dwellers

OSGOOD'S LUCK: A TALE of the GRASSLANDS

NOW HEAR THIS; Living in the Cold War Navy

PHOTOPEOPLE;
COMING OF THE GREENBACKS.

PAUL W. RICHARD

To Dan & Linda,
    May you take a look
at saving the world.
    Sure appreciate you good
friends.
            Cheers,
            Paul Richard
            2020

Order this book online at www.trafford.com
or email orders@trafford.com

Most Trafford titles are also available at major online book retailers.

Print information available on the last page.

ISBN: 978-1-6987-0163-9 (sc)
ISBN: 978-1-6987-0162-2 (hc)
ISBN: 978-1-6987-0161-5 (e)

Library of Congress Control Number: 2020909750

Trafford rev. 06/01/2020

www.trafford.com
North America & international
toll-free: 1 888 232 4444 (USA & Canada)
fax: 812 355 4082

To the five thousand students I taught over thirty years in developing open minds and positive attitudes concerning life, biology, and our earth's future.

CONTENTS

ACKNOWLEDGMENTS

Many kind people waded through my pages of manuscript for this science fiction book. Their unselfish help and ideas alerted me to the many gaps in logical thinking as well as my other shortcomings. They will never know how deep my appreciation is for their work on this story about the earth's future.

Thanks go to doctors Jim Gliozzi, Marshall Clough, Joyce Lackie, Steve Mazurana, Charles Olmsted, Julia Richard, and Jhelene Shaw, Cyndy Giauque, Dick Riner, Emily Richard, Cathy Olmsted, and Helen Williams for giving ideas for improvements.

INTRODUCTION

When the tipping point of CO_2 in the atmosphere was reached in 2031, and despite strong efforts from many nations to stop it, climate changes were slowly impacting the world. Seashores, coral reefs, weather patterns, and enhanced deserts around the world were forcing vast changes in the quality of human life. The health of the earth's ecosystems and the ten billion people were facing a slow decline in quality as never seen before.

Myriads of industrial solutions were tried to reduce the release of methane and CO_2. It was a slow losing battle. The new energy release technologies to capture, stop, and remove the CO_2 gas created more CO_2 than was being saved. Thus, no new technology was able to stop the worldwide decline of quality in the increasing human populations. Humans continued placing huge demands that spewed off CO_2 heat damage on the earth and most living things.

Could this world disaster be stopped? What would it take to change how humans lived and thought? Could the world be saved by science or political actions since it was really human thinking that prevented the possibility of human life remaining on the overheated earth long term?

Could some hope for the troubled human future and their planet home be found, of in all places, deep inside their reproductive cellular DNA?

By 2010, an ongoing genetic project had mapped the human genome vastly improved technology, opening the doors for new changes in humans.

Every living thing has a huge DNA code uniquely making it function, change, and reproduce new generations. This code can be altered by new technology involving complicated chemistry, computer programs, and genetic instruments. Few people understand the details of this vital research that can identify human and other life forms using only a tiny sample of their DNA. And genetic researchers can alter human DNA to help treat some diseases that are unique to our specific code by changing parts of it.

We are our DNA. It makes us all what we are and can be edited to make changes in all kinds of ways. This can also be done with other living things on the planet Earth. We humans have our own specific code of DNA made of the same chemical compounds that are in other animals and plants. However, our code does vary, making us unique as are all other plants and animals on this earth.

Genetic engineers now go into cellular DNA and find sections they wish to change. Then they use chemicals and computer technology to snip out sections they wish to replace or alter. Also, they can splice in new DNA codes to replace what they removed. This is called gene editing and works akin to when a teacher removes a word or section of a term paper and replaces it with a different word or sentence.

"*Photopeople*" deals with the consequences of how DNA codes can be replaced, altered, and new ones inserted. The science of doing this is so terribly complicated that only highly trained people can understand this work. This book, however, does *not* take the reader down the details of that complicated science path.

I deal with the changes that may result after moving DNA sequences from one gene site to another, and what might result from doing this in both animals, plants, and humans. Will making these changes in DNA in the long term save the earth?

Most everyone who has taken biology in the last thirty years knows these basics of DNA or at least has been exposed to them in our public schools. So *Photopeople* moves forward with how people can deal with gene editing work that changes living things for the better or worse. What kind of changes can these possibly be, and how will they work for humans on this degrading planet in our future?

—PAUL W. RICHARD, 2020

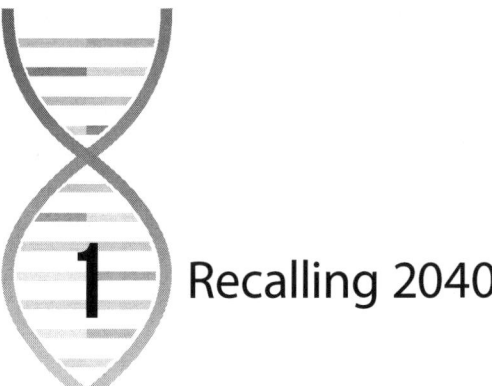

1 Recalling 2040

Our human ancestors of a dozen different varieties roamed Africa for over several million years. They all shared a majority of the same DNA. Yet they varied in a few ways as their genetic codes changed through mutating over the ages. But eventually all the many varieties except one became extinct. We are the sole survivors of the many kinds of ancient humans.

We are the only way life can understand itself despite all other living things being made of the same basic DNA structure; the only difference is the codes inside our cells. Some human scientists can understand the basic plan of life inside cells; however, this coded plan is very tiny, beyond the microscope, and is slowly changing over vast time through mutations.

Homo sapiens' DNA changed bit by bit over millions of years. Amazingly these many gene changes have given rise to thought and memory. We are the only creatures on earth whose cellular genes, holding our DNA codes, give us a brain that allows us to understand life itself, to think highly, to learn complexly, and to remember long term and then—of all wonders—to be able to pass on our memories, new ideas, and thinking to future generations. We are such special creatures, but we have our many shortcomings.

In spite of being able to understand life on the earth, by 2040 humans had fouled their own nest because they abused their personal right to have too many offspring for generations. Their numbers had far exceeded the carrying capacity of their earth by the 2040s. Land, water, and air were slowly degraded by this bursting human population. People mostly ignored that dangerous situation despite dire warnings from scientists, leaders, and educators.

Humanity failed to act as their environment changed around them in drastic ways: degrading the planet's ocean coral reefs, increasing the earth's deserts, losing vast lowlands to ocean expansions, suffering intense droughts, and tolerating hotter temperatures, and suffering extreme storms and floods worldwide. These and other climate changes uprooted massive populations, plunging them into poverty and hopelessness.

Yet most people kept producing several hundred thousand new humans each day, which meant eighty some million new people each year in the earth's crowded nest. This was devastating, adding more misery to the already suffering and hungry humans in the poorer failing nations across the globe. The impact of people had become the greatest catastrophic force on earth, slowly degrading all forms of life and the planet's future. New human numbers sapped up dwindling resources worldwide. Because of religious thinking, traditions, greed, and ignorance, little was done to limit the human desire to extend their own kind.

Scientists had long raised red flags about the creeping environmental fouling, but governments didn't change policies, fearing a loss of power politically. Humans continued to smother the earth with new people. Combustion byproducts were the humans seemingly incurable addiction as fossil fuels degraded the environment slowly. The environment declined before their eyes. Beyond all logic, they continued producing more and more people to consume the earth's declining resources and adding to the chaos.

It was a losing battle worldwide trying to educate the bloated earth populations about the coming and worsening disasters. People still wanted new young for many reasons and to make their lives more meaningful.

Would the earth be saved from the mounting human defiling, or would humans disappear as had the huge megafauna of elephants, sloths, and thousands of other beasts in the last twenty thousand years of earth history? Would human extinction make way for the next wave of new evolutionary nonhuman life as people vanished by their own hands?

Now instead of lamenting the past human shortcomings, let us follow a new trail in starting changes in humans and their two million years of ancient thinking.

* * *

Twin Starks, Zita and Erick, had tried to act as responsible scientists in Texas and California. Now in her mid-fifties and slightly graying, Zita sat back recalling how the revolution began for her way back in 2040 after she and her brother left the space agency. It had been like a fairy tale with an innocent beginning in her new West Coast job. At least her role in it originally had been pure science work. But now, those research results were unlocking a future that was dividing the United States. A weak president had tried to mollify those who preferred to the old ways and protect the new ones at the same time. Zita had doubted if any president could do either very well.

Always socially concerned, Zita had wanted to do pure science to protect her endangered planet and improve life. She now wondered, could all have been done differently? She thought not, retracing past events in her mind. It was as clear as if it all had taken place yesterday as she awaited her brother.

Zita on that warm spring afternoon in 2040 had sat on the back step of their new condominium soaking in some warming rays of the California sun. She wondered about her brother, Erick, who was hauling their furniture from Houston across the roasted Southwest devoured by intense drought.

Distracted, she watched a small red ant crawl lazily across her foot and up her chalk-white leg. Laboratory work didn't allow much time for tanning, which was harmful anyway, she supposed. When the ant topped her knee and hurriedly scampered toward the inner thigh, she felt its six tiny claws in the more tender area. As it skirted her blue shorts and headed toward the sidewalk, she contemplated its transformational possibilities.

Could a rearrangement of the DNA controlling its thick chitin armor be done in such a way as to decrease its weight, allowing its size to increase until it resembled the giant ants in the old movie *Them*? She mused at how those film monsters had dominated the Los Angeles drain system and terrified the population in the 1950s. Yet she knew it was possible to alter the ant. Perhaps make it longer-legged. Let it be the size of a small puppy. But how would it feed, and what problems would it cause? Perhaps it would live on people's pets and small children. Not a good idea. But as a molecular geneticist, she loved to ponder intriguing possibilities.

At least the climate wasn't as damp and sticky here as in Houston. The air was a dark brown unlike black Houston's, having been chemically altered since historic auto emissions had produced most of this LA pollution. Oil refining had poisoned the air in Houston for a hundred years. How some sunlight penetrated the brown gunk here in LA, she never knew. The California sun's rays initially felt good on her ivory skin, but now it was too hot. She had to live wherever genetic research was taking place. Why hadn't they located the genetic Quotech engineering labs in Wyoming or Idaho where better air could be breathed? Most of her colleagues wanted the culture of a polluted city more than the isolation and pure air of cold windy Wyoming. She didn't.

A sudden moist breeze from the Pacific stroked her face as she thrust her sharp chin up, taking full advantage of the cooling air, allowing her long blond hair to extend halfway down her back. She closed her gray eyes and wondered where Erick was with their belongings.

She drifted in her mind to the growing-up days in Hill City, South Dakota, where their parents worked for the National Park Service at Mount Rushmore. Theirs had been a delightful childhood in the Black Hills where their parents directed their focus into the sciences and natural history. Since childhood, she and Erick had been inseparable and strangely allied as only twins can be.

If it hadn't been for their parents sending her to the same Colorado science program, that her brother Erick had won a scholarship to during their junior year of high school, she might have taken a different path in life from his. After that exciting summer with those science whiz kids on the Northern Colorado campus, she had never felt satisfied outside the sciences. It was as if she'd been married that summer to the ideas of futuristic research and improving human capabilities. That Frontiers of Science Institute experience had brought her closer to Erick in her thinking and actions.

Erick, straight and tall, with shining blond hair and granite brown eyes, had always loved the sciences. They appealed to his innermost imagination and desire for perfection. In high school, he had won the award for being "Practically Perfect" at the awards assembly. He was brilliant in mind, had a distinguished manner, and was years ahead of his classmates in maturity and wisdom. Zita dearly loved her brainy brother because of his intellectual bent and the consideration he had always shown her since childhood. He was the only young man who had treated her with total respect. She felt doubly blessed having a career she loved alongside a brother who inspired her to her fullest potential.

A large green dragonfly darted past her head. Instantly, it reminded her of the research project she had done with the iridescent insects, as a junior in high school. As a budding scientist, she had captured them with a net along pond banks. Then she had force-fed them mosquitoes infected with a virus. She had wanted to see if the virus could infect the dragonflies via their digestive tracts. The results were inconclusive, but she'd enjoyed working with virologists, entomologists, and disease ecologists; she'd had her own white lab coat just as if she were a real scientist. But her love of genetics in college had swept her away from the fun of working with insects.

She felt good about her life, but the headlines of the morning paper concerned her. The general wisdom was that she shouldn't worry. Change was a part of science and the earth. But "Ocean Level Still Rising" had grave implications for the world. Because of the impure air and elevated carbon dioxide levels to 460 parts per million, the Antarctic ice cap was warming each year, resulting in over a foot increase above the ocean levels of the 2000s. Already, New Orleans was under water and abandoned because of the decade-long trend and several killer hurricanes stronger than Katrina. Other low areas were following in its wake. Zita knew there was little she could do about it and felt helpless. The buildup of carbon dioxide had been ongoing since the industrial revolution and had worsened in the early 2000s because of industrial development in China and India. It shocked the world in the late 2020s when the greenhouse effect caused a more rapid melting of the Greenland and Antarctic ice. This had been expected. Where would it end, she didn't know, but it appeared to her that people were confined to a planet with a shrinking landmass as the oceans slowly expanded worldwide.

Why should she worry? Change had been the order of the day since the time of prehistory. The longbow hadn't wiped out the earth's population, nor had gunpowder, atomic weapons, computers, or the new space lasers. She had to live with change, and once the fossil fuels were totally exhausted, perhaps the trend of melting would slow and eventually reverse. At least that was the general wisdom in which she held little faith. She wanted a perfect world, but instead buried herself in science research to avoid thinking about it.

She and Erick had lost faith in experts and their predictions while working on their doctorates at the University of Colorado and had become even more dismayed during their four years of NASA in Houston. Scientists-turned-administrators had been the most incompetent of all as they struggled in jobs for which they hadn't been trained. The correlations between good teaching, good researching, and good administrating didn't exist in her mind. Few people could perform well at all three jobs.

At NASA, she and Erick had developed a self-contained food pack for astronauts and space station workers in less than two years. They were both young and filled with energy and scientific ideas. Over several years, their engineering teams under Erick's leadership, and with her ingenuity, had hit upon the exact combinations of fluids, optics, and genetically modified green algae to help feed people in space. Their stellar science research work developed a food source that met carbohydrate requirements and cut down human wastes and expensive bulk foods needed by workers at huge space stations high above the dank earth.

Most importantly the biopacks provided food and oxygen while working well in conjunction with NASA's small O2 generators.

It had been highly satisfying watching films of workers at space stations using the equipment she and Erick had big roles in developing. They both wanted to help the earth become healthy again as it had been before they had been born. Biopacks were helping space workers in assembling the vast solar collecting arrays high above the earth. These space assemblers could work twice as long, have more freedom of movement, and were speeding up vital construction.

These giant sunray collectors would soon beam solar energy straight down to the world's power grids, helping reduce the burning of fossil fuels and CO_2 release on the earth surface below.

Their enormous success had opened corporate doors to new leading-edge research positions here on the less-polluted West Coast. Zita continued enjoying the cool sea breeze, reveling in her increased salary, and wondering how their new research work would involve her and Erick—hopefully continuing to make the world a better place.

2 Surprises

Despite Zita worrying about his travel and not always keeping in communicator contact, Erick suddenly drove in with their belongings. He had fooled her on his progress. She rushed out to give him a huge hug and teased, "Glad you're safe, you trickster."

"Traffic's a nightmare when you're pulling one of these trailers with this powerless compact electric car you insisted on." She ignored his jab at her insistence on energy efficiency.

She was so happy to see him even though having talked infrequently by communicators; everyone on the planet could be in contact if they wished. She made cold drinks of flavored tea, and they sat on the front steps in the now dimming sunlight fighting its way through the opaque air. Later, Zita helped him unload their possessions.

Zita chattered, "Thank heavens this stuff is all inside and we're a bit settled. Now we can arrange. I would have dreaded starting work next week with this place in chaos."

"You're just that ole perfectionist. Have to have everything in proper order, and that doesn't bother me. Just happy bein' off the road," replied Erick as he turned to his willowy sister who had always led in looking after their household needs. He was the relaxed and laid-back one with a mind like a steel trap. He often wondered what might happen if either married. For now, they had been so intensely involved in their work that other relationships were a luxury for which no time existed.

"I think you're the same as I am, Erick."

"Perhaps so, but it's worse here than at the labs with you."

"Well, I'll try to adjust my habits, just a little bit. With what they're paying us, we could hire a cook and housekeeper too."

"I'd hate that type of hotel living. It would be like attending those big meetings and conferences."

Changing the subject, Erick asked, "Think you're gonna enjoy working with green pigmented primates?"

"Erick, we are not supposed to discuss details outside the lab! This is not like NASA."

"Yes, I know, I know, but we're at home, and I doubt another company would have this place bugged."

"You're right, I suppose, but we can't include anyone else. This will sure be different from working at CU or with NASA where everybody freely talked about their research," said Zita as she rose and went to start unpacking more boxes.

Erick soon followed, helping as they continued talking about their new jobs. "Hopefully," he said, "this is where nobody could possibly use a long-distance listening device to intercept what we say."

Ignoring his concern, she said, "Think I'll like the primate work since it's all at the cellular level and I'm not involved in the handling and cleaning of them. Hope we have competent laboratory technicians for that. I've never had a large staff before."

"Never have I, but I don't want to spend all my time overseeing techs. I need to do my own thing with some experiments and reading the journal data too. That's who I am."

Zita said, "Me too. I still can't believe they've spliced green plastids and vacuoles into the primate genetic systems. Maybe next week we can see the little greenies and meet our laboratory staffers."

"I'm curious too. Sure do hope the little guys are getting humane treatment."

"Just the thought of it all blows my mind. When I spliced in desirable metabolic between algae for the biopack system, I thought I'd done something unique in gene editing. But for these guys to splice between plant and animal kingdoms codes is a huge DNA leap," she said. Their newly hung NASA framed awards now hung on their white wall, and she wondered if they really meant anything since molecular science and chemistry were racing along so fast in a new troubled world.

"You know," Erick commented, "when we really consider that plant and animal cells came from the same basic stock of cell types hundreds of millions of years ago, maybe it's not too surprising that they're more compatible than we'd ever supposed. If that's so, the chemical systems to utilize photosynthetic materials may still be inactive in animal cells unchanged from that early prototype. What's wild is the possibility that animal skin cells would be able to use the sun in making food much like a leaf cell; it's something I'd never dreamed of. But you'd know this better than I. I'm just a biochemist."

"I know there is a lot of inactive old junk DNA in the cells left over from eons of mutations. But this is so far out there. I hope we both don't limit the research by thinking too narrowly," Zita replied with a grin.

"You never think small. If it hadn't been for your enzyme work, we'd never have gotten the new algae for the space station workers, and we'd be somewhere less advanced and less prestigious now. Instead, look at us, here with Quotech, the best genetic engineering company in America, about to begin secret jobs we can't even disclose to our parents up in Hill City."

"We don't really know what we're doing yet. Does that bother you, Erick?"

"Not a lot! It's like the work on the first atomic bomb with everyone doing their part in secret and only a few seeing the whole picture. I'm excited for a new challenge . . ."

"I hope Quotech doesn't keep us from seeing the entirety. Working in isolation wouldn't be much fun, and I want us to still work as a team of sorts."

"We'll see, but I don't doubt it's possible," replied Erick.

Zita again remembered their achievements. Both she and Erick had been instrumental in changing the biopack from a shunt feeding sugars into veins in the human neck to a port feeding into the upper back of the workers. Food entry from that area was more stable and secure during activities that involved so much neck turning and arm movement in outer space.

Yet it was because of Erick's enzyme chemical unit forcing the algae to release part of their sun-produced glucose that set things in motion. A sharing of sugars from algae allowed workers to live nicely in the constant sunlight in space, a stunning step in the space program.

Together she and Erick had redesigned the enzyme systems that encouraged the DNA-engineered algae to give up and extrude half of its sugars. It had been simple to then circulate the algae through an enzyme chamber after it had produced sugars. There it chemically surrendered half the sugars and circulated back to photosynthesize more. Medical personnel finally mastered how to drip the collected simple sugars into the veins of workers as space food. All told, it had been a great advancement of twenty-first-century space science. A big team of scientists—including the Starks from a small town in rural Dakota—had put it together and opened their door to Quotech.

They both decided to go out and have a good meal and continue the unboxing and arranging the next day. At a nearby family grill, they speculated about what might happen in the next year's research. Erick kept yawning, so they returned home arm in arm and retired early since he was exhausted after his long drive. Zita felt more whole having her brother with her again. He had always been her comfortable sounding board.

When their apartment was in total order with newly purchased furniture and food, they took a tour of the huge smog shrouded city. The smog was terribly brown since solar power had not been enough to keep from using hydrocarbon fuels that released gases now trapped over them and LA.

The following week, they reported to the tightly guarded and beautifully designed laboratory of research. Quotech hung in black letters above the entry arch leading onto vast green grounds. Jutting up like a courthouse in a small country town, the research lab dwarfed all the other buildings on the campus.

Dr. Charlie Proud, who had interviewed them and was in title the onsite research director, happily greeted them, giving the grand tour and first look at where their secret work would be conducted. His tiny mustache was bushy, and he was bald, but otherwise he looked like a little banker rather than a scientist. His looks and prissy manner made her wary of this pompous man who seemed all wrapped up in himself.

"We want you to understand our position in working with these green pigmented apes," said Charlie, "It's pure research to see how they produce food, how much is produced, and how to enhance production metabolically and genetically. To be honest, we don't really know where we are on this and what was done to get to this point."

That remark troubled Zita since she assumed they knew exactly what had been done with the chimps. But she said nothing. He was a traditional administrator in a gray suit orienting his new scientists in the spotlessly cleaned research cubicles with glass-like polished floors of tile bounded by vast electronics and banks of computers.

Next, he led them into the isolation laboratories. Erick and Zita were fascinated by the verdant pigmentation of the three primates. The color was extremely bright on one who had been recently shaved. The tiny chimps had the appearance of the "green man" space traveler that writers had long sought and written about in science fiction.

"They are amazing," said Zita. "How many do you have?" Suddenly she felt sorry for them in their pods with a color that would have made them outcasts in their African native habitat of the Congo.

"Three, and the females are pregnant now. We have harvested and cloned eggs and embryos so we don't lose the traits. It's enough for the breeding we want to do connected with the research," replied Charlie as he led them past the germ-free animal room. They followed Charlie to the work areas. He introduced them to their research associates, assistants, and a host of laboratory technicians who would do the bench lab experiments. Finally, they were alone with him in his office.

Charlie placed a huge packet of records on the new desk and said, "Erick, your first priority is to determine how much energy is coming from the primate skin and how much from their outside food. Some of the data in this folder may help. Biochemically we're somewhat in the dark on the exact quantitative measurements of what they can do."

Erick nodded, not asking if the research was to lead to any practical result. Of course, that wasn't even a consideration in pure basic research where knowledge was to be obtained for the sake of knowledge. This would be far different from the NASA applied research where people did something with the pure research data to solve a specific problem. This was a rung up on the snobbery ladder in the scientific world. Pure research was the pinnacle of research science.

Charlie paced back and forth with his hands behind his back as he instructed Zita like a professor lecturing. "Now, Zita, you're going to lead a team to explore how this pigmentation is transmitted. It was a fluke when it happened. Honestly, they were expecting something else, or so they said. We need to back up and see where we are with the DNA involved. Seems like the cart got ahead of the horse. Suddenly this female chimp gives birth to these twin green babies. All hell broke loose around here and people got fired.

"Dr. Moby wasn't supposed to be fooling around with plant DNA in animals. He's gone and now history. But we have this breakthrough, it's important to see where we can go with it. And of course, you and Erick understand the confidential nature of this undertaking. Someone suggested yesterday that we might eventually be able to produce cows that give milk but don't eat much grass or hay. But enough of my rambling about someone's speculations."

After watching how this little man moved and acted, Zita knew for sure that Charlie had an extremely high opinion of himself.

Erick said, "I'm really excited to work on this." He knew how great it was always having a scientist sister at hand to confer with him on projects.

"I'll second that," added Zita who knew Erick's mind was always hers.

Charlie said, "I'm delighted to have you both aboard with Quotech. We were lucky to lure you away from NASA. I've never had twin scientists working before. I think you both can really help us." He briskly spun on his elevated heels and led them to the side-by-side laboratory vast rooms they had requested. After he excused himself and swaggered off down the corridor, they both turned to their work areas to eyeball the changes they needed in exploring green chimp DNA.

Their new equipment was all brand new, highly computerized, and the perfect state of advanced science. Spectrophotometers, analyzers, and other gleaming instruments stood in a glistening row on blacktopped laboratory benches and against their walls. The microscopes were the most advanced, and a reversed air circulation system was in working order. There would be no mistakes of cross-contamination floating into the adjoining laboratories. On each office desk rested several large manila envelopes outlining every procedure from ordering supplies to communications and security codes.

After inspecting their labs, Erick and Zita again met in the hallway. Erick said, "They didn't leave anything to chance or cut on costs. This is wonderfully equipped and staffed."

She replied, "I couldn't ask for anything better. Except, they have no windows here."

"Secrets, sis, and to maintain a secure environment. But remember our huge bonuses to come here. I'll not expect it to be perfect since humans are in charge." He always tried to put a positive spin on work life and encourage his sister in any situation.

"I think there's a lot more going on here than determining the energy input and output controlling the DNA codes involved. This is an open door to unimaginable possibilities." She tended to look far into the future and at the ramifications of events that would open new issues.

"Could well be," replied Erick who had no idea what they were getting into or the long-term outcomes of this covert green animal research. This was his biochemistry love, dealing with unknowns.

3 Green Chimps

After their tour and introduction to the grandeur of Quotech, their working lives settled into a busy new learning routine; they then led many detailed meetings showing their staff workers exactly how they wanted things done. She and Erick often conferred about new procedure, research ideas, and results.

"I didn't realize there was both pure and applied research here at Quotech, and they farm out most of the applied work to universities," said Erick. He was learning the inner ropes of a company that had sprung up ten years before with funds from billionaires who wanted to help make the declining world a better place and also to make a profit.

Zita replied, "They sure have done amazing genetic engineering with crops around the world with that approach."

"Not much though with animals other than goats and sheep."

"As a pure researcher, I'm glad not to have to think about what they plan to do with my results."

"That's what I like about our work as pure science."

Each day on the Los Angeles Transit System (LATS), from home to her laboratory on High Tech Drive, Zita was vaguely unsettled by the stern unsmiling faces of fellow passengers; they seemed to make the oppressive smog, blown in from Asia, even more depressing. Yet at thirty, she wasn't going to shoulder all the world's problems. Let someone else work on the smog, she thought; she and Erick were now on the leading edge of critical research.

17

She considered her role in science as the railcar raced along. After millions of years of separate evolution, the plant and animal cells had now become recombined in part of one higher animal. Because someone didn't follow protocol in experimentations with DNA, Moby may have changed the course of history. Intellectually, Zita was excited about working on these staggering breakthroughs. She pondered if all this could make a higher animal self-sustaining as was the case with Euglena, a primitive animal. It could engulf food while carrying on photosynthesis in its green body.

Zita also knew the exact date in the late 1880s when Theobold Smith had worked with veterinarians and discovered cattle ticks could be vectors, carry and transmit disease-causing organisms to another animal. It turned a corner for humans, allowing the conquest and treatment of dozens of theretofore mysterious diseases that had plagued the human race over the eons. But would this green chimp breakthrough eventually have that kind of impact, she wondered? But she knew her role was only to experiment and discover, and not be personally concerned with what to do with the results. That was for the social sciences, politicians, and the public to decide, but as a concerned citizen, new possibilities for society stunned her mind.

Soon after her badge and retinal screening permitted entrance to the Quotech lab, she joined her teams. They took skin cells from the green chimps for growing in tissue culture containers. Nutrients were then circulated to feed the tiny green cells. Laboratory technicians cared for them and did the repetitive work of transferring them to cultures for experimenting.

She and her brother designed a series of experiments, and they examined the data and results that were neatly recorded, plotted, and graphed by the best computers. The technical grunt work was done by their exacting laboratory people. She felt like Louis Pasteur when he designed the experiments to conquer rabies. Just as Zita and Erick were now doing, Pasteur's brainpower directed others in the tedium of laboratory experiments and the analysis of the mad dog virus. Science to Zita had always been how to ask the right questions as Pasteur had done in saving humans from rabies.

The twins had frequent meetings with other Quotech science team leaders in a boardroom where results were hotly questioned, defended, and new directions probed. There were endless chemical formulas and math equations filling the boards and screens around the scientists as they worked together probing differing aspects of this unfamiliar green chimp molecular biology.

Months later, in a team meeting one Monday morning, Erick excitedly reported, "These results are startling! These green chimp cells are producing far more sugar than any plant cells so far studied on this Earth."

Raising his eyebrows in surprise, Charlie asked, "How do you account for that?"

"Perhaps the increased temperatures of the animal body skin or the genetics of it make the production of glucose a hundred times greater. It might be some plastid improvements Moby inserted into the DNA code somehow."

"Good heavens, it's that much?" gasped Charlie who had been hearing science results for ten years as head of research at Quotech.

"These are first results, but I think there could be a many-fold increase in photosynthesis in these skin cells. I believe we're not dealing with just some green apes, but we now have super glucose food-producing animal cells."

"My god! That could be a blockbuster. What do you suggest in moving forward?" asked a stunned Charlie, willing to jump on any idea that could eventually have a commercial use. Such thinking irritated Erick who saw profits as clearly unethical and in contrast to his devotion to pure research.

Overlooking Charlie's greed, however, Erick went on. "For my unit, two things: First, we continue refining these production results. Then I'd like us to start using the little apes under varying light and food conditions to see what a growing animal can do, not just these invitro cultures we have been testing. Of course, we will need a waste product and an analysis team to carry out the chemical job too."

"Go for it! I'll try to set up a team as fast as we can hire them. But you and Zita have to be in on the selection of the new people with me."

"We'll be glad to help in the interviews," said Zita who liked being in on the team selections since it enabled her to know the people before they set to work and to also know their background experience.

"End of meeting." But Charlie added as he left, "Can hardly wait to tell our board of directors about this one."

Erick nodded, picked up his papers, and left the room. Both Starks moved into their labs and lost track of the outside world as they buried themselves deeper and deeper in their grueling research work seven days a week. It was a hectic pace. They didn't want to miss anything, as results were rapidly advancing.

One weekend they decided to rent a boat and take an afternoon off. They sailed on the fishless bay outside Long Beach. It allowed them to escape the dense smog that hugged the mountains to the east and clung over the city like death's angels, billowing up in ugly brown forms from emissions.

"This work's lightning fast compared to anything I've ever done. We are nearly complete in the genetic analysis, and the picture is markedly clear," remarked Zita. "But let's not talk shop out here in partially clear skies. Please remind me if I bring it up anymore, OK?"

"Fine with me," replied Erick. "I've been thinking that our social lives are nonexistent—reminds me of the NASA days."

"Me too," responded Zita, thinking how complicated being involved in a personal relationship would be. "I'm honestly not interested and wouldn't have more than thirty minutes a day to give anyone."

"Wouldn't work for me either!"

"Giving one's life to science has rewards, but I hope we both don't spend forever at this high-pressure, time-consuming pace. It will change, don't you think?"

"Everything changes; we couldn't keep this up forever. But it's so damn exciting. And one of the best things is all the help we both have. Good people. I really enjoy my work."

"OK, no more shop talk, Erick. You know five years ago, some of the trees on those mountains were still alive. It sickens me knowing they're all dead now." Murky water spread apart as the boat's bow plowed through it like a dull knife. A dingy-yellow cast from the water reminded them how wastes from the overpopulated cities along the coasts had driven away most close to shore marine life, and it had increased water temperatures resulting from decades of slow climate changes.

"Yes, sis, we can't even see trees from here. Twenty-five million people produce lots of crud, and look at the plastic we're plowing." He wished he could be in South Dakota stream fishing instead of guiding the blue boat over the lifeless water.

"No, but I can make out the faint mountains outlined behind that yellowish smog. Just knowing mountains are there is the problem for me."

"Well, you don't know what's in your own genes, and that doesn't bother you, does it?"

"Of course not, because I know we can do something about genes the way things are going. And maybe someday something can be done to clean up this bay and filthy air so I can see the mountains too."

Erick looked at his sister and wheeled the boat toward the hazy shore. He enjoyed challenging his twin. They were so much alike, he thought, yet he seemed to have a wider view of worldly matters and public policy. He dreaded the time when she would leave, but her happiness was terribly important to him. He didn't want his demands to lessen her opportunities in the future. Yes, with her grace, beauty, brains, and good sense, she'd been the perfect supportive sister, but she probably would not be the same in the future. Everything evolves.

As for him, Erick gave little thought about married life. Biochemistry was now his challenge and his life's blood. He sought to learn all that was knowable about the chemistry of life. There was far too much work ahead to allow thinking beyond that.

As the boat approached shore, he smelled the repugnant city odors and thought to himself that no man should bring into this crowded world more humans. He swore he would not add to the sad state of human affairs; it was his mission to help or at least to try to solve some problems. Basic research opened the doors to let people have a better life. He had seen it all his life. There had been so many diseases and defects corrected by science, but ironically the total human condition had steadily gone downhill because of overpopulation. Their boat had plowed through clusters of floating plastic debris, causing him to wonder why people destroyed their own home. Yet could science alone better the world? He was still wondering as he cut the throttle and Zita connected the rope holding the boat to the marina's rental pier. It was the first relaxing day they'd had in months.

They were highly refreshed and ready when they went to Quotech the next morning. Charlie had asked them to present progress reports to the board meeting. Zita and Erick detailed what had been taking place in their research. The audience had few questions and didn't seem to grasp the long-range implications that the twins had envisioned.

Jack Wilson, who had introduced the Starks to the Quotech board of directors, turned to them. "As president of this company, I need to know exactly how we can profit from all this green ape research? Are we going to sell the critters as pets? Starks? Charlie?" asked the silvery-haired man in seeming jest.

Charlie replied, "It's that spin-off research syndrome. We have no idea exactly what will come of this. This could go big, or it might fall on its face. One thing I know is when we unmask what we now have to the world, our company will be on the cover of every magazine or media. This is big stuff; our stock could skyrocket."

"I know you're right, Charlie, I'm just bogged down by budget concerns for the present."

"Well, we need to enlarge our nitrogen utilization team. A breakthrough there could help save the soils and feed twice what the world does today. This costs now, but we could rake in profits we never dreamed of in the future."

Wilson said, "Go ahead and build up your nitrogen bacterial team. At least that project has practical possibilities for our bottom line."

"One thing about this company, if we need to recapitalize and sell stock, this green ape thing can bring in a million investors if we issue new stock," said Charlie.

"Perhaps that's our ace in the hole. But let's all keep a lid on it 'til sometime when it's needed," responded Wilson.

"I understand."

Six months later, the Starks eagerly awaited the birth of the first offspring from an earlier cross between a green brother and sister chimp. The mating had been done before Zita and Erick had jobs with Quotech. Such an incestual cross didn't seem to alarm anyone, as it might have in humans, but the Starks were involved in science, not public ethics. The cross was needed to see if the green pigmentation traits would be carried to a third generation.

On the big day of the birthing at Quotech, a select group of scientists were gathered around the operating room. The birth—a cesarean, so not to risk damaging the green mother—produced two normally pigmented chimps, without a tint of green rising from the thinly haired bodies. Even Charlie was stunned into absolute silence. The traits had vanished or had been masked, and the whole project, it seemed, was a stunning disaster.

However, two days later, an animal care unit worker noticed a darkening on the backs of both the male and female babies. In another few days, their backs were a bright green in the highly lighted nursery.

The astonished scientists couldn't believe their eyes. Obviously both chimps had a glucose-producing plastid-like area on their backs, much like plants have in their leaves. Why had the skin's green pigments accumulated, expanded, and migrated to the backs in such a tight arrangement? Everyone pondered the significance of the new pigment distributions. Some of the scientists felt it was a setback for the project and they feared future crosses could produce even stranger patterning. Zita could not understand what had happened in the genetics, or was it all a set of new mutations?

Over the next few days, Zita watched the greenbacks in the nursery and wished she knew exactly what Dr. Moby had done. How had he inserted plant genes into the embryos during DNA splicing?

Charlie had earlier revealed that upon his dismissal, Dr. Moby had fled the USA. Yet his notes were not to be found, and he had refused to discuss his unauthorized procedures since Quotech had immediately fired and blackballed him in genetic research. What a rogue researcher he must have been to do such work, and how had Charlie not known about it? Zita was baffled and terribly curious.

Zita surmised that somehow plant DNA must have been transferred in huge sequences to involve the entire back in green. It had to be! But what kind? What plant genetic materials had expressed themselves in this chimp generation gathering all the green plastid pigments into one back area? It was not unlike a tree having only green in the leaves while the trunk, branches, and roots were subtle browns and grays. Also, she pondered why some trees had green trunks and no green leaves, making distribution varied in many floral species.

She speculated that the patterning might also be the result of the animal DNA causing dark backs and light undersides characteristic of fish, penguins, and many sea mammals. It was a stretch of her imagination trying to account for all the pigment gathered so suddenly in the backs. How she wished the notes of Dr. Moby were at hand to disclose how and what plant genes were spliced into the chimps' fertilized eggs. What bothered her most were the surprises lurking ahead over which she had neither control nor forewarnings.

The work would have to be done the hard way since Dr. Moby refused to ever talk to his former employers from South Africa to where he had had a new position for several years. Zita felt it had been a serious mistake to release Dr. Moby without knowing all the details of his gene-splicing experimental notes.

In the weeks ahead as tensions eased, she struggled through the publications on cross-species gene transfers, finding little to help her understand the situation she had at hand. Then one day she walked into his office and focused on her brother's research efforts. "Erick, you have been struggling along for months now with your food production. Are things working?"

"No, Zita"—her brother smiled—"I am still not confident of the results. I need more data. The big problems are a shortage of the animals, Quotech's protocol restrictions, and more researchers wanting samples of tissue, blood, and also electronic hookups for other measurements."

"Perhaps I'll just clone you a dozen or so of the little rascals," she replied.

"Did you meet the new people on that nitrogen bacterial team today?"

"No, I was in the germ-free lab where we are working with tissue culture. Were they interesting?"

"They seemed excited to be with us. Except they aren't to be told anything about our work on the chimps. One of them, Harold Harms, is a rather handsome man. You might be interested, sis," he mused, gauging her reaction.

"Don't be silly; we are closing in on identifying the genes responsible for the redistribution of the green pigments. I don't really have time for even the cutest guy. Besides, all the bacteria people I've ever known were obtuse." She really didn't trust most young men after what had happened to her in Boulder when her future husband dumped her.

"You make me laugh, Zita. One of these days the ole love bug will bite again, and all the biological forces will overcome your resistance."

"I hope not until I'm in my late thirties and have a laboratory of my own. I need a man now like I need a second belly button."

Erick laughed. "Do you still really want a lab of your own?"

"Anything to get away from Charlie; he's putting requests, restrictions, and silly report writing on me. Most of the time, that man drives me crazy."

"Yes, but without the likes of him, you'd need to raise grant money to run your lab at the same time. There just isn't an easy way, unless you have funds from a big private foundation or the NSF." Erick was surprised that she was thinking about a future. But he understood her dislike of Charlie's rigid controlling ways. At times, Erick had those same feelings as he pondered Charlie's motive.

4 Experimenting

A full year passed in intense research producing more green-backed chimps. They bred true, all having the greenback trait that encouraged the scientists at Quotech.

On the social front, Harold from the nitrogen bacterial group had shown an interest in Zita. He would often move to her side at meetings, or in the cafeteria. During the Christmas party, he danced with her, and she liked the male attention. Yet she was cautious.

He was a square-jawed man with stove-black hair and a fine sense of humor on social issues. His interest in her work and the future attracted Zita more than his good looks and nice build. They continued visiting at lunches and seeking each other out during big meetings. Erick watched the adventure with interest but didn't dare mention it because Zita might see what was happening and bolt. During lunches in the cafeteria, Zita enjoyed the attention. It was nice having a friend at Quotech. At first, she didn't think of anything beyond friendship. Then coming to work each day, she found herself looking forward to seeing him at noon.

Harold invited her out several times, and finally, she accepted an invitation to see the indoors botanical gardens. She felt that he was a safe companion. It was an exciting and refreshing afternoon with all the green around them. She saw flowering roses of a hundred types that had long been absent around the city that lacked trees and even lawns. Their many showy petals hugged together delicately around each rose flower's center, inviting her to smell them. It was exhilarating like the first day of spring, something she had not seen since living at home in South Dakota. Harold was funny, alert, and very interesting and seemed to enjoy what she liked, impressing her. Their lunch visit focused on their favorite foods, media programs, and dream vacations. On their return, she accepted a dinner date for the coming Thursday.

Numerous times during the week, she wanted to cancel it but couldn't make herself call Harold and disappoint him. She wondered if she could trust him.

That evening he took her to a place called the Honky Tonk, which had wonderful food, and they enjoyed dancing. She hadn't danced much since college, and it felt good being with someone who did.

"Say, you're a great fast dancer. Did you learn those steps at a dance studio?"

"My mother helped me, and my brother and I danced a lot growing up. It was nice having partners right in our dining room. How about you?"

"Girls taught me after classes in the middle-school gym. And I never passed up a chance to do what we called 'Hoofing It' up in Montana."

She had never dated much since working for NASA, and time had always been short. But she liked Harold and decided the evening felt right. A friend beyond her brother appealed to her changing needs, and Harold was neither pushy nor too serious. Yet she was fearful of change and didn't trust men since they all seemed to hold a hidden agenda, hiding who they really were. She tried to be fair and not paint all men with the same brush.

Later that evening at home, Zita's mind wandered back to her university relationship. Mike and she had dated for two years while she wrote her dissertation. He was in physics, was exciting, and never tried to control her. She always remembered her father telling her, "He who loves the least controls the most." But then the unthinkable happened. By accident she discovered Mike had two other girls on the side and was sleeping with them when he wasn't with her. She knew in reality that he was dumping her. She dropped Mike instantly. It was difficult since she had planned to marry him.

Since that time, she had suppressed her love and sexual desires, being fearful of taking chances. She plunged herself into work. But later that night, she thought about letting go of all her inhibitions with Harold but was torn about trusting any man again.

That following week, he had planned their evening date with dinner and wine at his place. It wasn't too obviously romantic for Zita. They had already shown some affection in the relationship. She found herself happy with it all and tried to suppress any concerns about Harold's character or intentions.

They laughed a lot during dinner, both sipping several glasses of wine, and Zita enjoyed it. She admired the paintings on his walls of Western history, something she had always loved because of her South Dakota past. After dinner, as the empty wine bottle sat abandoned on the table, Zita watched Harold finish washing the dishes. She felt excited when he turned and held her against the sink, kissing her warmly. Her lips parted and slightly opened, responding to his. His lips moved slowly over hers as they extended the embrace.

Harold said, "You're the nicest woman to ever come my way. I think I'm falling in love for the first time."

"Really?"

Zita vaguely wondered if he was truthful since few men ever were when dating. She moaned slightly as he kissed her, and the wine helped release her buried passions. Moving in tiny bites up the inside of her long neck, he nibbled down her shoulder. She let him lead her to the fireplace in front of the couch. There he pulled her to her knees and again embraced her. She returned his kisses with savagery and probed his mouth with her tongue in short flickers. She wanted to lose control and didn't protest as he untied her blouse and underclothes. Soon his lips and tongue were exploring.

She loved the feeling of his body against hers and wanted to totally surrender. Never had anyone she'd slept with in high school or Mike in college spent such time in foreplay.

Soon they were in their underclothes and locked in passionate body contact on the soft rug by the flickering artificial fireplace. Zita felt as if she would explode when he gently thrust his hand, touching her in all the right places.

"Harold, Harold, that feels so good; I can't stand it." She abandoned her fears and totally began to yield.

"Be patient; enjoy yourself. We have loads of time. And I want you to be happy."

"Yes, yes!" she whispered.

He did everything just right. She was highly excitable as he played with her. Soon she was ready and told him she would not be ovulating for a week.

She rolled over on top of him and raised herself over him, offering her breasts as he slid her panties down her slender legs.

He kissed her lips forcefully. She again raised herself upward toward him, releasing her pent-up emotions with him.

When Zita was home later that night, she thought over that evening. It was a part of Zita's character analyzing it as she would any experiment to be sure of her deep feelings.

She asked aloud if it was right, and she decided it pleased her being with him. What a difference that night had made, giving her more than genes and DNA codes to wrap her mind around. She was happy and wanted to see him again to gauge his reactions since the relationship had moved into the physical realm.

* * *

By that next July, Erick's team had finalized the data showing glucose sugar production had increased ten times greater than expected from the light-tinted green apes. The greenbacks, on the other hand, had half again as much production from their concentrated dense back areas. The results were startling since it was as if super chlorophyll worked in the plastids. If so, these chlorophyll genes could be transferred back into plants, and the yields could be fantastic for food production. Erick's mind raced over the possibilities when telling Charlie about his findings and the potential benefits.

For many months in the rearing area adjacent to the labs, the caged apes had been fed small quantities of protein, water, vitamins, and roughage. Erick's figures confirmed their need for fewer amounts of carbohydrates, provided they were exposed to direct sunlight. Both green chimps and the greenbacks were storing the oversupply of sugars they produced in their livers as glycogen. All primates store carbohydrate from the food they eat, but in the lab, it was from the sugars they were making from the sunlight instead of the intake of complex food.

All the housed chimps seemed to gaze hopefully with soft brown eyes at the scientists as if seeking to be elsewhere. Erick thought that they craved the freedom of the jungle even though they had everything they needed to be healthy in captivity. He knew they would be better off in the wild free with groups of their kind. At times he regretted caging them inside as it forced him to shift away to avoid seeing their plight.

The greenbacks seemed to have no idea that they had to have sun to get their energy. Teams of scientists were convinced that sun-seeking behavior for the animals to survive was not present, but it abounded in plants. This physical change in their energy gathering was ahead of any behavioral evolution needed for their survival. Cages with banks of light duplicating the sunlight spectrum had to be used during the day. With the light coming from all directions, they seemed to thrive as they ate little and carried on photosynthesis.

Zita had her teams concentrate on isolating and studying gene sequences that controlled the plastids on the greenback chimps. When the testing was finished, the DNA codes were placed into bacteria that replicated it perfectly. This DNA was then introduced into chimp's embryos to double the population of greenbacks for the laboratory experiments. Soon they had large-enough numbers to produce solid outcomes. It was an exciting time to move ahead with such a large sample.

On the home front, Erick had been pleased that Zita and Harold had been seeing a lot of each other the past months, and he liked the man. Since she was gone from home at least half of the time, Erick began missing Zita, but would never say so to her.

The only objection Erick had was when Zita told him that Harold had asked her to disclose work details. It instantly made Erick see a red flag, questioning Harold's character and ethics. Most scientists at Quotech had some aspects of their work classified. And Harold knew Zita's work was secret, so why couldn't he leave it at that? Erick decided to speak with Harold about it should Zita bring it up again.

That very next week, Harold said to Zita, "We have so much to share with our love. Why can't you share your work to me too? It would give us a lot to talk about and would deepen our relationship. I feel strange being totally open with you about all I do and learn. It's just a one-sided deal, Zita."

"Mine is too secret, Harold."

"Well, if you really loved me . . ."

"That's not fair."

"I know, but I can't help how I feel."

"You're not being rational, Harold!"

"What on earth could it hurt?"

"My professional ethics and my career."

"No one but us would know."

"I'd hope not. Just be satisfied with what you're doing with your bacterial work."

"I'm just curious like you! I might get some ideas that would help us both. You know two heads are better than one."

Zita could feel herself weakening slightly as she became more involved with him. Their relationship was fulfilling except for this one issue. The next day, she found her brother in his office and closed the door.

"Harold asked me again about my work last night," Zita said.

"The heck he did!"

"And when I tried to change the subject, he said if I loved him, I would tell him. Imagine! If I loved him!" She shook her head. "And everything's wonderful with him except this."

Not wanting to show his deep concern, Erick said, "This may be a self-correcting problem."

Then Erick revealed that Charlie and the company president were going public with the green ape information after the first of the year to help raise money. She was elated; this news should relieve the pressure from Harold. But in the back of his mind, Erick remained suspicious why now Harold was so pushy.

Later that evening at his place, Zita told Harold that after January one, he'd know all about her work. He weakly agreed to wait the four months, yet she wondered if he really would drop the pressure.

A week later in the cafeteria, Harold excitedly related to Zita that a competing company had successfully transferred the nitrogen-fixing genes from a bacterium into a green Euglenoid species. This allowed the single-celled green animal to produce its own nitrogen-based proteins instead of ingesting them from the protein of others. It was major news. Harold was sure this step could work in plants and other animals as well, thus someday saving much of the world's food supply and rendering self-sufficient many newly engineered organisms.

Later at home, Zita discussed the idea of splicing such genes into the chimps, allowing them to take nitrogen from the air to make their own proteins. Then all they would need in addition was water, oxygen, and sunlight. Erick was at first amused by the idea. Jumping from Euglena to primates was too large a quantum leap for him. Zita reminded him that such DNA-spliced material was of the same composition in all organisms, and it might work since only the codes were different. She let him know that it was not nearly as large a leap as from plants to chimps. He laughed aloud, agreeing with her.

That night she visited at length with Harold about the nitrogen genes. He seemed highly knowledgeable about the techniques and methods used. He knew information far beyond anything published by scientific journals she had scanned during the day. And Zita had read the most current literature too. She wondered why he was so well versed and why he was telling her. After all, bacterial nitrogen was his field, and he was not keeping it secret.

Their love life had advanced and also taken on new dimensions with Harold, leading to new pleasure positions and techniques. She felt this must be the zenith of physical happiness for any two lovers.

Often, she asked herself how he could do everything just right, so perfectly. Zita sensed that he must have some genetic program for lovemaking. Or perhaps he was trained for it. She let those silly thoughts go and enjoyed him totally. She lusted after him and could hardly wait to spend some time each weekend at his place. She considered marriage in the back of her mind, yet he seemed too perfect and calculating.

5 Crosses

Two months later, there was an unscheduled team leader meeting at Quotech. The twins reluctantly left their research work, grumbling as an assortment of geeks, some in long white lab coats, others in suits, and many in sports outfits, seated themselves at random around the long conference tables. Erick was surprised at how many team leaders were at work on projects related to the green chimps.

How was all of this work going to come to an end and advance Zita and himself in their careers? And was this going to make them happy in the long run? He sat asking himself questions about the future at Quotech, pondering the intense work he had going on. At least his sister was now involved in something besides DNA sequencing. He felt down in the dumps watching her having such a good life beyond work. Was he jealous? He sure didn't want to be.

He had never seen all of this many people at one meeting before, and it ended with blockbuster news. Charlie made a shattering announcement. With his half-balding head, wrinkled pinched cheeks, and puffy red lips protruding around his tiny mouth, he spoke, "We just received big news from Italy. They have created a new subspecies by crossing human sperm and chimpanzee eggs in vitro and implanted the embryos back into great ape females. The offspring are now months old, healthy, and doing well."

After a moment of silence, the anthropoid expert said, "I'm really underwhelmed, Charlie. We have been expecting this for years. If our regulations weren't so archaic in this country, we could have done it right here to learn the potential. Now perhaps we can get some decent guidelines and accomplish something substantial in the USA."

"Yes," Charlie nodded, "but what are the implications of this for our greenback studies? You people have to help me here. What are we paying you for?"

"Surely we're not being paid to help design some super race or some subhuman animals," said a team leader in a blue lab coat who ran a primate lab.

Ignoring Charlie's last comment, Zita responded, "You know, Charlie, this could lead to a working class of subhuman laborers. We have no clue what is happening outside this country in laboratories around the world where they're not hamstrung by our tight regulations."

"Yes, yes," came from some of the scientists.

"If they're this far along now, it's more of an economic and social issue than a scientific one," added Erick. "Someday we might splice into these subhumans our green pigmentation genes, which would allow them to work in space stations without biopacks, but I can't see a future in that for Quotech. I think we should stay out of designing lower-class intelligence creatures or dull strong workers. Others will do all kinds of things, but we should not engage in research reaching toward social engineering."

Zita added, "Ethically, we need to keep our noses clear out of this work and let policy makers guide it."

"Yes, yes, Zita and Erick, we don't know the future or demand for this at all," said Charlie, seeming to have lost his usual sense of direction. "But maybe the congress will loosen our guidelines."

In private, their research director was the object of ridicule by some of the scientists seated at the meeting. Many didn't see him as a true scientist since he was also their chief administrator. In their view, he wasn't producing any important work—researching the unknown. He was mainly viewed as a housekeeper, maintaining things in order for real researchers. Charlie was at the bottom of the pecking order to many researchers who wanted his help, at times, yet looked down on bosses and administrators. All they wanted was to be left alone to do the work they had been trained to do and use

Charlie when they needed him. It was the burden all bosses seem to carry on their shoulders even though the team leaders sought his help and support all the time, making it a two-faced relationship.

Around the huge wood glaring table, a lengthy discussion continued about the Italian development of ape-people and became generally more theoretical and social than scientific. Charlie seemed to lose his patience. "This is degenerating. Off the cuff, we scientists don't know crap about these social and political ramifications." He ended the debate. Then he asked the leaders to rethink the problem until their next meeting and write down where each of them thought Quotech should go with future chimp development.

Zita refused to write anything knowing it was a waste of her energy. Such matters were not her field and should be left to the board of directors of Quotech. She was not paid to speculate, but Erick loved doing it since he felt science should take a stronger role in speaking out on social issues, especially since their work would impact the future. He did ask if an artificial placenta had been used in the Italian experiments.

Nationwide, the Italian ape-human accomplishment hit America's media, resulting in mixed reactions across the country. Many responded asking ethical questions regarding the sanctity of humans, while others opposed it on grounds there was high unemployment across the globe. Religious leaders opposed it as scientists playing God. Many citizens didn't see how it would help the crowded world with land and cities facing rising sea levels with polluted air blanketing most nations. All scientists, however, supported the freedom to experiment and inquire. Overall, it seemed akin to science fiction in another country that would have no impact on America. After all, America had no genuine need for subhuman workers as they already had an overabundance of migrants from Latin America.

Yet the debate raged in the media after the breaking news. And Charlie and his bosses on the Quotech board were watching the debate closely. Was this the environment into which they would release the news of genetically engineered plant genes in chimpanzees? They were afraid of the negative publicity in this nasty media climate, and especially after Moby had done his deed they were now using and having fled to Africa. Yet the media didn't know Moby had opened that new door in changing chimps. So there was no action from Erick's or Zita's bosses.

That evening at Harold's place, Zita said, "Harold, my personal feelings are that these new human apes or ape-humans could do the world a lot of good in the future. I'm now for it regardless of what people say."

Harold replied, "This has really shaken up the religious right across the world."

"I really don't care what they think because there are more mainstream secular unbelievers worldwide. All I want is for science to move ahead without restrictions. Otherwise, we could end up like today's Muslims or fifteenth-century Europeans where progress was blocked by religions."

"Zita, I couldn't agree more. But right now, I love you and want to show it."

Boldly, she said, "Well, do it instead of talking about it."

Harold quickly with fumbling fingers unbuttoned her blouse, unsnapped her bra, while kissing her neck. After some time caressing her, he pulled her to the floor and said, "Why are you so interested in the Italian ape stuff? I wish you'd talk about your work as freely."

She ignored his comment. Their conversation gave way to Zita's pleasure groans and moans. She pulled savagely at his arms, digging her fingernails into him. Her face contorted in the anguished passion that caused her neck and chest to redden. It all ended with two sweaty bodies moving into conversation.

"You're so damn good. You can have me anytime you want me, Harold."

He held her tenderly and kissed her with frequency on the lips, cheeks, and eyes. "Oh, Zita, why do I have to wait? We are good together. Maybe I can help your research too."

Zita rose sharply to a sitting position, looking him squarely in the eye for a long moment. She spoke, "Harold, I have given you everything, it seems to me. Why do you want to destroy my professional self-respect? This is a matter of my integrity and ethics."

"I don't want that, Zita. I'm sorry. I just—it's maybe—I'm hurt that you won't share it now when you're soon going to share it with the world."

"You only have to wait a couple of months. I can't and won't do it," she replied coldly, rising to her feet and walking to her clothing.

"That's it? I share my life and work with you, and you share only part with me. What a relationship."

"It's not my personal life. My work is top secret!"

"Big deal," he said, sinking down onto the bed.

"Harold"—she turned as she slipped on her blouse—"that's not fair and you know it. Your work is apparently not top secret from what you tell me."

"I think you enjoy keeping me in the dark."

"I'll pretend," Zita said angrily, turning to the door, "that this conversation never happened so my opinion of you won't be dashed." She slammed the door and walked rapidly into the hazy smog blanketing LA.

Her long strides carried her like the sharp edge of a knife cutting the muggy night. She'd lost her temper and didn't feel badly about it because she'd taken enough pressure. What did he want that couldn't wait a few short months?

A low-slung electric car silently slipped past her, and three teens whistled and shouted obscene come-on remarks. She pondered why men were so impatient in love and control. It seemed they had to have it all their way, and right now. What was it that her father used to say? Oh yes. "He who loves the least, controls the most," came to her mind. Was Harold insecure because she had secrets and he had revealed all? As a researcher, he should be able to understand her ethical duty.

On the other hand, she pondered, the entire thing would be revealed later. Maybe it didn't make that much difference—it was probably just academic anyway. After all, she did love him, and he'd been so good to her; yet she resented that last final surrender of her work. She wanted Harold to know she couldn't be pushed around. But she could feel herself giving way on the issue a bit. Maybe that was why she was so angry. She contemplated what might happen when she next saw him, if she'd open up. It would probably give them a lot to talk about. She could just see the shocked look on his handsome face when he learned of the tinted green and green-backed chimps totally hidden in the secure bowels of Quotech's research complex.

She enjoyed the long ride on the LATS back to her place. The city's night workers and cleaners again intrigued her with their somber and tired faces. What secrets did their lives hold? Life seemed hard for them. Did they really enjoy their work? She wished she could touch each with a magic wand, sending more money and total happiness their way. But she didn't believe such things made people happy in the long run; her life was that of a realist.

As the train pulled up to her stop, she observed with disgust the smoke shrouding the public lighting. There were many things she would change if she could just have the power. But her job was to tend to science. Maybe the workers she had looked at were happy since they didn't have such complicated lives and high-pressured work. She stole into the house and slipped into bed thinking more about the world's climate change and its plight than her personal troubles. That had always been a way for her to put the problems of life into perspective.

She took her lunch to work to avoid Harold the next day. At a meeting, she learned that herpetologists and other genetic engineers at Quotech had spliced chlorophyll-producing genes into iguana egg cells and had them fertilized. These little lizards were bright green and grew rapidly while eating very little. Zita was surprised to learn that such work was being done. It made her keenly aware that she knew only part of what was going on in the huge complex and other universities.

Later in his office at Quotech, Erick told her how this could someday lead to a positive food revolution worldwide. Put the genes into animals such as iguanas, cows, pigs, and they could live and be used as food without the costs of expensive feeding of grains or forage, and there would be little waste products. They would still need water, vitamins, and minerals. Erick, who was always looking for global improvement, said, "Such a step could help save the African midsection where desertification has been rampant for decades."

"But it could increase the world population. I just cannot concentrate on that social issue. I need to concentrate on my chimp work," said Zita. But she sought out and enjoyed playing with the tiny green iguanas and questioned if the trait could be passed on in them as well as it had in the chimpanzees.

She could see no practical end in her research on the green-skinned apes. Indeed, they were unique, but what could come of it all? Perhaps as a pure research scientist, she shouldn't answer such questions. Just to gain knowledge and edit gene were the goals. It was up to Charlie and others to direct it to profits. One must not get ahead of him and past official approval as Dr. Moby had done when starting this green chimp problem for Quotech. Yet Moby's work was most fascinating even though she still knew none of the secret details.

Since having isolated the genes responsible for transmitting of the green pigments in the primates, Zita was now searching for a new project direction. Charlie hadn't been a lot of help. She tried to see him over the next two days, but he was indisposed with some big crisis—as his office secretary told her. Zita hated just spinning her wheels, reading scientific papers, and not knowing what new research thrust was ahead.

After their past personal spats, Harold had usually contacted her in a day or two. But this time, she was taking the initiative with plans to put the dispute behind them. She hated being in limbo with both work and Harold. She waited three days and then called.

"Hello, is Harold there?" Zita asked the secretary at his unit's office in the far end of the complex.

"I'm sorry, Harold no longer works here."

"What do you mean?" questioned Zita. "Where did he go?"

"I can't answer that."

"Why not? I've got to know."

"I'm not authorized to give any more information than what I've told you, I'm sorry."

"Thank you," replied a deflated Zita, lowering the phone to her neck for a moment. Then she slammed it down and raced into Erick's office.

"They told me Harold doesn't work here anymore. Can you feature such a thing? Do you know anything?"

"Gee, sis, I haven't heard a thing. Charlie's the man to see. I hope it's not true, but they do make sudden changes."

"Yes, but why would he leave without a word to me? We are in love, Erick!" She gasped, sinking dejectedly down into a chair.

"I know. Let's go see Charlie."

"Lot of good it'll do. I've been tryin' to see him for three days and he's too busy."

"Come on anyway," Erick coaxed, extending his hand.

Together they walked into Charlie's office since his secretary amazingly indicated he was free.

His baldhead could be seen above the long table stacked high with journals, reports, and assorted papers. At the other end of his office, a clean and well-organized desk stood in naked contrast.

"Good morning, Starks," he said, his eyes coming into view. "Let's move over there where we can get this work out of my sight. I never get caught up on these cussed proposals and reports you people grind out."

"But don't you ask for most of them?" asked Erick. There was no response.

Zita followed him to the clean desk and waited until he sat down. "I just want to know the status of Harold Harms."

"I can tell you he's no longer working here as of yesterday," responded Charlie, squirming in his high-backed chair.

"Can you give us more details?" asked Erick.

He didn't answer immediately, placed his hand under his chin, and seemed to think deeply. "Under the circumstances, it would be extremely awkward. Why the interest?" probed Charlie, raising his eyebrows.

"Well, we knew him, and we're surprised he's suddenly gone and didn't even tell us goodbye," replied Erick.

"Yes, and the secretary down there won't even disclose where he went. Isn't that odd?" questioned Zita.

"Well, I think you'll have to leave it at that. If he wants to contact you, he will," muttered Charlie.

Zita burst out. "You've got to tell me, Charlie. We were very close."

"How close?"

"Well, if you must know, involved," she replied sheepishly. She knew well the old saying, "You shouldn't have your honey where you make your money."

"Oh! I see," Charlie said, his eyes opening widely for just a second and then his gaze falling to her knees, "Well." He paused and pursed his lips, his eyes seeming to inventory the room before he looked back at Zita. "Well, all right. But this can't be disclosed to anyone else. Cannot be! Understand!"

"We agree," said Zita, "but what's the big deal if he no longer works here?"

Charlie sighed. "Harold wasn't the man he seemed. By that, I mean he took advantage of the company and may have done the same with you."

"What was he then?" Zita asked. Her knees felt a little weak, and she slid back into the chair beside Charlie's desk.

"I can't give you details, but we think he's a biotech spy for another company. We noticed it when he became overly interested in other people's projects. And then our security people filmed him photocopying secret files. We have filed theft charges against him. This kind of messy thing needs to be kept quiet for now."

"We understand," said Erick.

Zita sat silently, feeling a numbness creeping into her, and wondered how this could be happening.

Charlie turned to her. "Zita, Harold may have developed a relationship with you to gather information. If that's the case, you may never hear from him again. But I need to know if you disclosed anything about the greenback research?"

"The jerk, he must be a spy!" she hissed. "He tried every way he could to get me to tell about my work. What pressure, Charlie! But I swear to you, I didn't tell him even what I did. So nothing was compromised." She was totally furious.

"Well, that ends that for you. Sorry! But we're in better shape than I expected." Charlie stood, shaking their hands. "Thanks for your integrity—it means a lot to the company. And remember, this doesn't go beyond my office. I'll let you know what happens as we continue contact with the louse."

The twins departed the office in silence. Erick knew Zita needed some time and didn't talk about the subject again. A few days later at dinner in their apartment, she emotionally unloaded as she could only to her brother. Finally, she dried her tears.

"You know my confidence has been shaken. To really have trusted a man and loved him. I'm so hurt. But using me for evil purposes makes me feel the fool too. He just played that role of the romance catalyst making things happen for me and not entering into them himself. It's all so unfair, Erick. I really cared for the guy."

"I know."

"He was too good, too perfect. I still can't believe he was a spy. Why, why, why?"

"It probably revolved around money and greed, Zita. Usually does."

"I suppose, but how could he have used me and totally discounted my feelings? Boy, was I a fool! To have actually trusted and loved him only to be used makes me ill. This is the second time in my life. Why me?"

Erick stood up and placed his hand on her shoulder. Hers soon grasped his. "At least you're strong enough not to let him destroy your ethics. I'm happy about that. In time, it will only seem like a bad experience and you learned something."

Getting up from the table and heading for the sink with the plates, she replied, "I learned that lesson the first time in Colorado. Perhaps now I'll never trust another man, or a scientist?"

"You can always trust me and our father. And there are still some other honest and decent men out there."

"I know. But I let myself love this guy. I was nearly to the point of telling him everything he wanted to know. I was just that close and getting so weak."

"I understand your frustration. You won't run into anyone like that again, and he can't be found. It's the kind of thing we usually read in fiction."

"Well, he was real to me. It makes me so mad how he took such a chunk out of my life by making me feel something—I was so happy."

That very next day, Charlie stopped her in the hall asking her to come to his office. "I need you to help me out with our board of directors next week."

"How might I do that?"

"Well, I need a short presentation after introducing you as one of our top female scientists in DNA work. Some new board members aren't up on the history of genetics and splicing work, and I need to fill the agenda. Maybe just ten or fifteen minutes would do on the background of big stuff, hitting the main points."

She wondered if he only wanted to show her off as an attractive female to those old men. "Do you want me to run my comments by you first?"

"No, it's your field, and I'm not very up to date with that changing stuff now. Will do me some good too."

"I'll just give an overview."

"Fine."

In a huge boardroom with a long oak table surrounded by gray-haired men, Zita began with basic DNA.

"Once a woman scientist, Rosalind Franklin, in England figured out the ladder structure of DNA, it all made sense. We understood that the A, T, C, and Gs are the base pairs making up the ladder's rungs of the genetic code for all plants and animals on earth. We then knew how genetics worked in a simple code of four bases in our genes on chromosomes, and some DNA in the mitochondria." She showed the codes on a power-point screen, and then continued. "But what the codes do is highly complicated inside the genes of all living things on earth. Then the Human Genome Project had top scientists spend ten years mapping the twenty thousand protein coding functional human genes. They have now an estimated 3 billion base pairs of coding in those twenty thousand genes in all of us.

"And today, we in genetics have mapped those in many other living things, all having the basic DNA with only differing codes. Even in its highly complicated codes inside cells, this was a starting place to work with genes, codes, and the DNA and RNA in any living thing. Genetics is the perfect tool to use to study the differing codes in all creatures and plants that control life structures and functions with proteins and enzymes. Mind you, this is all horribly complicated chemistry in a world beyond any microscope.

"Are you with me? Then years of strides were made by scientists around the world trying to work with the code to alter it and help change living things in all kinds of ways. That work was vast and slow as understandings increased about the tiny codes inside cells and genes, one heck of a job for sure probing nature's secrets is so highly complicated. I won't bore you with all the equipment and computer details we use, but I'll jump to the next big steps getting us to today's major work.

"Sharp scientists found and recovered nucleotide sequences in bacteria that could alter DNA in fighting viruses. Then they discovered these same chemicals would do it in the cells of plants and animals. Astonishing!

"It is called CRISPR, and these special nucleotide sequences can be used to alter DNA and thus edit genes. These special sequences serve as guides for an enzyme called CAS9, a molecular scissors, that cuts DNA at specific points. CAS9-cut DNA sequences can be removed from genes inside cells or added to other genes to create different gene forms. This new technology allows us to edit virtually any gene by altering its DNA sequence. That is how we can change DNA in living cells and change life.

"That, gentlemen, is exactly what we do in our research and have done to edit and change the genetic code in plants and animals. It has opened a new world, allowing changes in animals and plants that all have the same material in their genes, but only differing codes. We can now edit and change those codes of life. That is what I do for you."

She answered many questions and shook hands with some board members.

Then Zita scurried back to her office preparing to be gone for eight days to a Molecular Congress of leading-edge genetics. She had now been with Quotech for two years and some perks were coming her way. This was a trip to a small unpolluted paradise called New Zealand near the opposite end of the earth. This trip would alter her life in ways she never suspected.

6 Unexpected Ventures

Zita had something new to occupy her mind venturing on her first international trip to one of the most beautiful and pristine countries left on earth. She felt glad to get away to somewhere else and put Harold thoughts behind her. As the plane's wheels gently touched down on the concrete runway, she felt it surge a bit from side to side. The power slowdown phase thrust her forward in her seat even as she was restrained by the tight seatbelt. She hated landing and taking off, but while high in the sky, she experienced only the personal joy of escape.

After such a long flight, Zita wondered if she would enjoy her stay. Just prior to landing, the Southern Alps had impressed her, poking a string of snowcapped heads upward below the aircraft on its decent into Christchurch. The greenest of emerald plains surrounded New Zealand's second largest city. She had never had a desire to see the islands, but Charlie insisted on sending her. He felt the World Congress of Genetic and Molecular Engineers would give her a leading edge and updated research ideas. She hadn't resisted but would have preferred having someone along.

As she waited at the airport, a large wall mural of an ancient bird caught her eye with the information that it was a meat eater and grew seven feet tall. She paused wondering how such a creature, being flightless, could reach these isolated islands fifteen hundred miles from Australia with no large islands in between. Although now extinct, the carnivorous bird was alive and thriving when people in canoes found and first settled the land.

Her mind raced in speculation as she waited. No bird that size could reach the island naturally. Thus, it must have arrived on the islands ages ago and in a different form, and it must have flown and had both male and female pairs to survive. Hence there must have been millions of years of mutations to render the animal wingless, huge, and a meat eater. Most likely it, similar to penguins, underwent gene transformations reducing wings yet not hindering its survival. Back then, food must have been so abundant that changes in size to larger did not matter as the DNA mutated for eons of time. The bird may have moved from a plant diet to animal tissues since there were no other huge competing predators on the landscape at the time. They may have roamed the landscape as the top of the food chain on both New Zealand islands.

Millions of years later, humans from faraway islands entered the scene as top predators, eating the bird's huge eggs and slaying them into oblivion for meat over many recent decades. Humans then had to turn to the seas and rivers for fish protein since no other large animals inhabited the land. That genetic code for the huge birds sadly would have been lost forever. Suddenly, the bus appeared, halting her thinking.

The bus ride to her hotel showed her a city far different from Los Angeles. The air was as crystal clear as the city was spotlessly clean. Homes were small with highly flowered yards. In fact, she had never seen so many brilliant rose blossoms except in botanic gardens. It was a far cry from the dull yards in LA where few flowers could survive the stifling air and water was now too costly to maintain green lawns. Christchurch yards were filled with myriads of striking colors and strange species of trees, and the grasses below were refreshingly brilliant green. Traffic was light and buses were many as they raced along in the left lanes. She sat in rapt attention until they stopped at the Old Dominion Hotel, one of the city's oldest.

She noticed people drove in the left lane and walked on the opposite side of the sidewalks and in her hotel hallways. Such a small change it was, but somehow exciting. She was pleased with her small room in the ancient hotel. Everything was probably new back in the Victorian age. She loved the old bathtub with its clawed feet and archaic fixtures.

After a quick soaking bath, a good night's sleep, and a breakfast of fruit and cheese, she changed and walked the three blocks to the Convention Center to pick up her registration materials. Noting that people looked left to see the traffic coming as they crossed the streets reminded her to do the same to avoid being hit.

The registration area was packed, yet amazingly her packet of materials was there. Charlie's assistants had done a fine job in planning her meeting, she thought. Today was reserved for excursions, field trips, and visitations, and she wasn't yet signed up. She waited in the long line pondering which trip to take. There were big-game farms, laboratories, bird sanctuaries, botanic gardens, and national park tours, all looked inviting. Just as it was her turn, a tall silvery-haired man cut in front of her to exchange his tour ticket for one going to Mount Cook. She was a bit irritated but decided to let nothing upset her on this trip.

The man turned and apologized, "Sorry to jump line, but they gave me the wrong ticket, for the second time."

"That's OK. I hope they've gotten things right now," she replied, glancing up at his nametag. Her eyes focused in disbelief: Dr. Alexander Moby, Union of South Africa. She was aghast.

"May I help you?" asked the clerk. Zita stood staring at the man disappearing into the crowd. She had no choice but to take the same tour.

"I'll take a Mount Cook and Hermitage if you have any left."

"You're lucky. This is the last one. Bus leaves at ten thirty. They serve a lunch on the trip too."

Zita walked to the elevator packed with all men scientists. Someone behind her squeezed her buttocks. It made her extremely angry, but she decided to ignore it. She didn't have time for a scene and only hoped that New Zealand men were better mannered than these science conventioneers from across the world. Her mind was working overtime thinking of having met the elusive Moby face-to-face.

At the bus boarding area, she worked her way close to Dr. Moby and boarded directly behind him. He chose a window seat, and she settled in beside him. He quickly said, "Sorry again for line jumping ahead of you in my ticket mess."

"Glad you got what you needed. It was no problem for me getting the last one for this trip."

The bright green landscape outside seemed to hold his attention. He didn't speak again until they were nearly out of the city. Zita sat in rapt attention watching the beautiful verdant trees and grazing white sheep.

"It's going to be a beautiful day to see the glaciers," he finally said.

"I didn't know we could see them from the bus."

"They fly us up from the Hermitage lodge, or so it says in this description," he said.

"My name's Zita Stark."

"I'm Alex Moby. Nice to meet you, and I again apologize for back there. They had really given me the runaround," he answered, looking her directly in the eyes and shaking hands. His hand was warm and firm with no wedding ring. About forty something, she guessed. Gray hair must have come early for his face was not that of an older man. She wondered if this was the prudent course to be taking—yet her curiosity had the best of her. What luck, to actually meet the genius who had placed the plant genes into her chimps? She quickly decided not to identify herself with any company lest he brand her a spy from Quotech. It might be natural for him to do that and have nothing to do with her. She was curious about the man, only wanting to know more about him.

Zita turned the pages of the World Congress Program and started marking sessions worth attending. When Alex noticed what she was doing, he said, "I have a paper session there on page 22—I think."

She found the page and read aloud, "Recombinant Gene Editing of DNA and RNA Transfers Between Organisms of Different Kingdoms." She was pleased knowing he hadn't shifted his field of scientific endeavor.

"That's me."

"Sounds intriguing," Zita replied, "I've never worked between kingdoms in the laboratory." She knew it was not an honest reply, but she feared turning him away from her.

"It's a challenge. The results are sometimes startling—most unpredictable."

"Maybe I'll just attend your session tomorrow."

"I'd be honored."

"You sound very American, but the program shows you're South African."

"Yes, I'm a Yank. But I do work in Pretoria for an organization. It's a long story how I got there. Too dull for a lovely day on these Canterbury Plains. Aren't those beautiful hills?" They were extremely green and dotted with snow-white sheep.

"I've never been around such green and so many sheep. It sure is different than where I grew up in South Dakota. Yet I do love wool."

They made small talk and were awed by the New Zealand countryside. The topography changed rapidly from the lush grassy coastal plain to the upland dry tussock grasslands. It appeared almost Wyoming-like with scattered bunch grass but lacked Wyoming's common big sagebrush. Soon white Lake Pokekia filled the horizon.

"It's white as milk," exclaimed Zita.

"Yes, glacial origin," Moby replied. "Suspended particles from the glaciers make it look like satin, but the water stays cold."

"Interesting, but I didn't expect it to be so white like this." Above it rose the great peaks of the Southern Alps. The bus groaned along its shore on the narrow road.

A petrol and restroom break stopped them beyond the lake at a sheep station surrounded by evergreen trees. They walked around, stretching their legs, Zita marveling at the clean freshness, the big sky overhead, and the wide-open wild countryside. She could live here crossed her mind.

"This is so beautiful and unspoiled. You wouldn't even have to pull your shades," she remarked.

Alex replied, "Much like many places in Australia or South Africa. Think I like the southern hemisphere since it has fewer people and smaller landmass. Also, it's less polluted."

She sensed the loneliness of an unsatisfied man in his voice and asked how long he'd been in South Africa. It had been over two years, he said, adding how part of that country was quite similar to southern California. They visited most of the way to the Hermitage Hotel near towering Tasman Mountain, which was dwarfed by Mount Cook's rising snowfields far beyond. Ice fields capped Mount Sefton that blocked the valley to the south as glacial moraines covered its floor in front of them, reminding her of giant gopher mounds pushed up at random from below. Yellow greens dominated the landscape and emerald blue skies canopied above them, a breathtaking spot.

Alex invited her to accompany him on the flight up to the Tasman Glacier in the small airplane that held only two passengers. It was part of the tour for those who wanted to set foot on a real southern hemisphere glacier, one of the last in a climate changed world. He told her that he hadn't seen a glacier in years. How could she refuse? Her mind was racing with questions she dared not ask.

The takeoff on a dirt runway scared her as she sat frozen clutching her seat belt with both hands. Later she was struck by the length of the Southern Alps for they extended beyond her view from high above the glacier. Zita closed her eyes when they squared away to land on the shiny glacier's surface. How she despised landing. She could imagine it now, Erick and Charlie reading of her death with Dr. Moby. Was it insane being with him and playing this game? However, he was interesting and polite.

The plane bumped down safely on the snow and ice, gliding to a halt. Now she feared flying off the icy surface. Why was she doing this when she had no interest in glaciers? They walked about the glacier's slick surface admiring the view of the jagged peaks heaved to heaven surrounding them. It was the first glacier upon which she had stood with medial moraines and melt streams exactly as those she'd studied in introductory geology in Colorado. Blinding glare from the ice and the bitterly cold winds finally shortened their stay.

Within a few moments, they'd risen off the glacier. They hadn't crashed, so she again opened her eyes and enjoyed the scenery as they flew down toward the landing strip near the Hermitage Hotel.

"Fearful about flying?"

"Uneasy for sure," she replied, realizing he must have seen her clenched fists during takeoff.

Alex was soon pointing out red deer and goat-like Himalayan Tar on the side of Mount Tasman when the engine suddenly coughed, sputtered, and stopped. Zita's heart jumped to her throat, and she clutched Alex's arm as the pilot said, "Be sure your seat belts are tight. Hang on, and I'll land this bloody thing."

Alex clutched her hands as she sat frozen stiff with fear in the silent gliding airplane. Always she had been petrified about being in a plane crash; now it was coming true. She could see the pilot searching for a landing spot as he radioed his position reporting engine failure. In vain, he twice attempted to restart the engine.

But down they glided, narrowly missing a mountaintop, and entered the long valley with the hotel on the right side. Banking the plane to the left, the pilot headed for the road.

"Alex, do we have a chance to reach that road?"

"I bloody well think so unless the winds hold us back. It's much flatter down there."

"I've always been lucky," muttered Zita. "Maybe it will work for us."

"I pray so."

Like a winged maple seed in the wind, the plane glided toward the rough graveled highway. Soon it was apparent that they were falling short. Brush struck the wheels of the aircraft with slapping noises as they dropped to the cleared area alongside the uplifted road. The aircraft bounced once, came down with the wheels against the road's shoulder, and upended. Zita could feel the plane in slow motion standing on its nose in the road skidding along vertically. Suddenly it was upside down, a hail of shattering glass and metal felling about them. Then all was still.

She unbuckled her seatbelt and slid to the roof among debris. "Alex, are you all right?"

"Yes, but I can't find the buckle on this damn seatbelt." It was twisted behind him, and with her help, he was soon free. He kicked the small door open, and they crawled outside. There had been no movement from the pilot.

They raced around the upside-down plane, seeing a cement highway post protruding into the cockpit from below. They reached in and unbuckled the pilot, easing him down and pulling him free.

They noticed blood trickling from his mouth and nose. Perhaps the post had struck him as it came through the top of the cockpit.

"I can't get a pulse, and he's not breathing, Zita."

"Let's do chest compressions. Someone will come by soon."

For fifteen to twenty minutes, they took turns doing chest compressions and breathing into the pilot. Then he resumed breathing on his own and showed a heartbeat. A medical doctor and helper from the hotel arrived in a van and rushed the pilot to another plane now waiting on the dirt highway. He hadn't regained consciousness, but was still breathing as the plane headed for Christchurch.

Then the medical doctor insisted on checking them out once the pilot was airborne in the rescue plane. Seatbelts had prevented any major injuries from the crash according to the doctor, but now they were both shaken thinking what might have been.

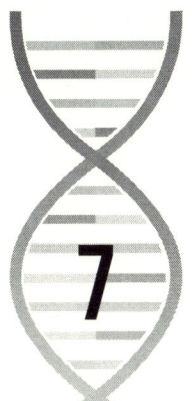

7 New Zealand Insights

When they finally reached the Hermitage Hotel, a crowd of people asking questions pushed in surrounding them. Alex finally said, "We've been through a lot, so please leave us alone to collect our wits. Later we'll talk with you in the lobby. I promise." And they all politely left.

Hotel staff found a quiet guest lounge for them. Zita sat on a couch with muddied knees, torn blouse, and ripped skirt. Her hair was in disarray and one shoe was missing. Tea was thrust upon them in fine New Zealand style, milk coloring it to a light rusty brown. In the following hour, they were better able to compose themselves and review the crash. A hotel maid found Zita some shoes and clothing in the park's lost and found. Thanks to their tight seat belts, neither had more than minor scratches.

Later, after cleaning up, they sat in the Hermitage's grand lobby, viewing Mount Cook beyond the giant picture windows. Just hours earlier, they had been enjoying it up close during their flight.

Zita turned to Alex. "Just shows how precious and fragile life really is. We are so lucky to be here. That pilot did a fine job for us, don't you think?"

"Yes, I agree, and we need to thank him. We do rush about doin' our important work as if we're immortal scientists."

"It could've been all over for us if he hadn't found level land."

"I know. First engine failure for me."

"Maybe we'd better cherish every moment and enjoy our lives, never worrying about death."

"Or better yet, live as all other animals do, unaware and incapable of thinking about death. Let it come as a total surprise— it does anyway, I suppose." Alex looked at his watch. Just thirty minutes until the tour bus ride back to Christchurch.

"Please don't accept any more invitations from me takin' you out for a wreck."

She laughed and relaxed and enjoyed the tea.

"Let's not languish here and talk to these people. I want to walk. Let's start down the road after we ask the bus driver to pick us up."

"Great idea, I need to use these legs and get used to these new shoes."

Using their pent-up energy, they hiked nearly a mile, passed the crash site, looked for but couldn't find her other shoe, and were finally picked up by the tour bus.

"Now that was refreshing. You're a fast walker."

"Yes, I'm a faster lady than you realize," replied Zita, winking at him. Suddenly she felt foolish, like a teenager on a first date.

"I know you're excellent at chest compressing and walking. I wouldn't dare to race you," answered Alex, avoiding Zita's earlier implication. "Do you like to dance?"

"Love it."

"I was thinking, would you like to attend the congress mixer tonight with me?"

"Yes." Suddenly she realized to whom she was speaking. This was the secretive scientist of green chimp genetics who had knowledge of techniques far beyond hers. What would Erick think if he knew what she was now doing, and even going dancing with a great scientist?

Mixers are intended to bring conventioneers together socially. Alex and she needed none of that as they glided across the floor enjoying the music, the ballroom hits of the old times from their youth. They lost track of time and danced into the night. When it was all over, he stopped at her room door and politely bid her good night.

Impulsively she kissed him on the cheek saying, "You have been wonderful for such a wild day. I'll see you at your session in the morning."

He walked away, then turned, and said, "I'd like to pay a visit to the pilot in the hospital a visit tomorrow afternoon. Would you care to join me?"

"Yes, let's work it out after your presentation. Good night, Alex."

She closed the door and leaned backward against it. Why was she feeling attracted to this man? She had to gain control of herself, or else she was headed for trouble. Her urges had told her to invite him in, but that was too much for her following that crazy day and probably for him too.

After a continental breakfast in her room, Zita sat alone near the front at the general session. Everyone in the grand ballroom awaited the keynote speaker. The meeting's general chairperson came to the microphone with a paper in hand to make a special announcement.

"It seems," he reported, "that the American Congress Joint Conference Committee have just reached agreement on the Genetic Engineering Act. The new provisions allow changes in using primates and humans in gene research to improve human health and genetics. Most of us in genetics didn't see this coming in the US."

He paused and then looked up. "The American president still has to sign the legislation before it becomes law. But how timely this is for the work of many attending here today!" Loud applause echoed through the large hall from its nearly two thousand participants.

Zita was stunned. She knew the legislation had been pending but didn't think it had a serious chance of passing with any provisions allowing genetic engineering to improve humans. Perhaps the Italian human/ape development had hastened their decision, nudging them into loosening controls. This trip had been full of surprises, and she now felt grateful to Charlie for encouraging her to attend.

Later she attended the paper session presentation by Dr. Moby. It was highly theoretical dealing with nuclear and cytoplasmic DNA and RNA in editing, splicing, and recombining. He seemed deliberately vague in specifying which exact organisms were involved in cross kingdom transfers. She couldn't determine exactly if he was working with the cells of higher or lower organisms.

Perhaps it really didn't matter, but she couldn't help thinking it was all connected to his past work in producing green apes. Overall, as a speaker, he was brilliant and projected the image of an all-knowing and kindly Greek science god.

Afterward she moved to the lectern and congratulated him on his presentation. Appearing poised, he projected the image of a diplomat or chief executive officer of some multinational corporation.

After attending several more sessions together, they took the cab ride to the hospital. To their delight, the pilot was conscious and alert. He had suffered a skull fracture, shock, and some minor internal injuries along with broken ribs. Overall, he was lucky to be alive from how the post struck him. He embarrassed Zita when he thanked them for saving his life. They had come to convey that same message to him. And it embarrassed him since he said, "Landing you safely back from the glacier was my job."

The pilot thought the up-valley winds had prevented them from reaching the road where a smooth landing would have worked. From his point of view, chest compressing was not their jobs either. In his New Zealand accent, he again properly expressed his appreciation for his life.

Not wanting the pilot to have to incur any medical costs since he had saved their lives, they asked the hospital staff about paying his medical expenses. They were cheerfully informed that New Zealand had a cradle to grave health care system that took care of all citizens, even foreign visitors.

Alex had held Zita's hand in the taxi from the hospital. She responded by squeezing his in return. How comfortable she felt with this man as the common bond of nearly losing their lives now seemed to pull them closer. Before they reached downtown Christchurch, Alex had the cab stop, and they walked along the Avon River arm in arm.

A green belted area hugged the stream on each side. Ducks bobbed in water so clear they could see large rainbow trout swimming below. Also using the streams were children in small paddleboats and young lovers floating lazily along in plastic canoes. Verdant grass and numerous yellow flowers bordered the banks.

Young and old people walked, sat on benches, or embraced under the trees. Alex paused at a great spread of daffodils in their yellow splendor surrounded by soft pink roses. He sat and pulled her down to smell the flowers. Gently he held her and kissed her lips. She was a bit shocked, but relaxed slowly in his arms.

"Perhaps you think I'm forward. It's like I've known you a long time—not just two days."

Zita replied, "My thoughts have been along those same lines. It's a nice feeling, but scary to happen so fast." They embraced several times before stretching out on the grass surrounded by the daffodils.

"This is our own private world," Alex said, "We can hear the water gurgle and distant voices of other people, but the flowers block them all out except the blue sky."

"It's perfect."

On that late afternoon, they lay there close to the Avon River and talked of many things, how they were raised and schooled, their parents, and dreams as kids. Zita told him in great detail of her NASA work with the biopacks. She even revealed working for a genetic engineering company and how all she did was classified by her contract. He understood her position, having been in exactly that type of situation. They laughed at the silly nature of it all since top secrets today become public common knowledge sometimes in as little as a few months. It was nice having such rewarding jobs, but the profit motives of the companies caused them both to feel corporate research could end at any whim. Neither felt any conflict with the other since they were, after all, working in different countries.

Alex finally said, "Today we in advanced molecular biology and genetics are in a new world. How do you feel about where our science is going?"

"I sometimes worry about what will happen in the long run and if it will better the world," replied Zita. "But let's not talk shop now."

That evening they attended the big banquet together and enjoyed a drink afterward. The speaker was a Nobel winner who pointed to new directions in gene splicing for the good of the planet. Both she and Alex were impressed. Both knew hopes for improvement rested with political approval following scientific advances. In their views, international cooperation had long been supportive on insignificant issues but totally lacking on significant situations worldwide.

At her door, they kissed several times with increasing passion before she led him inside. Later, and as with most first lovemaking, both were a bit overwhelmed and nervous. But he had been a gentle lover and she accepted him with grace and passion. Spent, they lay in each other's arms and drifted to sleep in her bed.

Alex awoke seeming embarrassed that he had spent the night. Quickly he dressed and slipped out to his own room. She watched him with a slightly opened eye that he didn't detect in his haste out the door.

Later he called, and they breakfasted together, and attended several meetings. Alex seemed a bit aloof after their night together. Zita appreciated seeing him a bit off balance from his usually poised manner.

"I'm embarrassed about how fast things took place last night," he said.

Zita smiled and said, "It's all right. You have nothing to feel sorry about."

Finally, he leaned across the table. "I plan to take seven days following this congress as holiday on this island. Would you be able to extend your trip and join me?"

Zita thought briefly. "I could probably extend for that much time. I'll have to contact my boss. I'll just tell him this is a onetime opportunity to see New Zealand. But of course, being with you would be wonderful as well."

She then attended a presentation on New Zealand and its history designed for spouses of attending science people. Her aim was to learn more about New Zealand for the upcoming trip.

Projected images of Captain James Cook and his search for the long-sought Southern continent by England in the 1700s opened her mind. He was on these islands before other Europeans had influenced the Maori people. They had lived here a few thousand years after coming vast distances by sea from other distant islands to the east.

Zita was impressed by how Captain Cook had used onions and other ascorbic acid plants to prevent and cure scurvy on his vessels before other explorers had. His vast and accurate charting of islands in the Pacific had been a boon for later ships over hundreds of years. Additionally, his ship was the first to cross the Antarctic Circle, and he went on to determine no human inhabitable continent existed at the bottom of the world as it was way too cold for humans.

She was deeply impressed how accurately Cook had charted the two New Zealand islands and many others on several voyages with his ships *Resolution* and *Adventure* in 1773 and earlier on his first voyages. He was a true explorer who moved science forward as a man of the sea and not a scientist. And like most English sea captains, he could not swim since waters around his British home islands were bitter cold. Learning to swim was to be avoided because it would bring bad luck. That was a seafaring superstition of the time in England.

On his last voyage in 1773, Zita learned that his two ships were separated by storms of great winds in New Zealand waters. His second ship *Adventure* was separated from him and awaited as long as possible in a harbor missing him by a few days. His fellow captain, Furneaus, sent a working party ashore to gather supplies of wood and water. Those ten men never returned to his ship. All ten had been killed and eaten by the Maoris, and the *Adventure* departed once they learned of the cannibalism by finding the scattered crewmembers' remains ashore.

Captain Cook, upon his later return in the same port, suspected cannibalism and ordered his cook to prepare a meal of a freshly dead crewmember for a visiting group of Maoris on the *Resolution*. They zestfully enjoyed it, confirming their cannibalism to James Cook who soon set sail. He had wanted to be sure of his conclusions as a scientist would. This impressed Zita. The presenter speculated that the lack of large mammals and the extinction of the huge birds had left the island short of protein on land, but fish in the streams and ocean were abundant.

As she was leaving the presentation, she heard one scientist say, "You know what a cannibal is?"

Another asked, "No?"

"It's a person who likes his fellow man with potatoes and gravy."

Some laughed as they entered the elevator, but not Zita who headed to meet her new friend for a meatless lunch.

Over the next two days, Zita reached the saturation point of attending meeting after meeting. Charlie finally answered her request and granted additional vacation days. That kept her going to other meetings and spending the evenings with Alex.

She absorbed all the leading-edge information in genetic engineering her mind and notepad could record. If it hadn't been for Alex, she would have failed to see the meetings to their bitter end. She felt a renewed dedication and would bring the latest research and controversial thinking back to Erick and Charlie and her lab assistants. She was thankful, however, when the conference adjourned, giving her total freedom.

8　Travel Research

After having rented a hybrid car, they crossed the Canterbury Plains and drove on to Queenstown, a lakeside resort nestled beside towering snowcapped peaks and sharply wooded hills. It was pristinely inspiring in beauty, offering a relaxed atmosphere. Scattered tourists roamed the short streets, while vacationing New Zealanders fished the big deep lake adjacent the town.

They decided to stay in a small lakeside B&B where they could see exquisite wild ferns bordering the blue choppy water. At this visual paradise, Alex decided he wanted to go fishing. He then learned of a hot location from the fish depot shopkeeper. The man happily directed them to a small lake nearby after renting Alex fishing gear.

At the small lake, Zita watched from the shore as Alex, all decked out in his fishing duds, tried his luck in Moke Lake. Three New Zealanders were already fishing there, wading out in chest-deep water. Zita watched with interest as they flailed the water with their long fly rods. When they hooked a trout, they played it until it was tired out then brought it in close and whacked it over the head with a small Billy club. Their two-foot-long trout catch was then thrust into huge canvas creels that dangled from the men's shoulders.

Seeing Alex fishing in relatively deep water caused her to reflect on Captain Cook's demise in a Hawaiian Island harbor. Cook had returned from exploring Alaska's coast when one of his small boats went missing—apparently stolen by the natives on shore in Hawaii.

He and his marines confronted a throng of the native people and demanded his boat returned to the *Resolution*. Then violence set in caused by Cook's men firing guns.

Up to that point, Cook and his crew had been wonderfully treated by the Hawaiians who were all a head taller than James Cook and his European crew. Zita had learned at the congress program that the Island Effect had taken place in the population of people who had sailed from Polynesia ages before, making them isolated far from any visitors until Cook discovered them in the 1870s. They were a richly fed people in a tropical paradise that totally amazed Cook and his much-smaller sailors. Yet they were also a warlike people not to be pushed around.

Island Effect changes animals who come to a new land of plenty. Over time, these animals such as elephants, rhinos, and hippos have a population explosion on islands. And as time goes on and competition for food increases, the huge ones die off when food became scarce. This lets those with genes for smaller size to better survive while the huge animals do not pass their genes along for their huge size. Over thousands of years, mutations keep happening, keeping smaller animals alive, and they survive in balance with their reduced food supply.

Zita had been told that the opposite happened in Hawaii when there was unlimited food from the sea and land, allowing the big people to survive even as they became larger and taller from mutations over vast time. These were the large and tall islanders who turned on Captain Cook in their fight over a missing boat.

Cook and his few marines with rifles on shore fired at the Hawaiian crowd as it pressed in pinning Cook against the shore. Cook's men in small boats were only about fifty feet off shore supporting him with more gunfire. When the natives pressed in, Cook did not know how to swim out to the boats. He stayed ashore and was slain. She now worried that Alex might not be able to swim as he fished chest-deep water in his rubber waders. Then she thought he must know what he was doing.

Then Zita remembered how that speaker had linked the Island Effect to humans. It was first discovered on the Indonesian island of Flores where scientists uncovered twenty-thousand-year-old ancient human remains that measured only three feet tall. Genetic mutations had occurred for eons apparently altering the size of prehistoric humans downward. These reducing mutations made them a tiny half size, allowing them to survive. It was better than evolving twice as large when *Homo erectus,* their ancestor, had probably first populated Flores. She knew DNA is always slowly mutating in plants, animals, and humans over the eons of time. This history of islands and changed people enhanced her thinking.

She could never comprehend tens of thousands or millions of years as DNA mutated and changed life, and she could never get her mind around a million years, light-years, or even infinity.

Sitting in the car, she compared how DNA through mutations changed life in the natural world. That was opposed to how new gene editing was being done very quickly with all kinds of organisms, thus, bypassing evolution. Her and Alex's cellular work imitated slow natural mutations by fast changing life. She pondered if was too fast or too slow.

Alex was thrilled to catch two beauties over twenty inches long. New Zealand trout fishing was supposed to be some of the best left in the polluted world. Zita was happy for him, and he acted like a schoolboy displaying his garnered trophies. He recited a long-ago quote from American president Herbert Hoover, "Every fishing day is a day added to your life."

"Sure, a good way to justify a hobby." He chuckled.

They made several stops on the return back to Queenstown, one when she spotted a kea, big parrot-like greenish bird, and wanted a closer view. They also stopped and walked through a lakeside bank of thick tree ferns unique to New Zealand. Standing under tree ferns taller than Alex gave Zita a tingling feeling of being in the eon of great dinosaurs sixty-six million years ago. How she loved to imagine creatures of the deep past who are now extinct.

"Alex, this is a wonderful place. I could stay a week."

"Me too. But there is so much more to see on this island that we just can't."

"I know, I know. And these wonderful islands have no mosquitoes or biting flies."

"Nor poison snakes, but great trout."

That evening, their bed-and-breakfast hosts prepared Alex's trout as a delicious dinner. Fishing was a main topic with the two other guests. Zita hadn't imagined that catching fish was such a passion with New Zealanders as it was with Alex.

Later in a waterfront pub over glasses of dark ale, they relaxed, and Alex opened up.

"I had always wanted to be a pilot, but poor eyesight prevented that. So I ended up in genetic work at Stanford, did graduate work at Harvard, and eventually worked for several bioengineering companies. I'd detested the regulations and short-ranged goals that had limited research work. So I always had a shadow research project of my own beside my official work. This was to keep me sane, having something that was geared toward pure science rather than practical science for some later profit goals. Most of my bosses and people in the field had not been interested or sharp enough to spot what I was doing on the side.

"I had done tissue culture and gene-splicing work with primates for an upstart company. There my shadow project led me to engineer chlorophyll from algae into animal cells. This was a great feat, I thought, but because it came from shadow work and not my official work, the shortsighted administrators couldn't see its value and forced me out. They were, in my opinion, scared of regulations and couldn't see a breakthrough when it was right before their eyes. So I left that company without disclosing my detailed techniques, but left behind several green pigmented animals.

"That company blackballed me in the USA, preventing employment with other leading American companies. I resented their actions. So I'd taken a South African position with total freedom to work, but that closed state limited my avenues to communicate my results. South Africa had for the second time switched to a white-controlled nation intent on keeping black people as low-class workers. Somehow, they knew of my work in California and had offered me a gigantic bonus and super big salary to work there in total secret. I took the position despite its restrictions wanting to continue my green genetic work.

"Working in that country was safe and highly secret. That white government did not want colored people to rise up again killing off white elites, scientists, and politicians as they did in their last revolution. They were now intent on engineering genetic potential downward and producing new black people who could be worker bees and easily controlled. At least that was what I heard unofficially as the direction for their long term. And of all things, the UN has recognized the regime as a member, provided funds to help the colored people, but it is being detoured into ways to control or change them.

"I still couldn't seem to win for losing and am frustrated because I don't have a position giving me both freedom of research and open communications with the broad scientific world. They even had to approve my presentation at this meeting. I couldn't go beyond my paper you heard."

Listening intently, Zita knew the American company he was talking about, but said nothing. He had filled in details she always wondered about. He became more engrossed and spoke technically about how he'd done the work in California. Yet she noticed that he was guarded, never mentioning he had left green chimps behind. She asked only a few questions, nodded, and let him ramble on and on. He seemed to have the need to talk about his past work.

Alex paused, looked into her gray eyes, and said, "It's fine to tell you all this if I don't disclose the US company. That's an agreement I unfortunately made with them. And they can't disclose it properly, use it, or gain publicly since they don't know exactly how I did the work. They would be labeled frauds in courts if others couldn't do the same again. I've got them where I want 'em." He laughed.

Zita was all ears. Amazingly he went on disclosing that he hadn't introduced any chlorophyll-producing DNA or genes into the animals. Scientists had long known that hemoglobin molecules were usually present in many plant cells. Genes for the hemoglobin had first been found in *Trema tomentosa*, a subtropical tree. Finally, it was found in all trees, but difficult to detect in any structure except the roots.

From this finding, Alex told her he had remembered how similar in structure chlorophyll and hemoglobin were. Hemoglobin had an iron atom in the molecule center and the chlorophyll was magnesium centered, otherwise they were almost alike. Since plants had hemoglobin and that molecule was a cousin to chlorophyll, he deduced that animals could have a kind of hidden chlorophyll. He had taken a quantum leap assuming that all animals carried chlorophyll genes, which were totally masked except in green euglenoids and other one-celled organisms. It was known as the gene-junk in cells. His work involved locating these hidden genes and treating them with unmasking chemicals in the gametes—eggs and sperm cells. Once unmasked, they produced the green animals with plastids that carried on photosynthesis.

"I hope this isn't boring you."

"My god, no, it's exciting. I'm intrigued," she replied, hardly believing her ears. This idea had never occurred to anyone before.

"It all started way back when . . .," Alex said, "I don't want to take credit for early work done in our area. As you know, I think we stand on the shoulders of those people who came up with all the steps in genes after the genome work. After they finally finished mapping the human genome, molecular and genetic research really took off. We now know exactly what was in our human cells. And for that matter, we could and did map the DNA of other plants and animals too."

"Yes, Alex, that was a leap forward of huge magnitude, letting researchers know exactly what they were dealing with. All a bit before my time but so complicatedly wonderful. Bless their work."

"We didn't bless it, but we used it in all kinds of ways."

Zita replied, "When they came up with CRISPR, the door opened wider. I still can't believe how well the advanced gene editing has worked for medical research."

"And then came the cutting, editing, and splicing in DNA since all life has the same basic components. How stunning to help shape the future, now that we are able to switch gene codes large and small back and forth."

"As you say, piggyback CRISPR/Cas 9 on top of that, and we were on the precipice to change the genes of any living thing on earth—cut and paste—for better or worse, depending how people view it."

"But, Zita, that is sandbox stuff compared to what we're doing today in South Africa and with our chemicals and computer-driven work. What I don't understand is how people are fine with changes in other creatures, but they don't want it in humans to improve them? We all know that DNA codes are codes, exchangeable, and made of the same stuff in all living things."

"How about no more shop talk since we took this side trip to get away from science and enjoy New Zealand." She thought he would surely cover it all in the coming days.

"I just can't leave this alone."

"Neither can I actually."

"My biggest breakthrough on all this was finding the chlorophyll genes in two places. Some are in the nucleus, but there were others in the cytoplasm. You know that cytoplasmic DNA everyone supposes is a relict and not functional, but comes from our mothers. Well, I couldn't get green animals by unmasking the nuclear DNA genes alone. It took the unmasking of both the nuclear and cytoplasmic codes in the mitochondria simultaneously in the same cells. It was a real trick, and I don't think they will ever think to unmask it in both places at once. Who would ever think of unmasking both sites, even if they knew it was present?

"I've opened a real Pandora's box if that California group ever does anything with it. My bet is they are so shortsighted and scared that they have already destroyed my green animals.

"But with the newly proposed freedoms in that US bill, something might develop. On the other hand, they don't know how I did it, and that's their big problem."

"This is amazing," said Zita, thinking what a treasure trove she had just heard.

"It could be the catalyst of the future."

"What kind of animal did you use in this?"

"Can't tell you exactly because of my agreement. But it has a backbone."

Zita respected his ethics in honoring an agreement that was now probably worthless because of new guidelines.

"Holy cow! That's a shocker, and being in a vertebrate too."

"You can probably see why they fired me when these strange animals appeared."

"Of course, since it was a shadow project to boot."

Alex continued and explained exactly how he did the technical work with unmasking chemicals and enzymes in combination with the newest computer software. He became so passionate and excited that he seemed almost to hyperventilate. Finally, stopping himself, he declared, "I need a walk if I intend to sleep tonight. You with me?"

"I just don't feel up to a walk right now."

"I'll meet you back at the B&B."

Zita felt guilty doing so, but she hurried back to their room and, for an hour, took down vital technical notes on what he'd said. She hid them in her congress session notes. When she finished, she sat back and thought about what a marvelous passion the man had for his work. Yet she had a guilt knot in her stomach because of what she was doing. But she couldn't erase from her mind what she now knew.

The following day, they drove through a beautiful valley along a braided turquoise river and ended at a blue lake nestled in front of evergreen-laced mountains capped by gray rain clouds.

"This lake is immense," said Zita, gazing at Lake Teanu extending over the horizon before them. Teanu, the village, seemed a mere cluster of huddled buildings on the near shore.

"It's a much-larger lake than where we were at Queenstown, and this is the jumping-off place for the Milford Trek."

"What's that?" she asked, peering at the stark mountains lined up behind the lake as if protecting some great treasure.

"It's supposed to be the most beautiful walk in the world. Or so the travel industry claims. You take a boat here, cross the lake, and hike five days, staying in a different chalet each night. Then you're picked up on the seaward side by boat."

"Wish we had time to do it."

"Me too. But right now, I'm hungry."

In tiny Teanu, they stopped for a breakfast at a small teahouse where they had spaghetti on toast, fruits, and hot tea. Chattering high school youngsters with their backpacks crowded the teahouse. They had hitchhiked their country with abandon, freely flagging down cars for rides. Zita was shocked seeing how this tiny nation was still safe for such travel by young people on their school break. They would be taking a big risk doing the same in California.

In their Morris automobile, they skirted west along the lake over rolling hills of yellow grasses until they entered an evergreen forest.

Alex again talked freely of his research. Zita felt compelled to give him something in return and told him about Harold's work to insert the nitrogen-fixing genes into primitive animals like the euglena. Alex didn't see any problem with taking it into higher animals. If the non-nodule types could be transferred to euglena, it might be possible for other higher animals to accept the codes and produce their own internal nitrogen. Zita felt it was perhaps a future answer to world protein shortages. But Alex wasn't convinced of that. She didn't feel like revealing Harold's work would do any harm since he was no longer a factor in the company, or her life. She shuddered just thinking like the sneaky viper, but she feared her acting like Harold was not right.

Alex pointed out how animal hemoglobin was not a nitrogen transporter. It was only possible for nitrogen transport by plant hemoglobin when placed in animals. The unmasked plant hemoglobin was slightly different and did it. Zita knew that nitrogen was dissolved in human blood plasma but wasn't involved with their hemoglobin molecules. What Alex said to her made a lot of sense. Nitrogen could be made useable in animal blood via plant hemoglobin, not animal hemoglobin. This was a shocker, and something overlooked by scientists right before their noses.

Exiting the green timber at Gun Lake, they stopped the car and walked about. The landscape was evergreen forest and clear blue mountain water. It could have been Yellowstone National Park in Wyoming. This New Zealand was indeed a varied country, Zita thought. They enjoyed the breeze and changed the driving chore so Alex could look about at ease. But he still wanted to talk.

Zita listened and drove the car on dirt roads downhill through the temperate rain forest with a dense deciduous tree canopy. Soon bright green tree ferns as large as their car lined the underbrush. This was the habitat of the kiwi bird, New Zealand's national bird. It probed for worms in the moist rain forest soil and hid its flightless body among the dark and dense underbrush.

Soon they passed through a dark rock-lined tunnel. Before the entrance, a sign read, "One-Way Tunnel. Pass from half past to the hour from this end. Use your headlights." Water dripped down the walls on each side of the car in small rivulets. The road was frighteningly narrow requiring all of Zita's driving skill. At the far end, they emerged into a new world.

They had descended Homer Tunnel onto a tiny curving dirt road and into a deep canyon with glacier-carved towering walls rising a thousand feet above them. The lonely road snaked along the bottom. Soon the steady rain started forming hundreds of waterfalls along the canyon's rims falling hundreds of feet down into the evergreen trees. It was a breathtaking sight she couldn't enjoy much since she was clenched to the steering wheel fearing the drop off.

"Beautiful things seem to be happening on this trip. I feel you must be magic, Zita."

"This is a magical and wondrous place."

"That too, but you are a big part of it."

"It doesn't get any better than this," she replied as she started to worry about sliding off of the muddy road.

Soon they departed from the evergreens and enjoyed seeing broad-leafed trees standing stark in the rain and fog. The hybrid Morris slowly navigated the slick road and reached the hotel at Milford Sound. Soon they could see no landscape around them and entered the hotel, booking a room for two. It was the only hotel at the isolated resort and seemed empty in the midafternoon dampness. After tea in the spacious dining room, they marveled at the spread of gorgeous flowers surrounding the hotel. Pouring rain had interrupted their plans, and the desk clerk told them it usually lasted all day when setting in like this.

Once in their room, Alex kissed her repeatedly and settled on the couch to enjoy her. Soon he was on his knees kissing her passionately while she stretched the length of the couch. She probed her tongue into his mouth, and he met hers. Zita sucked on his tongue during the embrace. Alex returned the gesture, pulling her to the soft rose carpet.

There they embraced, and his hands found their way under her bra, unfastening it. She gave slight upward thrusts meeting his fingers and continued kissing him with great force. His lips moved from mouth to ears and down a sensitive neck, kissing with firm purpose. Next he lifted her green sweater and placed his lips on her. When he ran his tongue around, goose bumps arose all along her right side. He switched to the left side and was a bit amused when the goose bumps appeared only on one side. She forced her thighs upward against his lower chest and whispered, "Let's go to the bedroom."

"Are you sure you want to do this?" he teased.

"I want you." A connection was now there where she could be herself and not worry about consequences or the future. Zita had never felt so secure in her lovemaking and surrender since this was likely a onetime affair.

They rose from the floor and he half carried her, stumbling to the bedroom. There he unbuttoned his shirt. She kicked off her shoes and removed her jeans, setting her on the edge of the bed. Her long blond hair flowed down across her shoulders as she pulled herself back to recline on a pillow in the corner. She crossed her long smooth legs and watched him hurriedly remove his clothing. For a moment she saw Alex pause and look at her, naked except for white panties. She wondered what he thought, and if this meant a lot to him.

Soon he moved beside her and found her lips again and slowly removed her panties, then his own. Alex was pleasurable, so strong, apparently a veteran at causing such sensations. Zita sensed that he was determined to make her happy. Soon she stiffened, turned her head to the side, gave a slight gasp, and relaxed. Finally, he released his control and enjoyed his own pleasure.

"Wow, that was great; you're really some lover."

"Hey, it takes two. I loved sliding in our sweat." He taunted, "Want to try again?"

"Maybe later." Zita was surprised at herself in sharing such uninhibited sex with him so soon in the relationship. Her views of life's shortness since the plane crash and her unfettered sex pleasure had really surprised her, or was it this special man?

"What a great way to spend a rainy afternoon."

"You can't beat this." They chuckled in agreement. Soon they slumbered side by side, both wiser about the other.

9   2044 Revealings

Clear skies surrounded the Milford hotel the next morning as they looked out at the stunningly beautiful landscape. Mountains jacked straight to heaven rose from the deep blue fjord waters before them. Breathtaking!

During their breakfast, a stark white cruise ship silently came to rest alongside towering Mount Mitre across the picture-book fjord. Luxury liners heading from Australia often stopped at Milford Sound whose beauty matched anything else in the southern hemisphere. It was as if a bit of Norway had been stolen and placed on the southwest end of New Zealand's South Island. Passengers from the ship's small motor launches soon overwhelmed the hotel and its tiny gift shop, searching for trinkets for loved ones back home somewhere.

That afternoon, there was a hiatus in the rainstorms, as Zita and Alex boated down the fjord in the sightseeing craft, viewing a hanging valley notched high into the steep side wall. Its bridal veil fall spewed a snow-white cascade downward into the fjord. A canyon had been cut in half by their fjord long ago when it was filled with glacial ice. The waterfall was left high in the wall with its water helplessly dropping freely into the salty ocean below. Their craft circled in the great ocean swells and raced back down the sound for protection from the outlying ocean. Spray occasionally hit their faces as they marveled at the gorgeous scenery.

"This is the most striking spot on earth I've ever seen," Zita said as they neared the hotel boat dock.

"It's like a Yosemite filled with water. I'm so impressed. But with all these tourists from that liner here, I'd like to drive back out and see the canyon without clouds and rain hindering my bloody vision as we had on the way in."

"My thinking exactly. It's been delightful here in more ways than one, but let's not stay another night. There's too much to see." Quickly they packed up and left the tourist-inundated hotel.

On the long drive back to Gun Lake, they enjoyed the wild splendor of Fjordland Canyon while Alex openly talked of his future. "South Africa is a limitless research opportunity, but sometime I'd like to return to America. Perhaps my old company will cease blackballing me in view of the new freedom in US primate and genetic research. Think I'll find out, and in a few years, return if I can. Would you like that, Zita?"

"Yes, of course. I want you to be happy, and if South Africa isn't your niche, make a move somewhere else."

That wasn't exactly what she thought he had hoped to hear. She was intentionally cautious. She later told him of her breakup with Harold, the corporate spy. Zita indicated that it would take time for her to totally trust any man again after that betrayal. Besides, she knew Alex was fifteen years her senior, and he shouldn't be thinking of any long-term relationship, not just yet.

"So I'm on a short leash."

"After what I went through, any man would be."

Alex said, "Let's pass that subject. But I do know, or think I know, spies are in the company where I worked all those years. Other companies knew or quickly repeated our findings. Guys like Harold may have been there, but mark my word, there are bigger fish in that pond."

"Seize the day" seemed to be their vacation mottos. Yet she sensed she was more than a passing fancy to this Greek god–appearing man.

Beyond Teanu's long lake, the countryside opened into rolling hills of bright orange-yellow grasses neatly fenced into low hillside pastures. Black and white border collies worked the numerous bands of sheep along the way. Sheep stations were scattered about them when they stopped in Lumsden for lunch.

Alex enjoyed steak, eggs, and tomatoes while she had the fresh crawfish. No place in this country was far from the sea, and fresh fish was in tandem along with mutton, hogget, and lamb on every menu. In the half-abandoned café, Alex asked her how she felt about primate and human interchange engineering and the new regulations.

"I'm ready for anything to improve the human species. We have come a hundred years saving all the defective genes, defective people, and have allowed them to continue. It's time we did something constructive for the *Homo sapiens*. I want to improve people. Why do you ask?"

"Researchers in the laboratory complex where I work have already made successful crosses between gorillas and humans as well as chimpanzees and humans and did it well before Italy released the news. This, unfortunately, was done with blacks that my government considers less than human."

"My god, Alex, I've known about such things in Italy! What are the crosses like, and are they a real improvement?" Zita was shocked by his revelations.

"An interesting blend between the two as you might expect. I'm not privileged to give details, and its secret. I'm certain they are between apes and humans in intelligence and physical characteristics. Hair patterns are reduced. They don't seem an improvement over humans yet but are a jump over apes."

"Why are they doing it?"

"I suppose to create an ape to work harder in the hot and stifling mines. Maybe they can withstand higher temperatures and wouldn't have to be paid either. Maybe they will be more easily controlled than the tribal blacks they've worked the past few hundred years. I fear it could be a new type of slavery."

"Do they plan to reveal this to the world's scientific community?"

"I doubt it, and I think it will remain as the country's nuclear weapons do—highly speculated about, but no genuine confirmations."

"This seems to be the kind of thing Americans fear and have fought against by not loosening the engineering restrictions in past decades. I hope your company keeps this awful thing secret."

"You can count on it for a while anyway." It all now clicked for Zita. Alex must be involved in the green pigmentation studies to make these sub- humans photosynthesize. She didn't dare ask him, but that country would want a miner who could think little, work hard, and produce much of its own food. How perfect for that government to profit from lots of revenue in South African gold mining.

"As you might expect, these human embryos have been transplanted into female apes and brought to term now that an artificial placenta works perfectly. So far they appear normal."

"All of this is revolting, Alex. Yet it's exciting thinking of people in control of their own genetic possibilities." She now wondered what would be done in her company's new gorilla research laboratory, completed just prior to this trip. There was much she hadn't been told and until now didn't question. Was her company aware of what Alex said was happening in South Africa? Were they preparing to move ahead with this cross-species research? Her mind was overwhelmed by these ethically questionable procedures she had pondered for years on a theoretical basis. It all seemed so different now that it was a coming reality.

As their car moved into country reminding her of Scotland, Zita reclined her seat, closed her eyes, and thought. Were her ethics compromised since she was traveling with this charming man and loving it? Her curiosity had changed to passion, and now she could feel the upwelling of intense love. Was she a tart letting herself be used while learning more about his research and using his information herself? She didn't think so since he willingly told his secrets, thinking she would have no use for the exact information. But she didn't tell him that she wrote some of it down for later use. So she wasn't entirely honest, or a bit honest. Maybe he also felt it was only a short time until the world would know all this in view of the Italian ongoing research. She wondered about her conduct.

In Zita's mind, their relationship had blossomed not because he was who he was, but his maturity, manners, handsomeness, and gentleness with her was winning her heart. Life has its surprises, this being a huge one. She was enjoying the moment but knew they must part soon, and then what would become of it all?

She didn't want it to be only an affair, and how could she explain her role except as that of a spy? She hadn't really been a spy, but it had just happened, she thought. Still, she recorded notes. That's what she would have expected a Harold to do. Could she explain a personal involvement, least a love affair, with this man to Erick? Perhaps she didn't need to explain her actions to anyone. She recalled from her college ethic class the four most limiting and destructive words in the human vocabulary to be, "What will people think?"

Having always considered herself an ethical person, she now felt compromised and was in some turmoil about her actions; conversely, she felt so happy and human because of this newfound excitement. She decided not to decide; matters would take care of themselves as this was a self-resolving situation in the short run. However, she feared its long-term implications.

"Are you married?"

"No. I was once, and my wife died."

"I'm sorry."

"That was long ago. We never had children either."

"I've never found anyone honest with me. Most men are too self-centered, or they are just plain dishonest like my first boyfriend. And Harold was a fraud, so my men have been less than uplifting or rightly honest."

"It's difficult to find someone whose chime matches your own. I know. There are many good people, but their chime doesn't ring like hitting a champagne glass, more like the dull sound from a stone if you follow me."

"Yes, it's true."

Alex said, "I've had some who loved me madly, but as I grew to know them, I couldn't spend my time with their limitations."

"Yes, and they seldom change, Alex."

"That's for sure. My dear mother, bless her honest heart, always said to me back in Nebraska, 'If you don't like 'em like they is, don't marry 'em for they ain't agonna change.'"

"How true. I didn't realize you were from Nebraska."

"A tiny place called Funk, right in the middle of corn country and lots of Swedes. My father was a merchant there."

"Do you ever go back?"

"Way back in 2015, I attended a reunion. My dad's old store was a T-shirt shop, and the town was about the same."

"I think it's important to remember who we are and where we came from, don't you?"

"Oh yes, even though I haven't a lot in common with the folks there now. If events had only slightly changed, I might be a farmer there today. Strange how events alter these fickle lives of ours."

"I think you are making this lady's life much happier; just being with you has let me see something beyond the laboratory I've been so fixated on these last years."

"Yes, it's a big world, and our lives change. I really enjoy being with you, Zita. It's not like the awful dread I've had with a few women—just counting the time until escape—but not wanting to injure their feelings."

"Sometimes, I think it's all too much trouble."

"Zita, nothing worthwhile is ever easy."

"Yes, but I can't stand the trauma of interpersonal stress very well."

Dunedin jumped up at them from the seacoast. Its red-topped roofs stood stark against the ocean at the bottom of a large north-south running valley. It was pure Scottish in architecture and people. Later they learned the people had been brought directly from Scotland to settle here in the late 1860s.

Alex took her to a couple's pub that night. The floors were filled with sawdust, and huge barrels were used as tables. Dark European beers and ales were consumed by standing couples. They had a game of darts, and Alex bested her easily. A workingman's pub was next door where women weren't allowed.

Later Zita and Alex walked the seashore admiring the light pink sunset and wishing this could last forever. Hand in hand they strolled the brick streets back to their hotel. They dined in leisure observing the other guests, mostly New Zealanders. Zita noticed that they all used their left hand to bring forked food to their mouths. The knife was also used a bit more freely than in Europe. They joined a raucous freewheeling loud group in the bar after dinner. Their Scottish brogues and jokes about Americans and themselves lifted everyone's spirits.

As they reveled into the night, Alex consumed far too much beer, and at midnight, Zita had to help him to the hotel room. He snored heavily and slept dead to the world after she removed his clothes. She didn't know when she'd had so much fun in one evening. Her dart playing had improved a great deal that night, but she still preferred light American to these dark ales.

The following day, Alex was somewhat subdued as Zita drove up the coast and entered the Canterbury Plains. The landscape was as truly mystical appearing as King Arthur's lands in the midmorning haze. Hedgehogs crossed the road ahead several times. They were delayed by a large band of sheep crossing at a bridge. Their packed white fleeces seemed a moving rough carpet as far as they could see. Zita soon chose a side road to escape the white snaking band that filled the road fence-to-fence and streamed up the emerald green countryside.

"One of the interesting things we have done is add Vitamin C synthesizing traits to humans in our laboratories."

Trying to be coy, Zita said, "That's been needed for so long. I've always wondered how only guinea pigs and we humans are not able to make our own ascorbic acid."

"Yes, I wish those genes were in me. I need something the way I feel. Perhaps someday they will introduce a new code to eliminate the horrid hangover."

"That's a brain fluid problem, and probably not subject to gene action. So those who get carried away and overdo alcohol have to suffer." She laughed and reached over and patted his knee wondering why he had suddenly jumped to a science topic.

"I just wish South Africa could release some of the great work we've done in genetic engineering. It would just knock the socks off of genetic engineering. The Vitamin C alone is a great breakthrough."

"Maybe you soon can as this climate changes nationally."

"In the US, the underlying motive is profit, but in South Africa, it's for power."

"That makes South Africa worse?"

"Oh yes, they are interested in survival as a self-sustaining state and will do anything to maintain their system and operate it more efficiently. Crossing humans and great apes in the laboratory hasn't bothered them. They were interested in me because I could work on a self-nutritional dimension. Really you don't want to hear all this shop talk. We're on holiday—let's change the subject." She knew now the specific nature of his research; just that one remark in his hungover state confirmed her suspicions. Her mind raced as she drove on toward the largest city on the South Island.

That afternoon they had walked the seashore, watching the gulls and petrels in colonies. By evening, they entered Christchurch and spent the night in passionate embraces as if this was their last chance to ever be together. Then at the airport, they awaited his flight.

"I don't know what to say, Zita, or how to say it, but you're wonderful."

"I feel the same about you."

"It's been a long time since I was comfortable with and excited about a woman. I'll not flatter you, but I could get serious about you. Except, we are continents apart, and long-distance relationships are difficult."

"Let's give it a try," she said, looking him squarely in the eyes.

"Maybe I can manage a summer visit to the States and we could . . ." His voice dropped.

"Visit Funk, and see the corn?" They laughed and exchanged address and media information.

"I feel we have a lot in common, but I am older, you know."

"Things are better with age. This has proved it for me."

"Thanks! I don't really want to leave you."

"Keep your chin up; we both must try to maintain. This is the start of a future for us both. Take care." She kissed him and watched him slip away across the tarmac to his airliner. At the stairs, he turned and waved with the stout wind blowing his silver hair back. She wondered if they would ever meet again.

On her Air New Zealand flight over the Pacific Ocean, she mulled over the past days. What an adventure—totally out of character for her lifestyle. She had actually taken chances and gone wild in the southern hemisphere. She had made a major leap in knowledge of genetic research, much of it coming from Alex. Why did he tell her all those secrets? Was it that he trusted her or didn't think she could use it directly? Surprisingly, he hadn't even asked her to keep it all to herself. Her last thought was that he didn't care and just needed someone away from his laboratory as a sounding board. It must be frustrating doing breakthrough research and having no avenue for the scientific world to know of it. Perhaps she'd been his safety valve where he could release the pent-up developments freely.

She still had mixed emotions. As a female, she knew letting any man love her always released the subtle desire for partnership. Those were clearly there, plus he had given her a mind massage of the highest order. What a handsome perfect person. On the other hand, he was a blackballed scientist. However, it had been so delightful being held and loved. She missed Alex already.

She imagined Alex sitting in his cramped seat, questioning his wisdom of having revealed so much. He probably didn't think it mattered since he trusted her; besides, she wasn't a primate researcher anyway. His mind was probably imaging the July visit to California for that scientific *Elan* meeting. Seeing her would have to be high on his agenda in the plan. Perhaps, she thought, he might also be job hunting at the meeting too. Could be a good chance to size up his status with other genetic engineering companies. Zita hoped events would turn his situation around, maybe even remove the blackballing. She felt his exile. It was her goal to be most patient with this kind man.

She could see him sitting there and planning to make his reservations early. That would provide something for him to look forward to. He was probably now sitting with his eyes closed wondering if he really loved her. He would be mulling it over, uncertain. She knew she was the kind of woman he could grow to love. Zita then wondered if he would actually take a chance on a younger woman. That was a big risk for any older guy.

What the heck, she thought, he must know that life is one big gamble. Anyone who chanced changing animals for the better could surely risk. How would he, on an airplane, filled like a bomb with flammable fuel, and heading for troubled South Africa, be worried about taking chances?

10 Breakthroughs

After he met her at the airport, Zita talked for hours with Erick about the World Congress and glorious New Zealand. She didn't feel tired from the travel and wanted to move to that Kiwi land, but what could she do in her field there, she asked?

"Maybe if we ever retire, we can move there to enjoy the cleaner air and quality of life," said Erick, "You're sure sellin' me on the unspoiled natural environment of the place."

"You know my love of history and islands, and these are big ones with so much pristine land and lots to learn."

"Well someday let's plan for a long vacation down there to enjoy a sunny winter with little snow instead of all this polluted air."

"I imagine this filthy air and old age will get us before we can retire down under. Besides, you are no tea drinker."

"To live there, I'd gladly drink tea or anything else."

She avoided revealing information about Alex since she didn't want Erick to know unless the relationship stayed alive. Also, she made up her travel being with another woman and totally felt badly doing so. Oh god! She suddenly remembered giving Alex her home address. What if Erick saw a return address on a letter or e-mail from South Africa? She hadn't given Alex her lab address fearing he would know the company or they would know him. All this intrigue was too much since she had never been a person to hide and deceive on many personals, even to her brother. Could all this be done, or should she just confess to Erick right now and get it off her chest? She thought not just yet.

When she went back to work, she found team leader meetings abuzz with new ideas since the US president's signing of the executive order allowing human genetic research. Her fellow scientists talked about the change as if it were a new frontier. None had expected the turnaround in government policy that had been bottled up in congress for years. Now many other changes might pass when the final bill was finished in congress.

Surprisingly the detailed and quickly published national guidelines were rather open-ended. Could there be some sanity in her government after all? Was it possible for them to trust scientists with near total freedom to research and improve human life? It had not been a total wasteland, she thought, since Obama had lifted the stem cell limitations in 2009 that had been imposed for religious reasons by then president Bush in 2001. Things had improved but never fast enough for her or Erick. And now would the government only impose new restrictions if things got out of hand? These new guidelines appeared to be more forward looking than many in the past. Zita thought, as did her brother, that great progress always comes from allowing scientists to freely inquire. She knew that had been true since studying the dark ages of the 1300s.

Soon after her return, the company board of directors went on a week's retreat to set new goals for the future. Some greenback matters would be on hold until Charlie returned with a grand plan. She spent that time getting caught up with all the backlog of issues in her unit that had piled up during her New Zealand trip. Zita was amazed at how many decisions she was involved with in the genetic engineering. Ideas and information from Alex's work and the conference were also smoldering in her mind. She pondered revealing them and decided not yet.

Upon Charlie's return, she was called into his office. Zita's jaw dropped and she gazed in disbelief at Charlie across the desk. "Be in charge of gorilla and chimpanzee genetics? Why me?" she asked, not believing her ears.

"You're so good and this will best fit Quotech's needs. Our goal is to put competent people in charge. You will have several PhDs under you. Eighty people in all from here to research universities."

"Yes, but . . .," she hesitated and took a deep breath, "I'm not a true primate molecular geneticist." That was all she could come up with to defend herself from becoming an administrator.

"We know, but this unit will draw from all disciplines and the best minds worldwide. No one is perfectly trained for any of these things. We trust you completely, and you'll have two new assistants to keep up with it all and the paperwork."

She knew that in his trust comment, Charlie was referring to her behavior with Harold. She chuckled to herself. If he only knew how close she'd come to breaching back then, he wouldn't be offering her this post.

"I will only take it if I still have a free hand to be involved in the actual research hands-on when I so choose. That's essential to keep me sane in my field."

"Done."

"OK, I'll take it, providing Erick can work part-time with me, when the need arises."

"Done!" replied Charlie, shaking her hand.

"Please put it all in a memo."

"Yes, yes."

Alone, she walked the glistening white hallway with glass on each side separating her from the primates. There were now fifty chimpanzees and half that number of gray-tinged gorillas. Mothers with young were kept together in large spaces, while males, except for natural breeding time or semen collection, were kept alone or in small groups. Zita marveled at the wonderful spaces they had and how the lighting, humidity, and heat were controlled to simulate their native African ecosystems. She could not totally fool herself, regretting they were not still wild and free munching vegetation in Africa.

Feeding pods branched from all cages. A solid stainless-steel door could be lowered, dividing the pod from the main space. It was also air tight to allow silent administration of anesthesia gases to eating and drinking animals. It was much better than individual handling or the primitive tranquilizer darts used by early primate investigators. The great apes simply fell asleep while in the pods and a blackout curtain was lowered, preventing other apes from seeing what scientists did to them. When the animal awoke, it was as if nothing had happened. The pods were also designed autoclaves and were automatically sterilized when needed to keep the space nearly germ free.

She enjoyed watching her closest mammal relatives play. They were well treated and, except for the confinement, had a less hazardous life than in their natural habitats. Zita tried to see them as happy and content experimental animals. But she could not ignore their soft eyes that told her they longed to be free to race around somewhere in the African rain forest.

In the next wing, locked under tight security, were the green-backed chimpanzees in their highly lighted cages. They acted as normal chimps, but their back colors were shocking when shaved. Down the hall were the totally pigmented light green chimps. She felt sorry for them with their sickly light green–colored faces, reminding her of space alien characters from some old media offering.

Zita knew laboratory natural reproduction was too slow and uncertain in primates. It would take years to do research, waiting nine months for each birth. They needed to double up. So chimp production was accelerated using gorilla females as surrogate mothers for housing the developing chimp embryos. Since these females were larger, they could have twin baby chimps much easier and without midwife help from the scientists.

In her mind, she reviewed all the production procedures. Sperm was collected from anesthetized male chimps. Female chimps were then artificially inseminated during hormone-induced ovulation. A team would soon flush out the embryo and transfer it into a surrogate gorilla female; it would be attached to an artificial placenta. They then used hormones injected into ports to cause the green or greenback chimp to ovulate again, producing embryo after embryo to transplant. This increased reproduction while accelerating research upward with enough numbers of test animals. Over the next months, Zita felt that she was in charge of an egg factory. These methods would raise the population of greenbacks to the statistical required twenty-five by year's end.

Infrequently Alex sent her e-mails, letting her know he was safely back at work and would keep in touch. She felt relieved that he was safe and doing the work he loved.

Zita directed one of her new DNA teams to work on rendering the chimp lower digestive tract vestigial or with little functionality. Another of her groups of genetic engineers was busy trying to mask or delete the genes associated with hunger and the pleasure of eating by transferring in genetic codes from other animal species who hibernated. Once these were in place, the new green chimps would not be consuming vegetable matter they didn't really require. This would move them toward being true photoapes.

Quotech's board of directors wanted to establish these changes in primates and then insert them into other domestic animals consumed by humans.

Over the next six months, Zita buried herself in work with her increased responsibilities. She heard from Alex several times by letter, but thankfully he didn't put his full name on the address. They both were looking forward to his visit just two months away. She now told Erick he was just a friend she'd met at the congress in New Zealand. It wasn't a total lie, just a half-truth.

Alex's laboratory in South Africa didn't allow internet, email, or mail communications from the compound for security reasons. He had to go into a dangerous neighboring countryside village to contact her and avoid detection and monitoring by the government. His laboratory overseers did read all his other mail, deleting or redacting any science in his letters to her.

Soon a giant breakthrough came at Quotech. Engineering to allow nitrogen intake for inclusion in mammal cellular proteins from the atmosphere was working in hamsters. The fuzzy rodents could now be fed diets without food protein. Engineered animals breathed the air that enabled them to grow, to heal, and to function. The researchers waited for the side effects. This atmospheric nitrogen synthesis could now be a reality in mammals. Charlie wanted it placed in greenbacks if possible, and he enlarged that research group to focus on that huge task, placing it under Erick's direction.

Zita told her twin, "This whole thing is just going so fast that I can't keep up with it! Ramifications of all this is beyond my comprehension at times. These could change how the world works in so many ways. And the social implications have to be looked at beyond our labs."

"Maybe so, sis, but we can't be in all that public policy debate. It's not our role."

"I just want a perfect world. Is that bad?"

"No, but we have our hands full with the science involved."

One of Zita's top team leaders had come up with the idea of using the genes of a blue green algae. It could carry on photosynthesis in near darkness. He had collected it in Antarctica and was testing how it would produce in bright sunlight. He also found that *Nostoc* had unique nodules. In the nodules, atmospheric nitrogen gas was converted into usable nitrogen for the algae. Transferring those gene codes into hamster embryos had worked, enabling the mammal to take in the nitrogen from the air that could be used in making essential amino acids in the cells. With the earth atmosphere nearly 80 percent nitrogen gas, this unlimited source for amino acids building blocks for proteins, for energy, and for body repair was possible. It could then be used to make all the different dozen proteins animals need. Instead of eating animal or plant proteins, the bodies of hamsters in the laboratory could now feed on the atmosphere for protein building. It was a stunning achievement that was kept secret for the time being. It had to be repeated many times for accuracy.

Quotech's board of directors was ecstatic with this advance, feeling that they could someday change agriculture across the globe, if the *Nostoc* genes would work in mammals beyond rodents.

There were so many genetic teams working on projects that Zita had a hard time keeping them all organized. Despite having two assistants, she was so busy preparing reports, reviewing research log notes, and keeping her complex units going that her time at home and social life were nil. Events and breakthroughs were rapid fire and exciting. She didn't like being in charge and having to help solve so many complex problems; however, the progress was rapid and refreshing. It had been much easier and less stressful at NASA working on her personal projects instead of supervising so many.

On the other hand, she had the power to give Dr. Koob complete freedom to carry out the research at his university. However, she felt at times she was becoming like Charlie, an administrator to be disliked. Power was a double-edged sword. So she worked to be sure her staff of investigators were always involved in making the big decisions.

What made her job more difficult was that Quotech did not conduct all of the research. Much of it was farmed out to universities and research institutes worldwide in the form of highly specialized contracts and grants. Zita had two top-notch academic assistants who worked between these outside researchers and her Quotech scientists. There was all manner of secret agreements, selections of who should perform the work, and what should be done. For Zita, it involved constant meetings, constant grant readings, and the constant submitting of proposals to universities, rendering it a spider web of communication channels. It was a nightmare of details, yet it fast-tracked the efforts by a factor of ten since Quotech did not have to start as many projects from the ground up, something that could take years. Universities that had been doing similar work could move ahead rapidly as could research institutes. Success hinged on selecting the right institutions and scientists for the work. All unit directors in Quotech as well as Zita had to jump through the many hoops of justifying the work, writing the grants, and finding the very best minds for the outside genetic engineering.

Zita came home late one evening in July. Erick looked at her strangely as she dragged through the door. "You've got to stop working this hard. It'll be the death of you."

"I'd quit today if things weren't working so perfectly. We may have greenbacks obtaining their protein from the air within a year."

"That's progress," he replied, continuing to read *Scientific American.*

"I'll go change, and be right back. Seems like we haven't talked in a while."

"Good idea, sis."

She enjoyed her shower, put on her long flowing robe, and sat on the couch. "How're things with you?"

"Well, not too good. I had a call here for you from a Dr. Alex Moby from South Africa." Her heart sank. "I explained I was your brother, and he said he'd call back about 11:00 p.m." He looked at Zita who flinched and dropped her eyes, focusing on the floor.

"God, I shouldn't have tried to keep this from you! I didn't think I could explain and keep your total respect. It's turned out much differently than I expected. At first it was just curiosity with him— now more serious."

"Tell me?"

"Might as well, it's been hell worrying how to tell you. Never before have I tried to keep something important like this to myself. If I'd been smart, I would have told you—it's such a problem for me."

"Go ahead."

Before Alex's later call, Zita explained the entire episode including some genetic secrets she'd learned that advanced her chimp work. During her long explanation, he'd listened and made no judgments. Then his call came.

"Should I answer it?"

"But of course. I don't think you should change because I know." Yet she sensed he was hurt by her keeping a major happening from him.

She had a nice conversation with Alex. It was wonderful hearing his voice and knowing she would see him before July ended. She told him she'd been put in charge of the primate unit at her company and was promoted to oversee a number of new teams. Charlie had said that she could reveal that much. Alex responded by saying, "If that is the case, I'll bring along a bloody surprise."

When she finished, Erick looked at her and said, "I don't think this is such a terrible problem except between you and Alex. Everything can all be worked out on this end; let's think about how to do it."

"Glad you aren't angry."

"Course not, love you. You're human."

"Sometimes I wish I weren't. At the lab, I sometimes feel like I'm a robot going a dozen directions at once." She suddenly felt a new freedom. It was as if a ton of bricks had been lifted off her shoulders with her brother knowing about Alex.

Charlie came into her office the next morning and asked, "Do you have a minute?"

Surprised, she said, "Of course. What's on your mind?"

Taking a seat directly across her highly organized desk and looking her directly in the eyes, he said, "The powers that be and I are worried about the future of the company since stock prices have declined the past six months. Funds are tight, and I didn't want that slowing down our research. So many projects are on the verge of startling breakthroughs like the *Nostoc*. It could be exciting ahead.

"Potato research has resulted in grapefruit-sized spuds that may be a big money winner sometime. Also, the cherry tree cross which produced peach-sized fruit will revolutionize the fruit industry, someday, if we can find a way to increase the limb size of the darned trees to hold the heavy fruit. There are so many opportunities. Should we be working on photosynthesis in chickens—wouldn't work with the feathers, I suppose. Perhaps would with hogs since they could absorb the good sun, having such sparse hair. I dream that once the photosynthesizing direction is set, the chimp genes could be spliced into other animals. But there's a long way from the genetics to making money."

Uncrossing her legs and standing up, Zita asked, "Would you like a cup of coffee or tea?" Usually their conversations were on the walk down laboratory halls or in team meetings. She wondered why he was taking his valuable time now.

"Tea with loads of milk. Please."

"Coming up." She looked at the little man who seemed so confident in all situations, who seemed so overbearing with others, and who seemed to have little need for social interactions, and wondered what kind of a man he was.

He continued, "I wonder if this is the time to unveil the greenbacks to the public since regulations now allow it. We could then issue new stock to recapitalize and push ahead. Realistically, a year's time lag would be better. If it was done now, there might be a protest about the work having been done on the project prior to it being legal. I hate to take the wait, but who would scoop us?

"Probably nobody's out there doing what Dr. Moby started. Maybe that genius did us a big favor. I don't know about the value of photosynthesis in apes, but I do know there might be big bucks and opportunities for those mammal genes in other animals that people can eat.

"How can we get big bucks from the green chimps outside of using their genes for food production? Our board would like to know. The animals are expensive to raise as you well know. They must have other uses. Any eighty-pound chimp is stronger than a full-sized man. Oh, what is the direction?" His train of ramblings was broken as the secretary informed him of Erick's appointment.

"Ask him to meet us here in Zita's office."

Responding to Charlie, Zita said, "Most of the time I stick to pure science and put all the business stuff out of my mind. I'm tickled pink that you're questioning all that's going on. I thought you had all the answers, and that I was the only one in over my head about all this and the future. Welcome into the pool." They laughed. Then Erick opened the door.

"How are things goin' with you, Erick? I'm sorry not to have seen much of you lately. As many meetings as I have, even with six assistants, I need to be two people to do my job."

"Well, if you really want to be two people, I hear of this lab that is working on that down the valley," replied Erick.

They all chuckled and made small talk. Over the past months, the Starks had started liking Charlie a bit more.

Finally, Charlie asked, "What's on your mind since you made this appointment?"

"Well, it's a rather sensitive matter with Zita. I'm just here for moral support."

Zita was nervous about disclosing to Charlie. This could either ruin her job or it could help them all. "Well, it's a rather long story. I'll try to hit the highlights and can fill in specifics later. You'd better sit and brace yourself."

"Sounds serious."

"Very serious," she replied.

Clutching his teacup, Charlie sat as she spilled out the happenings with Alex. She skipped the details of the genetics, wanting overall reaction first.

"My god, this is a blockbuster. The implications here are serious."

"We know," answered Erick.

"What kind of information did you obtain on the original work producing the pigmented chimps? He didn't leave notes here."

"All of it," Zita replied, forcefully looking him in the eye.

Charlie gave a big smile and asked, "What kind of plant material did he use?"

"Potato, a tropical tree, and the unmasking of ancient genes."

"That makes a lot of sense since he was doing so much splicing and editing. Potatoes have that great production capacity too. The guy's good, but out of line with our policies."

Here it comes, thought Zita, that lecture on being with someone dangerous to her company. But the chiding didn't materialize.

"This could put us light-years ahead of other companies and make us tops." He stood up and walked around her desk and paced before the window, rubbing his chin with his palm.

"You know, Zita, we don't condone corporate spying on anyone's behalf—not even ours."

She bristled and responded, "Not once did I entice the man to tell me anything. I was just curious when I learned who he was and liked the guy. He told it all of his own free will."

"Yes, but you two were involved, you wrote it down, and you didn't tell him who you worked for. That looks suspect!"

"Charlie, you make it sound like she was a spy. I resent that," retorted Erick.

"Yes, I know, I'm just trying to see how this might sound to our board."

"If you have to tell 'em," said Erick.

"Maybe not; it's water under the bridge since all this is legal now anyway."

"But there are serious questions bound to arise if we put this information to good use in our research. Let me think on this.

Zita, please prepare me a report including all the specific genetic information, methods, and techniques."

In a split second, she said, "No, no, that would make me a documented spy on paper."

"Yes, you're right. Can't be a paper trail. Let's meet on Friday. This will not go beyond the three of us."

Zita felt ill after Charlie left.

Erick told her that he understood why Charlie's put her in a spy category. It was logical, but he did question Charlie then wanting all of her information for Quotech. "If you give that man all he asks, then he can hang you out to dry. I wouldn't be hasty in giving exact details to anyone for your own protection."

"I don't intend to. Not until we see my options. I've just got to remind myself that Charlie is a company man and self-serving. Yet I am not innocent in this mess for sure."

"Right on. But you can't give Charlie all the power since he's a tyrant and you could end up his escape target."

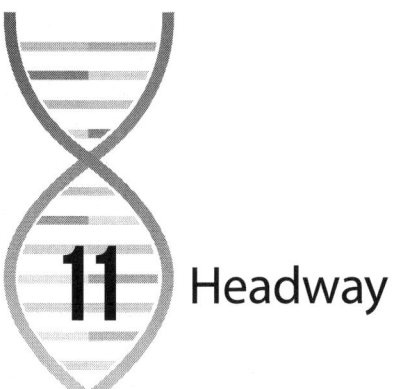

11 Headway

That Friday's meeting with Charlie was a disaster. He again demanded a full report. She refused and told him he couldn't have it both ways, condemning her as a spy and using the data. She also told him she wanted Alex's blacklisted label removed by the company since his work was now legal and the company still keeps using his modified chimps. Charlie was furious, accused her of blackmail, and refused to act on Alex's behalf. Zita stomped out of his office after losing her temper and telling him, "Go straight to hell."

Charlie continued yelling as he followed her down the hall, "I can fire you."

She hollered back, "Just try."

He raced to catch her, and at her urging, they each took a deep breath. Finally, they agreed to meet Monday to iron things out. Zita thought she had held her ground against him. He had some nerve accusing her of blackmail. It was he who was being underhanded wanting power and her total information.

Before the meeting, she reoriented some projects in view of her new knowledge gained from Alex. She didn't provide specific information but could eliminate redundant steps based on new data. She did switch from *Zea mays* (corn) to the Inka potato cells as the species of genetic origin in the photosynthesis research since that was what Alex had used. She told her lab technicians that new information required the big changes and details would be forthcoming.

In her many labs of researchers, Zita's teams actually worked on DNA material with chemicals of many kinds to edit the genes codes they were trying to understand and change. This was done with precision using established methods learned by great scientists over recent decades. Then after many trials to verify the lab people's work, they analyzed what was done to the DNA and mutations in the genes with complex machines using computer software. It was technical and precise, involving many steps with repeated trials to verify the results. All her people knew the results in science aren't acceptable until results are repeated many times to ensure they are repeatable and totally accurate.

Another letter from Alex awaited her at home one evening. It contained newsy items about the strife in South Africa. The struggle for equality between blacks and the white minority had gone on for generations. But Alex now feared coloreds might seize total control again as they had under Nelson Mandela in the mid-1990s. Whites years later had shocked the world as they revolted and again clamped an iron fist on the country and its black majority. The United Nations failed to do anything about it since South Africa soon had nuclear weapons. Sanctions didn't work either because the nation's natural resources were vital to starving neighboring countries.

Alex's letter also expressed concern about his own safety since his research was sponsored by the white government. Whites had been able to control the situation previously when the odds and population numbers appeared overwhelmingly against them. But they were experts in human control. Then he ended his smuggled letter expressing his longing to see her. She was deeply worried.

Later over breakfast coffee, Erick asked, "Do you know how Alex got the idea to look for green pigments in chimp DNA codes?"

Zita replied, "Sorry. Thought I'd told you. He was reading some old literature and came across a 2006 article where they found those teeth in a chicken's beak."

"Really!"

"They were stickin' right out and lined up as if they belonged there. But the significant thing was that they were reptile teeth. And we know birds descended from reptiles millions of years ago."

"So?"

"Well, it rang a bell in Alex's head. He knew then that genes from millions of years ago could be in all animals, yet remain inactive. He came to that conclusion earlier because he once saw a brain-mapping operation in a film."

Erick said, "This is gettin' really interesting."

She continued, "Surgeons, in this film, had removed the patient's skull cap and used electrodes to map what differing tissue responded to stimulation. The patient was awake during all this too."

"No pain?"

"Right, Biology 101. The brain has no pain neurons inside the skull. When brain mapping electrically probed one area, the patient said he heard a song from his childhood; in another area, he saw his high school swimming hole; and in another electric stimulation, he saw a Navy Day's drinking spree in a foreign port. So from that, Alex concluded everything we experience is locked in the pathways of the brain and stays there. It can be accessed by electrodes, but most of the very old memories can't be retrieved by ourselves."

"I see. If our brain can keep all this forever, the higher complexity of DNA could have past chemical trait codes locked away too."

"Exactly, but inactive, masked, and waiting to be unlocked as most of us know. We call it cellular junk."

"And with all the chemicals and enzymes we now have and CRISPR Cas9, it's only the complex matter of unmasking to find ancient genes for green."

"Correct! The chimp DNA holds all of their species' masked traits going back hundreds of millions of years when they didn't look at all like chimps and had probably lived in oceans before coming to live ashore."

Erick looked at his sister and was quiet for a moment. "Fascinating that anyone would make those connections. Brilliant because chemical DNA is much more complex than our brains and holds all that ancient data folded inside!"

"But as you know, there's more to it technically. How about my guy?"

"He is way out there with that insight."

That night at home and before she met Charlie again the next day, she was nervous and asked her brother's advice. While admiring her courage, Erick advised against too strong a battle. Zita felt she could easily get another job if Charlie pushed too much. But Erick reminded her that a blackball charge could be trumped up against her. She hadn't thought of that, and it made her more anxious since she hadn't been an official spy—perhaps a stupid personal spy.

He stood up and put on his jacket. "Where are you going this time of night, Erick?"

"I've got a date."

"Wow! Who is the lucky lady?"

"She works at another company nearby. I met her at a seminar—name's Kate."

"Well, be careful not to get in the kind of mess I have."

As he kissed her cheek goodbye, he said, "Don't worry. I don't plan to mix work and pleasure."

"I don't believe a word of it. You have so much pleasure in your work that I bet you both talk of it tonight. Wanna bet?"

"No bet; goodbye."

She was pleased seeing him socially active. It was maybe a response to her and a realization that she would not always be around. The thought of not always having him saddened her, and she hoped he wasn't exclusively responding to her recent behavior.

At Monday's meeting, Charlie was surprisingly sedate and ready to compromise; he agreed to drop his request for the report and to ask the board to clear Dr. Moby's name, and he gave her permission to fully implement the acquired information. She held out for one more demand—that there would no mention of spying to anyone or to the board.

Charlie told her that she was so valuable to the company now that he consented to all her requests and would put them in writing. She was amazed and wondering if he had some hidden motives about the secret data from Alex. Now, all she had to wait on was the Quotech board of directors' decisions.

Approvals came after the next board meeting, and she was free to work using her information. In a year, they had engineered a better chimpanzee with a solid green photosynthetic back, a reduced desire for food, and the ability to intake nitrogen from the atmosphere to make their own protein with protein synthesis. In addition, hair density had been reduced at least 80 percent, causing the apes to be nearly naked. If and when these changes were genetically spliced into other animals and if they could be carried to the next generations, the benefit could significantly transform the industry of animal husbandry.

In a big surprise at their next meeting, Charlie excitedly announced that Quotech was going public about the photochimps. A news conference was being set up to show three green chimpanzees to the US press. He gave the department heads a copy of the news release to ensure no one went beyond company policy in disclosing any other details of the actual work. Charlie was certain this event would later gain worldwide attention. After the first surprise showing, a second news event was planned for a few days later since a much-larger outpouring of interest was expected from huge worldwide media.

After the first release, newspaper headlines and media across the nation screamed about the food-producing ape story. Fully grown green chimp news was on every media network. Inquiries from around the world soon streamed into the company regarding the self-nourishing apes. It was a blockbuster, and they wanted more information.

Implications of the work were debated as no topic had been in years. Many groups feared the work in general, and some religious leaders were repulsed at the combining of plants and animal traits together, which to them was unnatural and playing God. Scientists, Quotech, and political thinkers countered that experimentation was the only road to advancement in science, agriculture, and society in an overpopulated, polluted, and sea-level-rising world. Most people around the world were intrigued by the idea of green animals getting sun energy instead of eating.

By the second news conference to show the animals, the quest for information and pictures had risen dramatically, nearly to a tidal wave level. Over five thousand reporters were on hand, forcing the event to be moved to a nearby field house. Reporters and cameramen spent hours at the large chimp display enclosure with its bright lights. It was like science fiction instantly spread worldwide showing the little green chimps with green bodies that made most of their food.

A Quotech spokespersons disclosed that a scientist in a foreign country had engineered photosynthetic DNA materials into the animals. Yet they wouldn't release any names associated with the project. Reporters hounded the company's employees, accosting them at all junctures of their lives for information. Happily, most workers knew nothing of the total project secrets, and those who did were above reproach.

Unfortunately, those opposed became vocal again, and bills were instantly introduced in national and state legislative bodies against freedom in genetic research. It would require money and time to fight these challenges on scientific grounds.

The company's stature was elevated overnight. There followed a great price rise in the stock, preferred stock, and bonds. Résumés from scientists wanting to be part of the work from across the globe poured into Quotech. Requests to share information came from hundreds of companies, universities, and research organizations worldwide. As Charlie had predicted, the response had been overwhelming and very lucrative, yet the strange little man didn't seem thrilled by it all, causing Erick and Zita to wonder.

A week later, Alex was due to arrive. Zita was delighted to see him step into the LAX terminal's waiting room. She rushed, embraced him happily, and whisked him to his hotel. She talked a mile a minute as if she were a middle-school child. At the hotel, he showered and changed from the long flight. Soon they fell into bed together for an afternoon of pleasure and rest. Their magic passion was still much alive as they enjoyed each other as if nearly a year hadn't separated them. That evening, they dined together at an exclusive inn.

"I kinda expected it, but was rather surprised when your company released the green chimpanzee research I'd started."

"So you know I'm there?"

"Yeah, figured it out from a friend or two I still have in Quotech, and your letters."

"Good. I knew my deceit had to be cleared up this trip. I never intentionally used you, but yet I did so never knowing we'd be together and what we are now. And I regret deeply acting to better myself. I hope you can come to trust me in the future. I'll never do what I did again to you or anyone else."

"OK," he said, mulling over her promise.

"There is something very important I have to tell you besides that I love you. I've been saving it specially for now."

"Must be science?" he probed.

"Of course, the best kind."

"Enlighten me," he said, resting back in his chair in the dim candlelight. She could see his silvery hair appearing nearly chalk white.

"My company today sent out confidential letters to all US biotech companies placing you in a favored status. You're now free to work in the USA again," reported Zita excitedly. She watched his reaction.

Alex sat quietly and thought a moment prior to speaking. "That's big of them. It does help. Are they going to give me credit for the breakthrough?" She was puzzled by his desire for recognition.

"I don't know. They allowed me to tell you only this good news."

"Don't get me wrong, your news is wonderful and restores my faith in you. But I want them to give credit where it's due. I should have a Nobel Prize in genetics. And they're using my chimps after releasing me for doing their work. What hypocrites, Zita."

"I know. I used that same argument to lift your blackball."

"Wonder how they'd feel if I held a news conference and declared myself the person who did the work. And offered exact procedures, methods, and techniques to the highest bidder?"

"They'd probably just shit."

"I'd hope so."

"Would you like to talk with Charlie about all of this?"

"Yes, and tomorrow regardless of what the little squirt has going. It's important."

"I'll see him first thing in the morning."

"Have him come to my room, here!"

Reluctantly Charlie cancelled meetings and took Zita with him to Alex's hotel. She waited in the lobby for two long hours while the two met one-on-one. Charlie finally emerged in rather high spirits.

"I suppose he'll tell you if I don't. We will be giving him credit for his work. He'll present it in Geneva to the World Health Organization. There are details to be worked out, but it should help Quotech and him. We'll be putting him on as a consultant retroactively clear back to his release years ago, so it appears he never left us entirely. He'll even get all that big back salary too, plus he will work here about a month each year."

"Do you think there's a chance he may return here to work permanently?"

"You're a jump ahead of me. You'd better ask him. But look at these!" He handed her two glass test tubes filled with a milky solution. Floating in them were two unmistakable embryos.

"Did he say what they are?"

"Yes, and I want them transplanted into two surrogate gorilla females immediately. The situation in Africa may come unglued anytime, and he wants these greenback improvements saved in case the worst happens there."

"Is what we're doing right, Charlie? I don't see us as ethical in this by taking South African embryos."

"There are no laws being broken here. Alex has it all figured out."

Zita was amazed at how pleased Charlie was with what could have been a nasty situation. Before the sunset, Zita's laboratory transplant technicians had the two embryos resting in the wombs of primate females. The implants used the newest artificial placentas that had recently been developed.

That evening over their hotel dinner, Alex filled Zita in on the details of the embryos and explained how they could benefit the company.

"I was going to give you the embryos as a surprise since I came to know what your work was. But instead, they came in handy in bargaining with Charlie. I have never liked or trusted that man.

Something about him just bothers me. Maybe it's that hair on his upper lip."

Zita laughed and said, "He has been a lot better in all this than I thought he'd be. Can't help but feel he has something up his sleeve."

"Could be."

Alex went on and explained how for years livestock transplanters had carried their embryos in tubes in and out of many countries. Zita said nothing but knew all about it. He'd simply used their technique keeping them warmly taped in his armpit on the plane and under a bathroom heat lamps in hotels.

The next evening, Erick, Kate, and Zita listened spellbound as Alex rehearsed his paper on introducing plant DNA materials into animals. Zita saw at once how he left gaps in order to protect the entire procedure from being easily followed. Both he and she knew some of the missing techniques. These omissions were expected in such generalized presentations.

Two days later, he presented his paper to the board of directors of Quotech. Alex had prepared most of the paper in South Africa and carried it with him for safety. They were spellbound and officially lifted his blackball status, shook his hand, and praised him for his great work, welcoming him back into the company fold. The meeting was secret and off the record to protect both Alex and Quotech.

A week later and in a new month, Alex winged his way to Geneva and revealed to the entire scientific world his great achievement. Alex acted as if no rift had ever occurred with Quotech. The press conference reporters asked why he was now working in unstable South Africa. Eventually, Alex told them it was a part-time farm-out opportunity too good to pass up. He was doing amazing things there, all of which were secret. Like leeches, the reporters tried to suck information from him, but Alex held firm.

This breakthrough publicity placed Alex in good stead as a world scientist of the highest merit. Without doubt, offers would come from around the world.

Soon Alex returned to his work flying directly to South Africa via London.

Zita felt so empty when he departed and couldn't figure out what he had to gain in returning to that troubled land. She ached to have him with her all the time, but threw herself into leading the fast-moving research. Time seemed to evaporate in her busy life.

Everyone at Quotech was stunned when a month later a French company unveiled the same green chimp types. What had happened? Was there a mole spy in Quotech, or had Alex given the genes to South Africa who passed them on to the French? The French could not have come up with this randomly out of the blue. This sudden development showed that competition was afoot in Europe as well as Africa. Despite all the worry and double-checking of security, there was no way of knowing what had happened in the closed world of biotech secrecy. Suspicions surrounded everyone involved in the chimp work, but nothing concrete had been uncovered. There must be a spy somewhere in Quotech working for that French company.

Months later, the two greenbacks Alex had brought to Quotech and implanted in surrogate apes were born and doing well. They were improvements in the areas of fat synthesis and digestive functions. Food intake could be greatly reduced, and cage cleanings were much easier with the newcomers.

Intrauterine-collected cellular DNA was inserted into the company's new generation of greenbacks. Duplicate samples were stored in the elaborate gene/embryo freezers banks at −70 degrees in Quotech's basement. The lab took no chances with these new gene treasures they had obtained from Alex. Hopefully the South Africans were not leaking duplicates to the French, but somebody was.

Charlie seemed highly pleased with Alex's reinstatement, even though he was part-time and now out of the country. Zita listened to Charlie and knew that he planned to capitalize on Alex as much as possible and lure him back from South Africa to full-time work. Zita knew landing Alex had made Charlie look good in the eyes of the board of directors. She was Charlie's ace in the hole to get Alex to leave South Africa and suspected that was why he was now being so great with her.

It all seemed too good to be true to Zita. There had to be a downside in all this. She wondered what Charlie was holding back. She tried to pass it off as just her female intuition or her scientific skepticism. Had she known what was ahead with the chimp project, she would have been shaken to her very soul.

12 Scientific Competition

After another nine months of intensive laboratory research work, Alex finally arrived back at Quotech where he was to spend a month working and consulting. Zita again felt happy, took a few days off, and enjoyed time with him after he recovered from jet lag.

Six months before Alex arrived, Kate had evolved into a faithful friend for Erick, and they gradually had fallen in love. She was a regular around their house, but still retained her own apartment nearby. She worked as a chemical researcher but was not at Quotech. Erick admired the peppy, positive, and energetic style of the dedicated Kate. Her quick smile and bright eyes told a zest for life. She was good for Erick, and Zita enjoyed seeing him in a positive relationship with another scientist. His new love was a fun companion in all kinds of way with her good sense of humor. She could make anything funny.

Since his outdoor childhood, he had moved to be a calculating scientist never too involved with anyone on such a steady basis. But he fell head over heels for his new lady. She loved to cook and waited on him hand and foot in an almost servant like manner. This bothered Zita, but Erick, who had fended for himself or had depended on Zita, wallowed in the attention. Zita couldn't figure out why a woman of science was so domestic. However, she liked her and didn't question Kate's hobby of sewing her own clothing. Kate was so fun and open for anything, which made her appeal to Erick who often needed some pushing to get into new things. He had enough drama at work to keep him occupied, and a new comrade put a new spirit in his home life.

At work, Quotech's board of directors responded to the French company Francone's unveiling of green chimps by having a big show of their own greenbacks, showing how far ahead of the French they were. Clearly, having engineered all the photosynthetic pigments into the backs was great progress. Worldwide, people wanted to know if fish, pigs, or cattle would be next in food-producing back patterns.

The big splash of media brought publicity, criticism, and numerous eager investors. Conservatives and skeptics around the world wanted to know what was going to happen if humans became part of this kind of change in animals. Was it moral now that humans could be used in genetic research due to legislation the president had recently signed? Quotech was evasive in responding to these questions, rendering critics outraged. Times were changing away from the days when a Chinese scientist went to prison for changing DNA in unborn human baby females.

At the end of that month and a few days before Alex's return to South Africa, the four celebrated at Kate and Erick's favorite spot, getting far away from the protesters who hounded Alex at every turn. Late in the night, the drinking got out of hand and loosened tongues. Alex described his first wife's habit of dressing and undressing in the dark or a closet. And how she liked sex in the outdoors in the bright sun under green trees.

"My ex-husband, bless his heart, wasn't able to hold an erection for more than a few minutes," offered Kate, "This killed his macho since he was of Macedonian extraction and a big college baseball coach. I think that, rather than me, drove him into grump hood. I was ready to divorce him, not because of sex, but for his grouchy moods. Didn't have to with him gettin' killed in the bus wreck. I felt guilty about it after he was gone—wondered what kind of a jerk I'd become."

"The correct term is 'Bitch.'" Alex laughed.

"Take this," countered Kate, flipping him the finger from across the table.

"Think you'll ever get married again?" asked Alex tauntingly.

"Only to someone who is really smart. Not a coach."

"Does he have to hold an erection?" asked Erick laughing.

Kate didn't answer and smiled. Finally speaking, she said, "He has to respect my career as well as his own. I never want to be a second stringer again."

"Speaking of second stringers, now that I'm a mighty consultant and can consult as I wish, let's all take the day off and roam a bit of California doing outdoors consulting."

"Desert consulting. Wow! With all those awful roads out there, let's not take any of our good cars and rent that one we got over on Pamona Avenue months ago," snickered Zita.

"Great idea to use it as we did on the last hill trip. I liked it so well. Great comfort," said Erick, "I haven't had a day off in a month of Sundays and will gladly drive."

"Charlie knows he owes me time off too, so I'll have no problem. I'll let him know we are all going. He'll have to live with it," added Zita.

Kate said, "I'll let you know if I can get off once I get to my lab in the morning. Now I just don't know. I need to get out of this dump before I really get zonkered clear out of my mind." Kate went to her apartment since she needed different clothes for the desert trip and asked them to pick her up on their way to the car rental in the morning.

"Hope I didn't offend her with my teasing sending her home, Erick," said Alex.

"Naw! She needs things if she goes with us. Just has to let her bosses know."

Charlie was delighted to give Zita the day off, but Kate called and had to stay at work. Erick decided to work too, letting Zita and Alex spend a day together before he flew off South.

"Sadly, I only have two days left. This month has really zoomed by. So what shall we do?"

"Let it be your choice, the desert or seashore?"

"The desert," he answered. "It has been years since I've seen the open spaces of inland California. That seashore is congested, and I hate the fetid waters."

As their rental car zipped along, Zita noticed the absence of vehicles once they reached the desert. Perhaps eight dollars a gallon for gasoline had something to do with it. Since the drastic decline in domestic and foreign oil production, Western Colorado's oil shale had saved the country. But it was expensive, and half of the nation's families had reluctantly given up their private transportation systems.

"I'm so pleased that you and Erick have gotten to know each other better on this stay."

"He's a prince, and by the way she looks at him, Kate adores the ground he walks on. I think they're made for each other."

"Yes, there's something afoot there. They've been seeing each other nearly half a year, and that's unusual for Erick. We've known each other longer than they have."

"Indeed, but damnit, the time together has been way too little. I regret my visits are so infrequent. Maybe you could come to Cape Town in July. It's lovely that time of year."

"Would they give me a visa with all that turmoil? And how safe is it?"

"Safe enough if you take precautions and avoid the black rebel–held areas. There are killer squads, usually political stuff. The authorities are leery of media people, but we science types are let alone. I might not leave you alone," he said, squeezing her hand.

"Maybe I'll just come see you. I haven't taken a long holiday since New Zealand." She leaned across and kissed his cheek, bumping her knees on the mounted cellular radio and GPS. "Isn't that a weird old radio to have in a rental car in this era, Alex?"

"Suppose so, but it was this tough ole car you wanted—so just watch those lovely knees, dear. South Africa is still a dangerous place since nobody knows what each side is up to. I'm directly in the middle of it all, but safe."

Zita could sense how uncomfortable Alex was and doubted if she would ever really visit him in such a racially contested land.

"Erick and Kate may be getting married. I can sense it even though he hasn't said anything. She's at our place nearly around the clock or else he's at hers."

"Sounds serious."

"They're a perfect match—both chemists and enjoy many of the same outside things." She looked at him, admiring what a slim and handsome fellow she had. Alex was a tall six-foot and maybe 180 pounds without any big midsection, and his face was way young for his age. Indeed, she thought he was most easy on the eyes.

"Would you ever consider linking your life with mine?" he asked.

"That's an awkward way of asking. I think there is definite potential there, but we must get in the same country."

He chuckled.

"I agree, I'd like to see myself out of South Africa in eighteen months. But I don't know if the USA is for me either. The falling standard of living, four hundred million people, and all this ugly pollution, plus the poverty and racial unrest in your stagnant cities." Alex bemoaned the downgrading of America, shaking his head. "It all sure happened so rapidly along with the global warming after George Bush and then Trump whose buddies let every safeguard vanish."

"I take offense to some of that. No country has the racial problems and poverty you do in South Africa."

"Yes, but I'm not a citizen there, just a working foreign scientist. With my new publicity, they now think I'm a saint. Some, on the other hand in this country, think anyone working in genetics is the devil. That includes you."

"That's true of the right-wing religious groups here. It all started getting worse when Bush and Trump were the anti-science presidents."

"What a mess they made of this country."

Midmorning they stopped for coffee at a small café. Three men soon entered and sat by the door. They were black and dressed in black suits. They appeared to be government agents or underworld functionaries. A heavy middle-aged woman with dishwater blond hair served them, chattered, and flirted happily. Few sleek travelers apparently came this far from the main interstate highway.

Soon after a coffee, Alex pushed the car at top speed beyond several small towns and headed into the more isolated desert on a graveled road. Suddenly, he noticed the gas gauge was low and wheeled the big black car around to fill up at the small town they'd just passed. Several miles behind them, they passed an oncoming tan car and the three men in a whirl of road dust.

"What do you suppose those guys are doing way out here?"

"They must be following us. The route I've taken is totally irrational. I don't like this."

"Maybe they're lost and just following us to find a main road or something."

"They surely have a GPS. Why have they stayed so far back? Most of the time nearly out of my rearview mirrors. With all the twists and turns, I don't see how they'd ever have followed us."

Alex filled up with gasoline and left the small town by a different road hoping to lose their trackers. After a few more miles, Alex noticed a dust cloud behind them.

"They're still with us I think, Zita. Must have GPS locked on to our car. I don't like this a bloody bit."

"Why us?"

"Who knows? There's everything from me being from out of the country, kidnapping, or maybe our work." He didn't mention robbery or the beautiful female beside him. He was having an internal panic knowing this was not normal.

"In about ten miles, according to this GPS map, we'll hit pavement again and can head back toward the freeway. You'll take a left there."

"I'm uneasy about this. It's not against the law to follow people either, so what can we do?"

At the blacktop, Alex turned left and raced at high speed for a few miles and pulled around facing the opposite direction in a scooped-out gravel pit with a steep bank bordering the road. Their car was neatly hidden. He planned to head left after they passed and moved out of sight.

"Now, when they come past here, we know they're after us. Once they pass, we just head the opposite direction." He clinched the steering wheel with sweaty hands waiting in silence. The car didn't pass. He couldn't figure it out, but they couldn't see the oncoming road over the high bank and gravel piles. They waited, watching for a passing.

Unexpectedly three men ringed the sloping north exit of the gravel pit between them and the road.

"Looks like they want to talk."

"Talk hell!" He slammed the car in reverse.

Alex gunned the car at full speed backward up the opposite bank, spun it around, and headed toward the open desert. By then those men had quickly drawn guns. Shots rang out and glass fragments showered the back seat as a hail of bullets pounded the car. He managed to avoid rocks and brush getting back to the road ahead of the men.

"Are you all right?"

"I've pain in my legs," she said coolly, "I've never been shot before. It's burning, and a little blood is oozing on my seat."

"Shit! I think they got me too, in my left arm, or it's the glass. But I can move it."

"How far behind us?"

"Just within sight, way back. I'm going to drive this beast for all she's worth for the freeway. Get that cellular car phone and call help. Bloody-sons-of-bitches!"

Calmly she reported exact details to the 911 operator and compressed the wounds on her thighs with her jacket, retarding the bleeding. She could move her legs.

Alex was pushing the car wide open. It was running well despite bullet holes. Yet he could see the black speck in his rearview mirror.

Zita crawled into the back seat, disregarding her bleeding thighs, the wind, and the broken glass. She placed a scarf around Alex's arm wound from behind; it didn't appear as if an artery had been hit. Soon she struggled back into the front seat and tended again to her own bleeding.

The powerful old rental car kept ahead during the wild chase, but the other car was gaining on them. Zita remained in contact with the California State Police and local sheriff who had set up a roadblock on the freeway stopping them. The close trailing car tried to run the roadblock, but its tires were ripped apart by the tire shredder stretched across the pavement. With satisfaction, Zita and Alex watched police drag the three men from the car and force them flat to the ground face down.

Quickly after some first aid, Zita and Alex were both heading for a hospital. The handcuffed men in black suits were still on the ground watched over by the California State Police as their ambulance passed them by.

"When I go anywhere new and fun with you, we end up in broken glass and blood," quipped Zita. They both chuckled as the ambulance sped along.

"Seems like it. I trust the police will find out why they wanted to kill us."

"Or maybe just you. I haven't an enemy in the world."

"Maybe you do and don't know it."

The emergency room team quickly cleaned and tended to their flesh wounds, gave them plenty of shots to ward off infections, and released them. However, they had to wait for the police interview.

"Except for my work, I can't think of a single reason anyone would want to kill me."

"Nor me," added Zita.

"Kidnapping is out too, I think."

The captain of the highway patrol and another uniformed officer entered, greeted them, and asked how they were doing.

"We're lucky to have flesh wounds, and thanks for helping us. Who were they, and why did they try to kill us?" asked Zita.

The captain replied, "We may never know. They have papers and diplomatic immunity preventing us from confining or questioning them."

"Surely you jest," snorted Alex.

"No, sir, what I said is the case."

Zita replied, "But they tried to kill us! Surely no immunity protects that."

"Not so, lady, and I'd love to jail 'em as much as you. My boss says I can't."

"What can you tell us about them?" asked Zita.

"Nothing!"

"Oh, come on, we have a right to know who the hell shot us!" roared Alex, his face reddening.

"I'll have to ask my boss!"

"You do that, and let us speak with him. Give him our wristband numbers. I'm leaving the country tomorrow night and need to know."

"Will do."

In wonderment, they tried to figure out why anyone would want to kill them in the desert, and how did they know where they were going, and in what car. Did someone at the car rental put a bug on their car? Or was it just a random incident? Alex feared it wasn't, and his anger boiled over as he suspected it related to him.

13 Immunity

It was a sobering ride back home for the bandaged pair. They felt at a dead end, frustrated at the blocked knowledge about the attack. Since his wounds were not bone breakers, Alex decided to return to South Africa because it might take weeks to actually learn about the attackers.

His work back in South Africa had been moved to a more secure secret new laboratory location northwest of Cape Town. Alex assured Zita that he could heal on the job and would have great medical care. Reluctantly, she agreed.

Later at the airport as Zita sat with Erick and Kate watching, Alex disappeared down the loading ramp into the airliner. Tears welled up in Zita's eyes seeing him go, but he'd promised to take care of himself. That would be easier now that he was an official consultant of an American company, Quotech, and had a newfound international reputation South Africa would surely boast of and closely monitor.

Zita's mind raced over those grim past twenty-four hours of frustrating events. State police officials came to her house and explained the three men were from the Namibian embassy and held immunity. Police did give their names, which didn't help much. She was told that a request could be made through diplomatic channels to have Namibia turn the villains over to the LA police. That was highly unlikely, and the paperwork could take months.

Back the next day at Quotech, both she and enraged Charlie tried to figure out why the Namibians would do such a thing to two of the company's scientists. Charlie was adamant that it was for political reasons wanting to get national attention by doing in a great scientist who was working for and supporting the white government of South Africa. Charlie was sure Namibia, which bordered South Africa, was a black government supporting the rebels across the border, but what interest might they have in Zita? Another question was how they knew where Alex was and where they were going. The police did find a homing device attached to the underside of the rental car, which explained how they were followed in the many spider-webbed and vacant desert roads. Was the device placed there at the café stop or earlier at the rental car agency? Nobody knew for sure. But the police would look into it.

Zita spent most of the next week healing and resting at home. She questioned if she was still in danger and extended that worry on to Alex. Maybe there would be another attempt. The mere thought frightened her. Yet still concerned, she returned to a light workday determined to watch for anyone following her. She now stayed with Erick going and coming from work.

She planned a trip to the embassy of Namibia, made an appointment, and had a representative of her United States senator's office and Charlie at her side. They were ushered into a sleek office by a polite and well-dressed man who appeared to be made of ebony. His sleek blackness and beautiful facial features were regal, womanly.

"Omar is my name, and I deeply regret this incident."

"We would like to know what is behind this shooting, and have those responsible held accountable," said the senator's aide brusquely.

"It is a most sensitive matter for my country," countered Omar. "I have no authority until orders arrive."

"Our State Department will be requesting a full explanation of this incident, a handing over of those involved, and an issuance of an apology to our government. We take very seriously the shooting of our top scientists."

"As do we. However, we must look further into the matter before taking any action. And as you know, your laws do not pertain to people in this African mission."

"We clearly understand that. At this point, we are seeking information that will allow this scientist to continue her life without fear of further assaults. The other scientist is no longer in this country."

"Then he is out of the picture since Namibia has no relations with his government."

Zita could see a coldness fall over the face of the official. She asked, "Can I not be at least given a clue about why I was set upon and shot?"

"We most deeply regret your injury, dear lady. I am not at liberty to speculate."

"Can't I at least talk with your people who were involved? They are right in this building, aren't they?"

"My government will not allow its mission members to speak on the matter."

Charlie erupted, "Don't you at least have the decency to set this lady's mind at ease with some assurances about future attacks?"

"I'm sorry!"

"What kind of a country is this Namibia anyway?" His face was beet red, and Zita thought he might be hyperventilating.

The aide took over. "We will be looking forward to your report on this matter. And you will be made aware of this country's actions over this incident."

"This is an outrage for you to give us literally nothing when my two great scientists could have been killed. Your damn country is so backward, what could you even know of their technical work?" snapped Charlie in disgust. Omar sat in stone silence.

Finally, the aide said, "Thanks for your time. It's time we left. Good day!"

They departed in deep frustration and anger with Charlie swearing to himself. Zita went silent wondering why Charlie was so overzealous. The senator's aide assured them the matter was far from closed, and they would be hearing progress from their California senator and the Department of State.

Doubt ridden, Zita and Charlie returned to Quotech. Zita sat in her office and thought about her situation. Waiting would be the name of the game until something came from Alex or the Namibians. It now seemed clear to her that there was some logical connection between the black rebels of the African National Congress and the attackers since the rebels were using Namibia as a sanctuary and supply area as they battled the South African government. How could this possibly involve her? The press had been told nothing of the attack because of its international sensitivity. Both Starks thought the attack was centered on Alex and the greenback genetic work, but they were not positive.

At their work, there was no need to fuel the fires of the protesters who daily chanted at Quotech's gate. "Quotech is playing God," their signs often read. The most active group, Those for Pure and Natural Gene Pools, started throwing eggs and tomatoes, forcing Quotech to hire buses to move several thousand employees in and out of the work compound. Executives were forced to ride the buses too after the protesters seized, rocked, and turned a board member's limo on its top.

Both Starks refused to consider they were doing anything wrong. It was a science undertaking, a pure and hands-off viewpoint of science work, although they recognized the social implications. Opponents saw these scientists as evildoers. Historically, it reminded many of the abortion struggles in the 2000s before the small "morning-after" pills and male birth controls defused the issue by severely reducing potential abortions worldwide.

A message arrived from South Dakota for the Starks. It reminded them of the sadness they had felt when their parents had been killed in a highway landslide six years before. After that funeral, their uncle Kenny had moved into their homeplace on the edge of Hill City. It gave him a place to live since he needed one in his retirement with only limited funds to survive. This new communication startled the Starks, saying Kenny had been found dead near the river on the property he was overseeing for them.

Closer to his maverick uncle Kenny, Erick decided to fly back and take care of the situation and the property now belonging to both of them. Zita was happy having him take on that responsibility and gave him power of attorney for whatever he wanted to do on their behalf. Surprisingly, Erick took a full ten-day leave and asked Kate to go along to which Zita happily agreed. She was happy not having to deal with the situation, knowing disposing of the wonderful river-bordered homeplace would break her heart. Additionally, she had never liked her recluse uncle because of childhood memories she endured from his verbal abuse and bad temper.

Kate and Erick arrived at the Rapid City airport and headed to Mount Rushmore National Park where they enjoyed a patriotic visit. Both of them became choked up seeing the huge faces carved in the granite and realizing how disappointing recent leaders had been in solving the nation's urgent environmental situations. Those in stone would have done a better job in their estimations.

On the short mountain drive toward Hill City, Kate shouted, "Look at the mountain goats there, a mother and baby!"

"Wow, aren't they stunning and so white. Reminds me of my zillion trips up here with Dad where he worked for the park. We'd see those goats at times too. What a treat. You are bringing good luck, Kate."

"Nice they're still here. I've never seen any before, and I love watching wildlife."

"Thinking of natural settings, this area was my wildlife paradise growing up. I was a nature boy in these river bottom wilds feeling like an early Native American. And Zita and I once raised a goat Dad brought home with a broken leg. When it grew up, we cried when releasing it. We had loads of pets from magpies, crows, woodchucks, and even a skunk once. That was a stinking mess. But you'll see how the old place has loads of habitat and with a nice river we grew up adventuring along. In high school, I even trapped mink and muskrats in the early winter for spending money. It was more fun than moneymaking following the river with our dog, and sometimes Zita came along on those frosty early mornings before school. Those special times with silent and stunning surroundings sure sent both of us into the natural sciences eventually. What a great way to grow up right next to a small town with the wilds just outside our back door. I was sure a wild nature boy growing up."

"What a growing up you've had. And having a naturalist father to boot. No wonder you went into the sciences."

"Yes, we had contact with most all the wildlife in these Black Hills with Dad, and then sis and I both went to Black Hill College in the sciences. That's where I fell in love with chemistry along with biology, and we both ended up at CU in Colorado on full-ride doctoral programs."

She replied, "My chemistry was an academic love without all your natural growing-up fun. My, you are blessed, and I love who you are and have been."

"I love you too, Kate, and can hardly wait for you to see my old home, but we have a lot to do taking care of the mess Kenny must have left behind. He was a semi hermit, but a responsible one."

The next week was full with cremation details, scantly attended funeral home services, and clearing out the family home with most everything going to the trash or donated to thrift and secondhand stores. Then they tried to find someone to list the place for selling. Neither of the twins wanted to sell, but decided they had no choice.

By the time they arrived back at LAX, the situation had changed because Kate had located tenant caretakers for the property. They were a local conservation group needing a headquarters house for managing several land areas already under their control in the local area. It was a perfect fit since the group had a good history. Erick had a twenty-year lease drawn up that pleased Zita. Now with the papers drawn up and the family property under lease to a responsible group, they could visit the issue again far into the future. Erick loved Kate as never before seeing her so helpful and engaged in a tough situation. He didn't tell her, but he was secure with her being his future wife.

Back at work in Quotech, endless meetings with charts, power-point presentations, and projected spreadsheets of chemical and genetic formulas cluttered Zita's mind, keeping her from focusing on her healing thighs and any intrigue outside of her building. Teams of geneticists and gene manipulation scientists kept her bombarded with new ideas and experiments for her to consider. She had to convey their proposed work to gain Charlie's approval. Much of it would be handed off to universities in long contracts. At times, she longed for the simpler days when she had her own complicated projects. Yet she felt powerful making things happen and having a hand in many pies, many of her own design.

Media messages from Alex told of his healing and the new marvelous laboratory, all positives. He avoided details of the political situation and speculated that in some misguided way it might have caused the attack on them. "After all," he said, "I'm a white scientist protected by and working for a regime oppressing the black majority." He did miss Zita and wrote her other lusty letters that excited her.

While sitting on the bus watching the protesters and waiting to emerge safely from Quotech, Zita was stunned with a thought that shook her deeply. She clearly remembered Kate knowing of their desert drive, type of old luxury car, car rental location, going to her apartment instead of home with Erick, and all on the night right before the dastardly attack. At first Zita scolded herself for such thoughts. But they kept coming back and back. She dared not share her thinking with Erick and pondered how to proceed but didn't have the time or know-how. She also wondered if her thoughts were some deeply hidden resentment about losing Erick to Kate. That did not seem a huge problem, but she would hate not having him as an always housemate.

After two days of stewing, she contacted Scott, the Los Angeles police detective attached to their desert case. She explained the delicate nature of her suspicions. The huge man with a deeply pockmarked face appeared more like a lumberjack than a detective. He listened carefully, took notes, and promised to check out Kate's background and connections on the QT. Zita was to contact Scott in one week and meet away from her home or work. She wanted no record of any inquiry in case it proved nothing. Scott agreed to keep it all off the record unless suspicions went somewhere.

That next night on the way home in a sudden brown dense smog, Zita felt guilty hating to face Kate and Erick over the dinner table. Keeping up a good front turned out to be easier for her that evening, and she was getting comfortable with personal and Quotech's secrecy.

The next week went quickly with news of some riots in South Africa. But happily, digestive tract genetics problems in the greenbacks kept her occupied. She worked hard to keep Alex and South Africa out of her mind. He was a big boy and had been taking care of himself for a long time. But her mind constantly drifted north of Cape Town when she was trying to find out where things had gone wrong with farmed-out gastric genetic work on chimp digestion done by a huge university in Germany. Her feelings were bounding back and forth between her work and personal life, making her stressed.

On the good side, however, progress was rapid in inserting the nitrogen synthesis gene system from hamsters into chimp embryos and plants. It had worked perfectly in the plants. These spectacular results had Quotech's best minds and consultants in constant meetings considering future insertions into potatoes, peanuts, and other crops around the world to feed the hungry masses in areas lacking fertilizers and having nitrogen poor soils. Having nitrogen from the atmosphere in more plants would be a boon for people trying to raise crops in the marginal soils around the globe. It could push back desertification and hold blowing soils on the edges of advancing deserts. And maybe less land would be used to farm, thus, also use less water, but would it slow down human overpopulation?

Zita, with her pure research view, resented and grew weary of Charlie always coming back to the economics involved. It sometimes dismayed her and Erick how the company brass downplayed the pure improvement in nutrition for the world's undernourished billions. They seemed to measure every advance with the yardstick of riches.

Erick usually said, "No lower can one descend than to measure everything in silver and gold," when they mixed economics and research science.

Heaped on top of all her concerns were the increasing press attacks and protests around Quotech. The attacks were now more violent as irrational ideas spread as scientific facts. The media was less than responsible in fanning the flames of the protests to make each event a bigger and bigger story.

Any layperson might conclude, from the media, that work being done at Quotech was sinister with goals of producing monsters and wanting to enslave humans via genetic engineering. It was way out of line and sensationalized as if science fiction hysteria had taken over some of the media. The company brass concluded the situation would settle down when the fickle press found some new story to cover. So Zita and Erick pretended nobody was throwing the vegetables and eggs that rained down daily on their bus when they entered Quotech.

14 Complications

Later one evening in a small coffee shop in chocking smog, Zita sipped cups of black hot coffee waiting anxiously for Scott to arrive. She gazed at the dense air in the hot night and fretted over what Scott had for her. He had called for a meeting not wanting to speak over any media, making her worry about what he had to reveal. Scott walked in and loomed tall as a redwood and finally settled into the booth across from her, his long legs sticking out into the aisle.

"Good evening, Ms. Stark."

"How are you, Scott?"

"Not worth a hoot, I'm tired! It was a rough day to say the least. Too many bosses and too many irons in the fire."

"I imagine you get overwhelmed." She liked the honest approach and downhome manner of the big man who had a kindness about him.

"Maybe I should have stayed unloading trucks at the warehouse. Just kidding." He paused, looked her squarely in the eyes, and said, "I have bad news for you."

"Well, for heaven's sake, tell me, Scott. I'm a big girl."

"I find no background information on Kate! She just appeared out of thin air takin' the name of someone who died back in Pennsylvania ten years ago, social security number and all."

"Are you sure?" gasped Zita.

"The FBI nationwide computers seldom give us anything but the truth. And there is more. Seems that a cellphone tower record from near her apartment shows calls to a foreign high-tech company and that embassy the morning you were attacked."

"Then she is involved."

"Appears so, and her own records show a cellular wristband call to a wireless phone before you and Alex rented that car just before you left Quotech for the desert."

"Suppose that phone belongs to some party with immunity."

"You catch on fast, and we had to notify the Namibians their records were being examined. Protocol, you know. It's probably only a matter of time until they figure out what's up and what we're looking for."

"What's the next step?" asked Zita, angry and unhinged. With this news, what might be Erick's reactions? This will just kill him. Under her breath, she said, "The bitch." Her mind raced. Kate, a spy and maybe with a foreign nation to boot. Zita wondered how Kate fit into this web. It was easier to see Alex in it, but not her. But why try to kill anyone, and even Erick who might have been along with them on that trip since he backed out at the very last minute? Did Kate know that?

"We have a judge looking to get us a warrant for the arrest. But we can't touch those others. The judge is also seeking a federal waiver of their immunity too. But that's rare, and he'll need approval of the country involved. Fat chance of that knowing what I do about them. Our government will probably eventually expel the whole lot in a few months."

"If we nail Kate, maybe we can get to the bottom of this. When do you plan to pick her up?" Zita was steamed, and angrier than she had been in ages.

"If the judge signs the warrant, first thing in the morning. I've let Charlie know, and the FBI will want her computer from her company too. I've said nothing to her company, just in case there is a nest of spies over there. Then we comb her office, search her apartment, and get proof of her connections with the Namibians. A live and involved witness is real good proof, lady."

"Don't know whether to thank you or not for this."

"Better Erick finds out now rather than later. Besides, she's the one who helped point the finger of death at you and Alex."

"She still doesn't seem the type. She never talked much with Erick or myself about our work or projects. It was strangely all social and fun."

"Lady, in real life, there are no types, and you may not know what she got from your brother, or how she was waiting to get it."

"Should I go home or stay away tonight? Don't think I can keep from giving this away."

"Just act normal, and it will be over by noon."

She stole into the apartment late, went straight to bed, and didn't have to face the two. She rose early leaving a note that she had an early meeting and headed to Quotech. Zita met Scott and Charlie there and rode in his unmarked police car to Kate's company. Once in front of Kate's building, they sat and waited for what seemed endless hours.

Finally, Zita called Erick. "Where's Kate?"

"Gee, I don't know. Haven't seen her since noon yesterday, and she hasn't answered my calls. Strange. Have you seen her?"

"No. I just have a question for her."

Later, Scott drove as if going to an arrest, squealing tires during the wild ride to Kate's apartment. They had first picked up Erick at Quotech on their way since Zita wanted him along because he had a key to her apartment. He sat in stoic silence in the back seat, stunned after what Scott revealed about Kate. Scott was careful not to bring Zita into the matter and made it appear that Kate had come up in his routine desert investigation and didn't check out.

"I don't see how she ever passed a check on her background. Some of it must be true since she could do her job at that company," said Charlie.

Scott replied, "These people aren't fools and have been trained a long time in high-tech spying. I wonder what's in this apartment. Maybe we'll surprise 'er."

"I hope she's there and all this is wrong," said Erick as the car stopped in the parking lot. Nobody replied.

No answer at the door. Keys opened the many locks. Scott said, "All of you stay out here 'til I check it out."

With his pistol drawn, he rammed into the room and soon reappeared. "Gone."

Everything inside was as Zita and Erick knew it; but her personal belongings were missing.

"Bet you a fin this stuff is rented from one of those places and was paid for in cash. They want to get out fast when the jig's up!"

Zita asked, "What now?"

"I'll get a team in here and maybe fingerprints will tell us something. As fast as she cleared out, I doubt there was time to wipe 'em all down. We'll find some someplace and of course her DNA."

"Then we just wait?" asked Charlie.

"Afraid so! Least we didn't find her dead or something. Now I can start with her company. They probably have it all erased and covered up by now, having had time to move her out. That's if her company was even involved in spying on yours. Damn the luck!"

"Or maybe her company had no role in all this," said Erick. "She never once asked me much about my Quotech work. What kind of a spy is that?"

"We seldom know the angles. If we had got her, maybe she'd talk and connect the Namibians to all this," added Charlie.

"Did she own a car?"

"No," replied Erick, "Why would she do this anyway?"

"Probably money," quipped Scott. "We'll eventually catch up with her, but it'll take time."

The investigation stalled. Months crawled by as Erick seemed to rise above his deep depression about Kate. With great difficulty, he finally accepted Kate being a spy, using him, and lying to him. Yet he never knew why she would betray someone she professed to love and wanted to marry her.

Kate had simply vanished, but her fingerprints were obtained from Erick's bedroom. Nothing new came from the FBI, and Scott urged patience, but he seemed distressed about how things were going. Even the expulsions of the three Namibians from the embassy hadn't made a difference. Quotech's rival company and Kate's employer did everything they could to help. It looked as if Kate's company had not been involved. It all seemed strange to Zita. Kate was gone, but whom had she been spying for, and who could have tipped her off to vanish?

Meanwhile in South Africa, Alex was outraged about Kate, and the country was deeply in the midst of a returning revolution. He was far from the front and northwest where the actual fighting was so bloody. Riots had prompted martial law to be imposed with dusk-to-dawn curfews across the land. Killing bands of both blacks and whites roamed the countryside, hunting targets and each other. These groups were pursued by government forces bent on stamping out all of them. According to the media, there was no safety.

Zita listened to the international news with an uneasy feeling that Alex was trying to keep her worry free. It appeared much worse than he let on. She concluded it was either that or the media was making tragic the entire situation, which was the usual case. She couldn't figure out why he was staying there when he could come and work for Quotech full-time and not be in such danger. His routine reply was, "My work is terribly important, and I'm far away from any fighting." Zita buried herself in the complex genetic engineering projects, trying to put Alex out of her mind. But she couldn't.

On the home front, neither Scott, the FBI, or Charlie's Quotech-hired private investigators could connect the Namibians with any high-tech companies outside of Kate's calls. After five months, the FBI matched Kate's prints to a passport application for Chile under the name of Wanda Fair from Boise, Idaho. That happened to be her real name, opening a floodgate of data on her real life. She really had attended BYU earning a PhD in chemical engineering and worked in research institutes on campuses. She then moved into biotech work with big companies.

Kate had no living family. Her parents had both passed away several years ago; she was also an only child. However, she had been married in college to a Hans Ulrich, divorcing him after finishing her final degree. Hans was an Argentine of German extraction convicted of corporate spying for both Chile and Argentina where he had been in and out of prisons. He was currently sought on charges of burglary in Colorado involving a high-tech firm in Colorado Springs.

The authorities were looking for Kate and Hans, but they had no current trail. They were checking biotech companies in South America and the United States. Scott assured everyone that something would turn up, saying, "Skunks never change their stripes. She has to have a secret long-term role in all this to be spying. I can't figure out how she got tipped off on us coming after her and fled."

In the next week, Zita and Erick focused on the deteriorating situation in South Africa. Several neighboring countries, Mozambique, Angola, Zimbabwe, Namibia, and Botswana, all of the Black Union, added troops, cutting off large portions of the South African Army. White panic and widespread rioting by local blacks were helping out. It was suddenly a three-front war with mercenaries from across Africa joining the fight to once again establish black rule in South Africa.

Even in all the news chaos, Alex often called from his off-laboratory compound local village, letting Zita know all was well with him. She knew he was putting himself in danger with his local-based calls and possibly getting suspected of sending science spy information to other countries. She hated the risk, but still wanted his calls, making her very unsettled.

Unknown to everyone, even Zita, Alex had made a secret agreement with the chairman of the Quotech board of directors. He could be picked up by a small corporate jet the company had in Cape Town anytime he needed it. The plane could also land on gravel runways. It was all in a secret escape option since even Charlie wasn't informed. The fewer people who knew the better since spies were suspected within South Africa and now Quotech as well.

Angolan and Namibian columns sneaked across Botswana between the Kalahari and the Gemsbok Game Reserves, taking the border town of Gabarone and seizing its airport. The Angolan Airforce utilized that landing strip and pounded the South African front lines and Johannesburg while ground troops advanced. Mozambique sent its forces south along the coast between the Indian Ocean and Swaziland. At the same time, Zimbabwe poured its tiny force into the battle crossing the border at Beirbridge, giving a big boost to the rebels who had been clinging to a small front in the north. These developments shocked the world.

Alex had revealed his location in Springbok north of Cape Town. The Angolan and Namibians had crossed to his north. Soon armies might strike south from Namibia straight for the capital, Cape Town.

He was at the moment safe, expressed concern, but had earlier already revealed his exact secret location to Zita. He had told her that he could get out if the situation became critical and, of course, not to worry about him. Alex would not give her details in case the call was unsecured. She was heartsick, worried, and stayed glued to the news, even at work as BBC media chattered across her office.

The situation worsened daily as every black nation in Africa seemed to dog-pile on the white South Africans with troops and support. Within a month, the country was reeling with its troops retreating south, losing the north of the country. The end appeared in sight as the United Nations was not inclined to come to the aid of such an oppressive nation. It wasn't one of those campaigns where the troops advanced with little opposition into the arms of a people happy to be liberated. Whites fled, locals looted, troops killed and rounded up the white population as the liberators were sweeping the country north to south.

Alex made a final call saying he was leaving the country. Death was everyplace as the bloodbath continued. Black nationals were pleading calm while radicals were killing whites to prevent them from ever holding control again. Whites who were heavily armed defended themselves and killed blacks in fear for their own lives. Zulus defended their own state against all comers, forcing the armies to bypass their homelands. The south and west parts of the country were still defended by the retreating white army. If the trend continued, Alex would soon be in the middle of it.

Without word, Zita waited long days fearing Alex may have been killed. Then, South Africa's white forces reformed as shiploads of hired mercenaries from India landed and cut off the invaders. It was a big setback for the black nation invaders who then fled to their countries in chaos. However, the countryside still had roving killer bands ravaging rural areas.

Both Starks could hardly keep their minds on their work at Quotech. The greenbacks from Alex's last trip were now born from the surrogates. Tests showed they had a suppressed desire to eat, seeming to get little joy from taking milk from their surrogate ape mothers. Although the thirst instinct was intact for water, it didn't seem to apply to natural milk.

This major advancement excited Zita. She knew it was her surprise from Alex. The little tikes cuddled and enjoyed being held and comforted by their gorilla mothers, but eating didn't seem a part of the equation. It was a bit frustrating for the ape mothers as their milk production dried up in their huge breasts.

One day Charlie called a staff meeting of all those involved with the greenbacks and related genetic engineering. Erick led the meeting. "We have some good stuff to talk about this morning." He usually would rather work than have what he called "useless meetings."

"What's going on with these new guys besides no drive to take in anything besides water? If for heaven's sake that isn't enough of a gift from Alex," he said, smiling at Charlie.

"Go ahead and lay it on us," replied an apparently happy Charlie.

Erick said, "For a starter, our chemical analysis of minute wastes coming out show mainly water, bile, plus a collection of enzymes, nor are they big important ones. Not a lot of E. coli either which points to the digestive tract now being 99 percent vestigial. But remember they do urinate."

Erick smiled and continued, "We don't know what's happening in South Africa with Alex, but this is one of the most startling developments in mammal engineering history. It must have taken years of changes in multiple genes. Whoever did this should get a Nobel. I think it could be Alex."

Everyone sat pondering what this meant. Finally, Charlie spoke, "Six of these little guys. We must get a huge cloning team to work at once. Isolate then in pairs; we can't take any chances of losing this to a lab infection or something."

"We could owe Alex on this one if maybe he is the one behind it. Think of what this can mean in pigs if we can transfer it. No more corn needed in their diet, just sun and water. Nebraska and Iowa corn farmers will use their fields to feed people for once instead of hogs. If we combine these greenbacks traits in the next generation along with air nitrogen fixation, then it's on to super domestic animals," exclaimed Erick to the astonished group. "My bet is Alex knows the history of all this, he is still over there in that African mess."

"This is far more than I ever expected in my lifetime in this science. Those South Africans must have spent billions getting the greatest minds to work in secret. Have you any word yet, Zita?" asked Charlie.

"None."

"Let's hope it isn't bad."

"I think they must have an escape plan for their scientists."

"Surely hope it works; we really need him here."

The next morning, a short call from an unknown party arrived, telling Zita conditions had changed and Alex was staying. She and everyone else at Quotech were shocked that he would keep himself in a war area even as the retreating blacks started a new offensive. Zita wondered if he really loved her, wanted her, and why was he still putting himself in such extreme danger. She was weary of the worry over Alex. However, now there were no communications of any kind from him. It remained an imposed total internet blackout. Much of the incoming news was speculation and couldn't be relied upon. She had to be patient and resigned herself to trust that Alex would take care of himself. Worry still tugged at her heart.

Late that evening, Scott called Zita wanting to talk about developments in the investigation. She met the huge man at an all-night café in downtown LA to avoid talking of Kate around Erick who was still hostile to any mention of her.

Scott opened by announcing the judge had issued a warrant for Kate's arrest and that the FBI was following new leads in Chile involving her former husband, Hans Ulrich. Current thinking was to find Hans or Kate and the other would be close at hand.

"Maybe we'll get someplace on this," she replied.

"Don't be too anxious. Things drag on forever; the FBI leaves no stones unturned. Seems like they'll want everything perfect before arresting," said Scott, apparently relieved that he had something positive to report.

"Anything on Kate's employers?"

"Only dead ends. They must have hired top people and those Namibians to cover their tracks. I have a couple of good people on it too. But without Kate pointing the finger, we'll never lay a hand on 'em."

"This is cause for celebration, anyway."

"Let's go have a drink. I know a little gin mill that's quiet," said Scott, raising his full six foot six out of the cramped booth.

Several drinks later, Zita was having a relaxed time laughing at Scott's stories. He told tales of police work with a bent for poking fun at his profession. He had scads of stories about police facing Saint Peter and trying to enter heaven. She laughed until tears ran down her face, never having known how funny he was.

"I want to see your place before you take me home; want to know how a real detective, not one on the media, lives."

"Nothin' special." He glanced at her, smiled for a long time, and finally released his gaze.

Their many meetings had drawn Zita to the big man with a gentle nature and quick smile. Scott seemed too nice to be a police officer, and she had often wondered what he was really like under it all. Or was what she saw what she got.

Being half looped on wine and feeling euphoric, Zita explored his spacious loft apartment in a warehouse district. The high ceilings made it almost barn-like. Walls were decorated with posters of wilderness area scenes, fish, and wild outdoor places. Hanging were actual framed paintings of Native Americans. She hadn't expected such interests from him. She poked fun at his clothes being arranged in full outfits by color. He seemed embarrassed and stammered at her teasing. She had expected clippings of cases adorning his walls. There were none. Apparently, his life wasn't his work. She hadn't known anyone like him, only workaholic science types.

She helped Scott fix another drink, and they bumped against each other in the tiny kitchen, causing a pause and the meeting of knowing eyes. He'd caught her hand to steady her. She embarrassed herself by wanting to grab and hug him, yet she retreated for the sofa sinking into its huge cushions. But she felt drawn to Scott. He settled into the sofa beside her and kicked off his big black shoes.

Eventually she boldly reached over and took his big hand. He reeled a bit, still holding her hand, and said, "I feel about you; do you return the favor?" He squeezed her hand, got up and turned down the music, and dimmed the lights before plopping down closer beside her.

"Maybe we should stop now."

Scott seemed to sense her lack of comfort, saying, "My rules are to never have a honey while in a case. When this business is all over, I'd love to see you 'cuz you're the best person I know."

"Thanks. Guess we have kinda grown on each other. And I've needed your support. Maybe too much drink."

"I couldn't agree more; sorry I was overcome."

"Thanks."

"Where does this leave us?"

She took his hand and continued, "Alex really has me up in the air now. Have no idea what's going on, and if he feels." Scott didn't answer and let her talk.

"He seems more interested in his dangerous work than coming back here to me, or even considering his own safety."

"Aren't all science types like that?"

"Maybe."

"Some people haven't time for anyone."

"Have you ever had someone?"

"Oh yes, but she was killed in an accident on a mountain."

"I'm sorry. How, if I may ask?"

"Heart attack in the Cascades."

They sat in silence for some time. Finally, Scott spoke saying, "Time to take you home."

"Good idea."

"Depending on how things work out in the future, would you give this officer a shot?"

"Without a doubt. I respect your dealings with me in this weird state of affairs." Then she headed home after he took her to a terminal on the rail line. Zita has a good feeling about her ethical friend.

That next morning, newspaper headlines from South Africa jumped out of the page at Zita. Rebels had again broken the lines of the government's forces and were plunging south in a drive to capture Cape Town. Everyone was fleeing the country as planes from around the world evacuated whites. She hoped Alex was among those. Still, time snailed by, without word telling her he was on the run, dead, or maybe a captive. She gritted her teeth in worry and plunged into work to take her mind off the situation.

At Quotech, they were working in secret and planning to set up clinics in many foreign countries to sell their future genetically engineered products, even though they were not all ready to market everything yet. They were going to start them at the outset as family planning and related medical centers that could easily be converted and enlarged for DNA distribution improvements, thus getting a jump on other firms as they built early long-term trust with their host governments. Zita thought it was too underhanded, but she was only one voice as planners looked ahead in a new world of gene codes and creature enhancements.

She and Erick were intrigued by the new instrument's inventive inflow bombarding their research efforts. These new inventions were long past the cell sorting/flow cytometer of their cell sorting college days since now they could order single cell types easily for all kinds of living things. The Human Cell Atlas alone profiled all the cell types in humans that make up the 37 trillion cells in the average human body. The secrets locked in codes in these single cell types and those of other living things keep being elucidated in fast-moving international genetics labs. Research and computer programs were unlocking gene changes over the 500 million years of living cell evolution on the earth, helping scientists anticipate more knowledge in dealing with the ever-changing future of the planet. New and better producers of human food as well as cellular medicines were dominating world funding research for the overpopulated and polluted planet. However, getting these changes into human populations was very slow since habits and traditions of the times still prevailed as if in stone.

Both of the Starks were enjoying their work on the leading edge of science, but their minds often roamed to the human situations of their own relationships. There were no gene changes to remove the stress of their unknowns about those they had loved and who were far away.

15 Newborns

Finally, a message came in from Brazil in South America where the Quotech plane was refueling. "This is Alex, and I'm out alive. Will be in LAX customs in ten hours. Lost all I had, and I have no money. Can you pick me up to get home?"

"Absolutely! It's so good to hear your voice. Are you OK?"

"Yes, but must run to get aboard. Love you. I'll see you at the airport."

"Love you too! Thank goodness you're out of there. I've been worried sick."

"Have a great tale to tell. Gotta run. Bye!"

Zita gave a great sigh of relief. Then she relaxed gathering her thoughts about her relationship with a man who had been absent most of the time as well as out of communication recently. She raced across Quotech's courtyard and told Erick the good news.

She didn't sleep well that night pondering her relationship with Alex and her growing feelings for Scott. Should she be involved with a scientist, or was it time to have more variety in life? Even after she decided on a "one day at a time approach," she couldn't sleep until the wee hours.

Anxiously she waited in the international section of LAX. Within minutes after his arrival and clearing customs with no luggage, a haggard Alex appeared. She hugged the rumpled and dirty man with all her might. Finally, her lips found his and all was well. When they finally moved apart, she saw tears in his eyes flowing in a clear trickle down each cheek.

"You have no idea how glad I am to see you."

Zita replied, "I wondered if I'd ever be with you again."

"Got out with my passport and these clothes. Just really a lucky bloke! I'm starved! Would a lady buy this destitute man a decent meal?"

She chuckled saying, "Only if he promises never to work in South Africa again."

"Fat chance of that now that the government is falling."

Zita wiped away her tears of joy and sat with him in a noisy food court. He ate and told his venture between bites. His harrowing escape tale included grabbing some of the latest embryos in culture tubes and fleeing northwest ahead of advancing rebels. He felt they might not kill him since he was an American white with a passport, if they would even bother to check before hacking him to death. He had a local man he trusted and much earlier arranged a vehicle escape plan. He had paid the man well. In fact, making the black man nearly wealthy to ensure his full cooperation. But to be sure, Alex had left half of the man's funds to be sent by a lawyer in Angola once Alex was safely out of South Africa.

Inside a tight and padded compartment under an old truck's bed, Alex bounced north of Springbok crossing desert Bushmanland. It would have been fatal to go south toward Cape Town. But soldiers, deserting the war, commandeered the truck, forcing his black driver to head into Namibia. None of the soldiers could drive. Luckily, they wanted to go to a small village near Kestmanshopp where they allowed the driver and his truck to go free. Alex helped the driver hide the truck in brush and waited for the deserting troops to move on south. It was only a short distance to a crude airport where Alex called for the corporate jet. Then he waited until the Quotech jet set down on the red dirt. No police questioned him at the landing strip when he boarded the jet since he was on an American passport and not South African.

"That ride bouncing over those terrible roads for days was the worst part. The dust was just awful, but here I am."

"Want to go to the apartment and rest?"

"No, let's go to your laboratory. I have something for you." He patted his armpit of sealed culture tubes. Once in her car, he handed over the tubes. He smiled from under a forest of gray whiskers and matted down greasy hair.

Zita held them up to the light, saying, "They appear in good shape."

"They had a rough trip too. Won't last much longer in these tubes."

"Ten this time. That last bunch put us light-years ahead in our work. What will these do?"

"I hope they'll give us another leap ahead of the competition."

"You always have a surprise."

"I don't mind being a human incubator for the little guys. Kept 'em taped in my armpit and the protein tubes held even in all that dust and rough riding. I just had to save them after all that work by so many other good people including me. Who knows what has happened to 'em in all that killing? Did mail you note copies of my work the week before I left. Maybe I didn't lose everything."

"Didn't lose you. That's what matters most. What is the surprise this time?"

"You'll just have to wait eight months," he replied, winking at her.

"I think it's highly irresponsible. We could be planning ahead and preparing for what's in these."

"You probably wanted to open your Christmas presents early as a kid too, didn't you?"

"Of course! Didn't you?"

"Indeed so, but you're just going to have to wait for these."

"You are the limit! Charlie will have a fit."

"Let him have so many fits that he doesn't have them right. I really don't care."

The embryos were rushed to the implant team at Quotech for immediate insertion into both gorillas and chimps using the newest artificial placentas. Zita didn't consult Charlie on the matter since he was on vacation, knowing he would want any advancement possible so they could later transfer the traits on to other mammals.

Then it was rest, consulting, and relaxation for Alex. Eight great months with Alex sped past rapidly. He and Zita were in deeper love than ever as her thoughts of Scott faded.

With no separation anymore, Alex asked her to marry him, and Zita accepted the proposal, having a little twinge of regret about leaving Scott behind. Zita was sure she was not entering a sympathy marriage, but one where they shared many common interests beyond the work they did.

They had a small wedding with family near the rocky outcrops of Sylvan Lake near Mount Rushmore followed by a long honeymoon in the Black Hills. Also, they visited her old homeplace and walked the pure river of her childhood near Hill City where they discussed someday retiring or living in New Zealand. But neither could predict a long-term future.

Life could not have been better for them both being in deep love. They soon bought a new home near Quotech and settled into work alongside Erick. All three led great teams working to change the biology of life in new ways.

Six months later, Erick had a newfound love, Emily. She was a museum director in the arts with business degrees, giving Erick a new insight into marriage and life beyond the sciences. They were a perfect fit and wanted to be wed in Hawaii. Alex and Zita accompanied them to Kona where they were wed on a beach at sunset as Emily wanted.

After spending most of the honeymoon together on the big island of Hawaii at Hilo, they traveled together. They enjoyed the heavy rains, great seaside sunsets, and pondered what the new generation of greenbacks would bring. Had they only known what was ahead for them, they would have been less lighthearted in the clear island air and on the stunning beaches.

Once back in California, they found a home for Emily and Erick near theirs. Life seemed to be settling down for the Stark twins in 2046 with mates, homes, and work on the leading edge of genetics and biochemical engineering.

They had waited the eight long months for the next generation, and now the first gorilla was in labor. Quotech teams were anxious to conduct tests on what Alex had brought from now-fallen white South Africa. He'd been stubborn about telling her or anyone what to expect. All he'd say was, "This is a gift. However, be sure I get the credit if it turns out right. A lot of people died for them and all the world should see it."

Charlie had bit his tongue playing along with Alex while at times trying to get tough to learn about the characteristics. He even threatened to fire him unless he revealed the details. Alex only laughed but assured him the press conference would be better than the last one on the first greenbacks. Charlie had stayed in a frantic stew for months. There was no other way of finding out since nobody knew if any other scientists survived the laboratory seizure during the black revolution. All had been secret, and probably few had survived the bloodbath in the African area. But Alex had been the lucky one with his planned escape.

Zita felt Alex had been playing some sort of game. He had been aloof over the recent months and even seemed depressed at times. Yet he and Erick made a fine pair drinking beer together and almost driving their wives crazy.

On occasion, Zita sought refuge with Scott, keeping a sound friendship. Outside of Scott, her off-work relationships were few. Alex had changed a good deal since his return, seeming preoccupied and terribly serious about the future. She was most patient giving him time to adjust since so many of his close friends had died.

Sometimes Alex would launch into long sermons on the conditions of humans in the poor countries, global pollution, and natural resource depletion of the earth from the climate change. Erick was 100 percent with him in these matters. At times, she thought her brother had been transformed a bit into a social scientist or an environmentalist.

There seemed to be a lot on Alex's mind that he danced around, but didn't share. She was patient with him, allowing time to heal and recover.

News lifting everyone's spirits involved Hans being found murdered in Santiago, Chile. FBI records showed he had been poisoned. What he was up to was still under investigation. Nothing on Kate to everyone's dismay.

Alex's big day finally came. At the first birth that weekend, Zita couldn't believe her eyes. She immediately had all the doors locked to the primate birth area, put her staff involved on emergency in-house duty, cut all their communication lines to the outside except her wristband phone. Then, she called Alex.

He answered on the first ring. "What the hell have you done? This is a black human baby with a green back, and I have seven more to birth this weekend."

"Don't panic, Zita. They are what I thought they might be. Get 'em into this world fast and don't tell anyone, even Charlie, until it's over."

"This stuns me, and I don't see why you didn't warn me."

"Just couldn't. Wasn't totally sure they were these. I'm on my way down."

"I'll have security let you in. I've locked down tight until we figure this out."

"Perfect. Maybe there won't be many protesters tonight and I can get right in. One more thing, give drugs to all the others to induce labor. There is no time to wait on this."

"This whole thing is your responsibility then?"

"Of course, it's all mine, and I'll stick with you on this whole thing."

"OK, let's get them birthed and figure the details later."

"Right on, be there in a flash!"

Zita felt a new excitement in his voice. Something she hadn't heard during his depression. Thirty-six hours were a blur of birthing and baby tending. Zita and Alex hadn't had enough time to talk in depth. One big surprise was the birth of white babies with greenbacks too. And the sex ratios were nearly even for the little white and black babies. All were eventually encased in incubators under strong light imitating sunlight. Their design seemed to be flawless.

When they had time to actually talk, Zita said, "You didn't miss a trick on these. Sex, race, and all perfect. Was this why you stayed 'til the last minute?"

"My group and I had a life's work invested. Couldn't just walk away and allow a bunch of racist savages to destroy everything. Actually, these are the wrong embryos, not the most advance greenback chimps I intended to snatch. They must have labeled these humans as chimp greenbacks as just hidden backups. We always do that for protection from the unexpected. I grabbed them not realizing they were something else until I saw the secret switch marks on the bottom of each vials at refueling. Why do you think I've been depressed thinking I'd lost all those wonderful greenback improvements I helped engineer? But these human greenbacks will be a challenge too, thanks to those others who did much of the genetics with me. Wish I could have gotten those guys out too. But there was no way."

"How could they do this with humans when we couldn't ethically clone back then?"

"Easy. That government wanted to start producing a worker requiring only water and sunlight and eventually one with low-level thinking, and ease of control. I'd heard those rumors in the lab. There were all sorts of experiments that must have gone up in smoke during the takeover. They must have killed the black surrogates in the compound too."

"You people used women as we use ape surrogates here?"

"Black woman surrogates who were paid very handsomely. They carried chimps as well as human embryos."

"God, Alex, you never told me that you had such free a rein doing anything you wanted. And we could never do that here at that time."

"Why else would I be in a secretive country like that to do free genetics?"

Changing the subject, Zita said, "I've sent some staff home. How soon before word leaks out about this?" She was very uncomfortable with the way forward, but she didn't really know any other way.

"If it does, nobody will take it seriously except the protesters."

"Charlie is going to have a cow."

"Let him," said Alex.

16 New Direction

That Monday morning, Zita could have knocked Charlie's eyes off with a stick when he saw the black and white photobabies. He staggered backward against the wall outside the nursery and exhaled deeply, rolling his eyes. Then he came unwound.

"What in the goddamn hell did you have in your heads getting us tied up with humans? There is no call for this, Alex. Don't you know a fucking thing? Have you lost your ever-loving minds? This isn't anything but trouble for Quotech. How'll we ever get rid of these? You both need to be fired!"

"Until you want to talk about this in a civil manner, I'm not listening," snapped Alex, turning and walking away down the corridor.

Zita stood trembling with rage at Charlie's lack of understanding when facing one of the greatest science achievements in history.

"What do you have to say for yourself in all this, Zita?"

"You don't want to hear what I'm thinking right now."

"Fair enough. We can all talk later in my office. How about one o'clock, and tell Mr. Alex." His disgust was violent as he swore to himself moving backward away from her.

"OK," was her stony reply. She was pleased to still be in control of herself considering the stress of the long hours from that birthing weekend.

She remained a long time at the incubator room glass after midget-minded Charlie had stomped off. She watched the little ones. All eight were quiet, on their backs, and in a row in their little caps and sleepers. Anyone would think them normal children were it not for the artificial light penetrating transparent backs of their sleepers from below. These designs had been developed and installed for the greenback chimps and worked well for the new greenback humans. Her feelings were different for them than the chimp greenbacks in the adjoining section. She cast it off to her instincts of human love for humans.

Alex was waiting in her office where he was in an unexpectedly happy mood. "It's been done. Charlie has no idea what's involved here." He chuckled.

"I guess not. Seems mad as hops right now, always flying off the handle any time he isn't totally in control. But we can cool him down, and maybe he'll see the light."

"Until then, I think you should lie down in this sleeper and get a little rest. I'll do the same in my office and see you back here so we can talk before meeting Mr. Charlie."

"That sounds good. I'm beat."

He grabbed her tightly and kissed her firmly on the lips. "Sleep tight."

Five minutes later, Alex entered the incubator room and said to the duty nurse, "I need to check out a few things with the little ones. You go get a couple hours' sleep while I do it. You have been up way too long."

"You're too kind, Dr. Moby, but I can stay," replied the attending nurse.

"I insist."

"All right, but thank you."

"Please be back at one."

"One it'll be."

He quickly set to work harvesting cells from the squamas epithelial areas of each of the eight babies. He made four duplicate sets of each culture, labeled them, "African chimps green 409," and destroyed the cultures in the Revco super freezers of that same number. He put a set in a backup Revco as well and another set in his lab freezer that remained unlabeled, but nicked on the bottom.

He'd hardly finished before the attendant returned and he met Zita in her office.

"I need your help in a united front on this. Charlie is only the start."

"You have it."

"I led him down this path, not you. Let me take the blame."

"He's in a box and doesn't know which way to jump."

"As long as you're with me, we can bring him along. I have his number."

They hurried to the meeting. A long time elapsed before anyone spoke in Charlie's office. Finally, his assistant broke the ice. "We feel betrayed by you people."

"This is entirely my responsibility. Zita was as shocked as you to see they were humans."

"That hardly seems plausible since you two are married," snapped Charlie with an icy tone.

"Well, it's the truth," answered Zita.

"It's all a moot point now. They are here," said Alex.

"Moot point, my ass! You have put us in the exact place the critics and protesters said we'd be, doing this stuff with humans. It will be an uproar, and all of us are on the hot seat whether you know it or not."

"It was my fault for bringing them here. So you two are off the hook, and your jobs are safe."

"I can see no use for them at all. Let's find some way to get rid of 'em!"

"What kinda Hitler monster are you? These are as human as you and I. I'll call the police the second anything happens to any of them," scolded Zita.

Charlie stroked his bald head and stammered, "I was merely suggesting maybe we give them to women in some isolated third-world community where they'd never be heard from again."

"Absurd," snorted Alex.

"Well then, since you take the blame, I'll keep this all under wraps until Wednesday when you two can explain to our board of directors how to make us not the monster company of America."

"Gladly!" snapped Alex.

"I'm looking forward to it; you'll be first on the agenda. And if it doesn't go over, I'll be washing my hands of the two of you."

"You're such a supportive dear, Charlie," scoffed Zita, wondering why he remained so upset and irrational.

When Wednesday arrived, Alex and a fully rested Zita waited while the Quotech board of directors met in executive session. Finally, they were called in and addressed by the chairman.

"Good morning, Drs. Moby and Stark. We have visited the nursery and discussed this matter before calling upon you two for clarification. Needless to say, we are shocked and worried about these unauthorized happenings. For our benefit, let's do this discussion in two parts. First, how these babies came into this facility and became our responsibility. Secondly, the future of this, and its impact. You first, Dr. Stark, and address the first point, please."

"Good day, Mr. Chairman and board members. The last time we met, you were thrilled because we had photochimps and all the potential they offered in mammalian engineering. I hope you leave this meeting feeling the same about our photobabies."

"I hate to break in, but please stick to the first point."

"When Alex arrived from fallen South Africa, all he had was a passport, dirty clothes, and five culture tubes taped under his right armpit. Then, we took the embryos to my unit to be implanted exactly as we had the photochimps from his last visit. Charlie was gone to a meeting and we couldn't wait because the culture solutions were near the end of their ability to sustain embryos.

"I didn't expect photobabies, and Alex didn't tell me what they would be. He told me it would be a surprise, and nothing more. My assumption was more advanced photochimps similar to the last ones he had delivered to our company. I was shocked at the first birth being human. I immediately called Alex to the unit."

"After that first birth, you made no effort to contact Charlie for instructions on how to handle the other surrogates?" asked a board member.

"Heavens no, sir. There are laws regarding preventing the birth of humans in the final trimester. If that's what you're insinuating."

"I'm insinuating nothing!"

"That's about all I know besides telling Charlie about this happening and facing you here."

"Looks as if it's time to move along to Dr Moby."

Alex paused a long time as if gathering his thoughts. "I have no idea why you are so upset about my doing the same procedure the second time, bringing embryos from South Africa. My only regret is that I couldn't have saved all the dozens of secret projects going on there and the lives of those great scientists who were killed, many friends of mine. It was a last-minute impulse on my part to try and save some greenback embryos.

"The rebels were only a few miles away, and it was pandemonium. I had a prearranged escape waiting at the edge of the compound. But it could only take one, me. I raced into the culture/incubator rooms and grabbed the wrong tubes and fled. Don't know how it happened, but they were labeled greenback chimps. With the gunshots closer and closer, I had to run for my life."

"So you're telling us this was all a mistake, and you thought these were improved photochimps?"

"Exactly, I suspected, but I didn't know human babies were involved in the lab work at the facility. One section was not told what another section was doing there. But we had heard rumors. My work was on the green-backed chimps, and it was unknown to me that some other unit was placing our efforts behind our backs directly into human embryos."

"How convenient!" snapped the chairman.

"I resent your comment. I was doing what any of you probably would have if you'd worked for years on a project and knew it and your own life were about to be destroyed."

A silver-haired board member spoke, "By making this all an accident, you have given Dr. Stark credible deniability, taking Charlie, us, as well as yourself off the hook. Now what do we do with these babies down there?"

"I suppose we are now ready for that second point, Dr. Stark."

"We have no choice in the matter. They are babies and protected under the laws of this country. First, I think nurse nannies are essential for them unless we plan to have problems with California social services later. Otherwise, we'd have to leave them with the gorilla surrogates, leaving us open to wider criticism. We need to monitor and check their functions, growth, and development from the view of good science and humanity. I feel the attention from the public will be enormous—much more than the greenbacks or multiple human births in past generations."

"This company can't exist on contention, media coverage, or a circus display. The costs here are substantial with no income benefit," argued a board member.

Another added, "Could we have them labeled 'orphans' and adopted overseas in some third-world country and dispose of this problem before the press dissects us?"

Zita snapped, "Certainly not. These are American citizens born in this country."

"But to a gorilla parent!" he countered.

"I don't think the National Immigration Service would see it that way."

"We digress, people," said the chairperson. "Let's seek Alex's opinion on all this since he's the initial source of our problem."

"If you will hear me out until I'm totally finished without breaking in, I'll tell you."

"Do we agree?" The chairman obtained head nods from board members.

"This is the greatest single happening to this company in its existence both in genetic engineering and economics. The publicity will outshine all competitors and the stock will soar as it did with the green and the greenback chimps. Most investors will think we are the leading edge, which will be the truth. Release the total story of how the photobabies landed here before we ever face the press. That will help defuse the entire difficult situation of what I've done. Then, show a photobaby to the press with its nanny as Zita has suggested. The hundreds of millions in stock price increase will more than pay for the care of these little ones.

"There are over a hundred and fifty thousand artificial fertilizations in these United States each and every year, and millions more worldwide. Harvested cells can be cloned and engineered to produce abundant sperm and eggs and embryos in company banks to aid people around the world who want these traits. It would be an ongoing business in our already setup clinics. And all of it is now absolutely legal." Alex paused.

"May I ask a pertinent question?" asked Charlie.

"Sure."

"Who would want a child with a greenback that was from an ape mother and might have low intelligence?"

"Probably a good many people who would like a child they didn't have to feed!" said Alex. A few members of the board nodded, and one even laughed an approving chuckle.

Zita spoke up, "What parent in their right mind wouldn't desire a child who required only water and sunlight—never producing a messy diaper. Just that alone and food would save the upbringing cost by a huge amount. And when you think about all the spin-offs, loads of people would want them, including me. Your assumption that they are of low mentality is probably wrong too, Charlie. I do not think these were engineered for that."

"I think we have heard enough. Maybe you've helped us past our fears and repulsions to a point of really considering this development's total ramifications. Earlier, I was reeling from seeing the little ones myself and was only thinking of the negatives.

"The board of directors of Quotech thanks you both for your work and will be seeking your future ideas and advice on this issue. We will now go back into executive session for further discussions. But all in this room know and are subject to forfeit their pensions, stock options, and accumulated bonuses as well as facing blackballing, if one word of this is released prematurely. All have signed that agreement as a precondition to working here or being a board member."

The board spent hours in endless discussions in the session. After leaving, Charlie was so put out over the outcome that he wouldn't speak to Zita or Alex; he locked himself in his office and would not answer their knocks on his door, nor would he answer his communicators. Yet the research went ahead full force being approved by Quotech's divided board.

What to do with the new greenback babies was a pressing problem since they had no parents or birth certificates, or any family to raise them. And by the time they were walking, something would have to be done. It had to go along with releasing the toddlers in a public media event. Again, Charlie was overruled by the Quotech board of directors who wanted the young ones adopted out to show the world what improvement they were.

Highly aware of the negative reactions they expected from the right-wing and some religious groups, it was still a go. Showing the greenbacks to the world was part of a highly planned thrust to enhance Quotech and reveal how the greenback clinics would work. The plan was also to educate how Quotech Clinics could add the greenback genes into eggs, sperm, and embryos to produce a greenback child of the future. Parents could have their choice of gender and many other qualities.

Unexpectedly that next week, Charlie pranced down the hall and into the weekly team staff meeting with a big smile on his face. "I've got big news. Alex has been nominated for a Nobel Prize for his work that produced our green chimps."

Applause erupted in the conference room, and a stunned Alex stood and took a bow saying, "Nobody ever mentioned a thing about this to me. I doubt if I have a ghost of a chance of winning."

"You deserve this, and what an honor for all of us here at Quotech. In a couple of months, we will know the results. And hopefully you'll be heading for Scandinavia."

It was the highlight of the meeting, and no release of the greenback babies would be made until the Nobel was announced. All the team leaders were again sworn to silence until after the Nobel selection concluded. Quotech did not want anything to influence the chances for Alex since they knew how the prize would help the company in a multitude of ways. Housing a Nobel winner was a big plus.

That evening the Starks and mates gathered for an evening wine celebration at Emily and Erick's place. "We'll know the outcome of this in a couple of months. I don't think I can stand the wait," said Emily.

"They won't select me since I worked in South Africa in an undercover situation. But how I would like it," responded Alex. He was still hung up on the great losses of research from all his colleagues who didn't survive, and he felt tainted and somewhat undeserving.

"It was not your fault, and you also saved our greenbacks. That will blow the minds of everyone when those are shown to the public," replied Erick.

Alex bristled, "Good thing they don't know anything about them now or my chances would be doomed."

"Dear, when they are shown, you should get to be our president. Nobody will ever forget you."

He laughed. "All those protesters outside our gates and science deniers will be enraged and want to string me up telling everyone that I am evil and from Funk, Nebraska. I think we need to talk about something else like our two families each adopting one of the greenbacks and raising them."

"Wow, Alex, you really go from the frying pan into the fire with this one!" snapped Emily. "If and when we decide to have a family, I want it to be ours, with our traits, our minds, and I don't want to chance raising a child out of some laboratory in Africa. What would it be?"

"Tell me how you really feel," he countered, realizing her strong feelings had never been revealed before.

Erick said, "I agree with not taking such a chance that could turn out badly for us with an offspring not really having our genes. All that matters to me, and maybe having to rear a child that is maybe not right and not our own would be really difficult for a lifetime. And I hope you realize that Emily and I have not had this discussion together."

"May I put my two cents' worth into this issue? I really don't want the risk of child raising unless it's your and my genes working together. I'd like to see what we produce and love the results, and not deal with some genes other than ours," said Zita, feeling she and her husband should have this talk without anyone else involved.

"I get the message loud and clear from you folks."

"Good," snapped Emily.

"I've never thought of adopting, and yet one might come up with a plan for them after we have all the harvested cells in tissue culture that we will ever need from them. And it maybe could be good for the little green ones. Have any ideas?" asked Zita.

Erick offered saying, "How about Quotech staff having a first choice to parent the greenbacks, maybe a lottery. I think the company could give a lifetime monthly stipend to go along with each greenback, removing any burdens that went along with them. And I think Quotech can easily afford doing it through insurance policies and living trusts."

"All sounds good, but what about the kids of these greenbacks if they have any children of their own?" asked Emily.

Erick ended the conversation. "This is a can of worms that our company's board of directors will work out according to Californian laws. We don't have to solve it all, and they won't blame Alex either since his bringing greenbacks and a Nobel nomination will place Quotech a light-year ahead of all our competition."

17 Surprises

Two months later, men arrived at Quotech to see Alex. They were speaking in a bit of broken English, which alarmed the security people. However, they were soon found to be from Sweden and sat down with Alex to talk in an isolated and secure reception lobby. After a nice greeting, Alex was sure they intended to convey the bad news about his nomination.

"Doctor Moby, you are now a finalist for the Nobel, and we are here to be assured, should you be the final selection, you would accept the award. Furthermore, we need to know if you understand having to come to Sweden to accept the honor as well as carry out a few public duties as the recipient."

Alex was dumbstruck and finally uttered, "But of course I would accept the award and do all in my power to respect and honor the duties and responsibilities involved. I am so stunned to be even considered as a finalist. I never actually expected to hear what you are saying."

"We Nobel people always visit our finalists to have a face-to-face involving the award should they be the selection. Nobel wants no surprises after the announcements so we can have the perfect ceremony in Stockholm. And please make no public statements about this visit or your standing before the final results are released to the worldwide media in two weeks. Here are written guidelines for you to follow should you be the one in molecular biology."

"You absolutely have my word of honor to do as you wish. I am stunned to even be in the top group of candidates."

Soon the men in black departed, leaving Alex wondering about his chances, but he sure didn't expect the award. He and other scientists always had joked about winning a Nobel, but that was all just in jest.

Alex was excited to tell everyone the good news, but ethically he couldn't. He explained the men in black to the front desk receptionists as embassy people wanting information on the long-ago attempt on his and Zita's life. That was that for the time being, and he didn't want to get his hopes up. Yet he checked on flights to Stockholm for himself and Zita. Then he plunged back into cellular genetic work.

Two weeks later to the day, Alex received a classified memo stating that he was the recipient and the announcement would be made in twenty-four hours to the world. He could not help himself and rushed to tell Zita and Erick that they were going to Sweden with him, but they had to keep mum until it was announced to the public. That night they celebrated as a family and planned for the trip, maybe extending it to a vacation in European areas.

It was a whirlwind after the news of his selection went public. Quotech had quickly hosted a huge news conference for Alex where a throng of invited reporters bombarded him with questions about his work on the greenback chimps. He was clever and honest in his answers but avoided going deeply into the controversial issues. He instead focused on what a great honor the award was for Quotech and those South African scientists who lost their lives in the greenback revolution. He was humbled when speaking about the award.

That spring when the award was to be presented in Sweden, the Mobys and Starks flew to Stockholm and enjoyed the pageantry of Nobel grandeur. Alex made several presentations after his honoring with top people from across the globe. They stayed another day and traveled on to Norway, giving another presentation at the Nobel Peace Center and later visiting the great fjords that reminded them of New Zealand's Milford Sound. They relaxed a day in Oslo enjoying Viking museums in a fossil fuel–free and totally renewable energy–powered nation, yet with dank polluted air from other countries.

"This city blows me away with its public transportation and everyone walking everywhere. Few cars," said Erick as the four of them enjoyed the striking and snow-clad city with the highest standard of living in Europe.

"Yes, everything people need is expensive, but those unnecessary things are really highly taxed, especially the sin ones that are not good for us or anyone else," added Alex.

"Do these people have any fun with those expensive drinks?" asked Erick.

Emily replied, "They just live in moderation and stay really healthy like we should be doing. This is such a stunning place. I could live here if it wasn't so darned cold in their winters, but they would expect me to learn their language too, and at my age, that would be really tough."

"Their Viking history has always amazed me with women being able to speak at their Athing big meetings and running their long houses with total control. Yet they had a lot of thralls. You know those slaves the men captured and traded for a thousand years ago. Thralls sure did so much of the hard work," said Zita.

"Those were the days of few people and a pure planet. I pray we can someday limit reproduction and have a better world," added Alex.

"Now with your big prize, people will totally listen to you"—Zita laughed—"but let's get our things and head to the airport and dream along the way."

At the airport in Paris, they were unexpectedly greeted by an angry crowd of egg-tossing protesters outside the terminal, many holding signs indicating science should not be changing what God had put in place. Emily was struck in the face by an egg, and Zita took one to the back of her head before police in bright green jackets shepherded them through the shouting crowd. Alex was furious about getting the opposite treatment to that they had experienced in Scandinavia. Yet they passed it all off quickly, enjoying the smog-bound wondrous city for two days with the most stunning art Emily had always dreamed about seeing. Then it was off to London by bullet train under the English Channel. It traveled without any big bumps all the way.

Erick told them on the ride, "I sure wish we had invested our money on these kinds of rail systems instead of on all those past senseless religious wars in the Middle East and Asia. We sure never changed the religious minds of people in those women-suppressing countries in the Middle East."

"Don't you know how you change the minds in those places for the long run?" asked Alex.

"Think it could be easy giving women the vote, equal rights, education, and birth control," snapped Zita.

"I agree a hundred percent," said Emily.

Their men shook their heads in agreement. There was no comeback since they all agreed on how the world should be fair to all people regardless of minor differences in genetic makeup.

Once housed in their hotel on Piccadilly Square in downtown London, Alex prepared to be honored by the British Royal Society where many great scientists had spoken over hundreds of years. Then all four raced about seeing the landmark tourist sites in the smoggy and odor-filled London.

When they headed back across the Atlantic in the fancy aircraft provided by Quotech, all were seated around a nice table with drinks and hashed over the events of the great trip. They were surprised by their overseas adventure and compared how they felt about what little they saw of Europe.

Erick said, "I'm just blown away how the British Isles are at least 90 percent renewables and release so little CO_2 into the world's air. Wish we could do that, and they import very little oil, only mining a little coal compared to their history of living way back in a coal smog with their country blackened by the emissions. That was a time so unhealthy with everybody breathing the chemicals of coal burning. But they still have some nuclear power plants."

"All that has helped, but they still get all the pollution from the world's air. At least they're doing their part by saving oil and coal," said Zita.

Alex added, "I've never understood how clueless we humans have been since the industrial age. You don't have to be very bright to see how nonpolluting sun energy and winds are. Add into that all these new renewables that are free energy and do not pollute. I can't get my mind around why, with the sun still shining and wind blowing, we humans are still using the polluting hydrocarbons of oil, natural gas, and coal."

"The sad thing about it all is when future generations look back at us, they will wonder what the hell we were thinking burning up all these hydrocarbons. Wow, they can be used to make a zillion products people need, and burning them in our homes, transportation, and everything else is as crazy as when Europeans cut down or burned the great hardwood forests in the eastern half of America just to farm more land," said Erick.

Emily added, "I once read that Ben Franklin wanted the wild turkey as our national bird because when the sun rose each day there were continuous gobbles from the East Coast to beyond the Mississippi in the treetops. But the founders went ahead and selected a bird that ate dead fish most all the time because of its beauty. Must have been men doing that selecting since they are still choosing things based on appearing beautiful."

"You do mean females, don't you?" said Zita with a laugh, knowing what a trap some men get into going for made-up beauty rather than character. She was very beautiful, but always downplayed her appearance and never tried to promote it with marketed cosmetic enhancements.

On and on the conversations went among the four far beyond the sciences as the corporate plane zipped them to California LAX. A large group of Quotech people greeted them, and Alex made a brief appreciative speech to all those gathered. Then it was home for two days' rest from the jet lag. Their worlds seemed to be going very happily as they returned to work the next Monday past the increased number of protesters outside the company gates throwing tomatoes and eggs at the vehicles. Some held signs of "Don't Change God or Nature's Works in Our Animals."

A few weeks later, Quotech set a date to reveal the photobabies to the world, inviting worldwide press with a large venue suggesting a big surprise was coming. The response was immediate as hundreds of media people wanted to attend. They were not going to miss anything like some had when the greenback chimps were first shown, shocking the nation. But Quotech knew it was all legal under the lifted genetic restrictions on using gene research with primates as well as humans despite some people opposing any messing with God's work. And this time, a Nobel winner would be making the unveiling. Alex was to head the program since he was advertised as the primary investigator of the work. And even before the event, stock shot up to its highest in years as speculators expected a moneymaking revealing.

On the day of the event, dignitaries and reporters received the stunning blockbuster, leaving them speechless and shocked. There behind Alex were two glass-fronted chambers cloaked in green hiding a nanny and a female child in one and a nanny and male toddler in the other. Both were greenbacks in cute outfits with transparent backs, revealing the green that was carrying on photosynthesis feeding the child.

When the photokids were revealed, there was total silence and gasps for a minute followed by a flood of reporters and photographers racing outside to post the shocking news none had expected. Then Alex took the stage and explained how advantageous these genetically engineered kids were for the future of people and the earth. That was followed by a press conference by public relations people from Quotech. They were evasive and intentionally vague on future details involving this great leap forward in genetics involving humans.

Seeing the photokids was in itself far more shocking then when the British had revealed the cloning of Dolly the Sheep decades ago. Chimps and sheep were one thing, but doing this with human beings was something even the protesters didn't expect to happen so fast. They then protested such human engineering was immoral across the world making Alex their monster and screamed that green-backed people should not be allowed. It was now legal to do such engineering with humans in America and many other countries, but many wanted to stop this kind of science in its tracks for many reasons. However, research with human DNA was still moving forward in hundreds of laboratories around the globe.

Back in California, Quotech had already harvested all the cells they would ever need from the photokids to sometime in the future engineer them into the eggs, sperm, and embryos of people around the world wanting greenback offspring. These cells were also kept in tissue cultures solutions where they could be mass duplicated. It was also decided to quietly let workers in the company who wanted to be parents adopt the greenbacks into their families. An in-house lottery was held in doing so with the winners getting a rich endowment to raise their greenbacks with the funds covering lighting, special schooling, solar clothing, and other needs for the kids until they were thirty years old.

The problem seemed solved, but Charlie seemed unhappy with everything involving the photochildren. He seemed sour and depressed with how the greenback thrust was going whereas the Mobys/Starks and Quotech board of directors were thrilled about its future. He signed off on projects, but he showed little zest in doing so.

A few nights later when events had settled down and over wine in Erick's home, Emily surprised both husbands with a striking plan. "Zita and I want you two to know that we each now want to have a child. And we want them greenbacks." A startled Erick and Alex looked at each other digesting the idea.

Soon Erick said, "I'm a hundred percent for it since we need to start a family. And what could be better than a greenback with so much of our work and dreams. A kid would add so much to our lives."

Alex looked at Zita, saying, "Wow, this sounds wonderful, and what could be better for us all than having little ones. We would be showing the world how greenbacks can come from great women. It would also be showing off our years of work. And I would love to have a child with you, my dear."

Zita then said, "I always wanted a daughter to rear."

Their topic then went far into the night as they hammered out when and how to get Quotech aboard. They wanted to be the first to have greenback babies as married couples showing the world how it could happen to regular women and show that scientists believed in their work. It would only take nine months after doing the gene changes once ovulations happened.

A few days later, the plan was pitched to the chairman of the board of directors at Quotech who immediately debated the idea.

Some thought what could be a better endorsement than having the top scientists and a Nobel winner kick off what the clinics would be doing worldwide starting in nine months and showing off the newborn greenback babies of the scientists who had done much of the work in the engineering. All had to agree to keep it totally secret until the births.

Charlie had been passed by since everyone knew he was cold to having human greenbacks developed at this early stage. He watched what was happening knowing he could do nothing to change what had been research and was now headed into actual human changes. Still he also had increased his stock holdings ever since the greenback chimps were shown publicly.

Then male sperm was donated by the husbands, and hormone-induced ovulations activated in both wives. Their eggs were extracted and engineered by gene editing the DNA for greenbacks. This was all done by teams of Quotech doctors. Then the fertilized eggs, now embryos, were inserted back in the uterine walls as a normal pregnancy. A boy for Emily and Erick with a female for Zita and Alex was the big plan. All went exactly as the implant team wanted, now it was a nine-month wait for the parents.

The next two months were filled with plans and total happiness as both women were pregnant and doing well. At Alex's insistence, they remodeled a room in each home to house and properly light the upcoming greenbacks. It was complicated getting the lighting for each photobaby correct even in the night. When it was all done and set up to accept the new arrivals, they celebrated and named the babies, Zona and Ian. Now all they had to do was wait for the birthing days.

Alex had been doing a lot of traveling and speaking at genetic conferences. When he returned to LA, he usually zipped to his lab to update his computers by inserting the newest programs, ideas, and information he had acquired. New techniques were fast coming from around the world, and he wanted his and Zita's staff to have the best leading-edge programs for their research.

On one return trip from the LAX airport, he told Zita to go on to bed since he would be at his lab for a time before coming home. And he was going to take the next day off to be with her for the weekend. When Zita awoke, there was no Alex, and she suspected he had crashed on his office cot for the night considering jet lag from his long flight. By noon that Saturday, there was still no husband or communication, causing her to be alarmed. This was not like Alex. She contacted security at Quotech asking them to locate her husband.

Later a call came in. "Your husband has been injured. He's in route to the Southwest LA Hospital by ambulance. I think you should get there." Those words terrified Zita as she contacted Erick.

They arrived at the emergency room together and were quickly escorted to a curtained cubical where Alex was prone on a gurney under a white blanket. A man in blue scrubs quickly told them Alex had passed from gunshot wounds. Zita fainted, but Erick broke her fall, catching and thrusting her into a chair. She soon came to and sobbed violently until a police officer arrived and escorted the stunned pair to a lounge. He explained how they had found Alex critically wounded and unconscious in his computer room. Doctors tried to console them, but nothing helped lessen the horror.

"How could anyone get inside our research area and do such a thing?" Zita sobbed, holding her face in her shaking hands looking at the floor. "He just can't be gone. What will we do, Erick? He was my life and my partner." Her tears flowed, and all Erick could do was try and comfort her. They were both totally stunned at what had happened right in Quotech.

Later, they learned Charlie had gone missing after a tech worker had seen him in the lab area with a weapon in his hand near the time Alex was murdered. Police and a host of investigators immediately worked on the case to find out what had happened. All they could come up with was that Charlie had killed Alex, but why?

The police probe was ongoing as the twins sank in disbelief and grief over their loss after a quick funeral. Then Zita dragged a chair into the center of her living room and sat in a dark silence for the next full day. She refused to speak to Erick or anyone. He respected her actions but kept a watchful eye on her. A day later, she returned to normal, apparently having come to grips with her earth-shattering loss.

Over the next months, grief lessened somewhat as they moved on into their new futures. And they followed up on work Alex had given them.

Neither Zita, Erick, nor Emily could understand why Charlie would do such an awful thing considering how the greenbacks had boosted him and Quotech. Was it something else Charlie was entangled with in a sick and murderous mind? And they wondered how both he and Kate had vanished without a trace.

18 Aftermath Years

After Alex was murdered and Charlie escaped without a trace, most of 2048 seemed a blur to Zita. Yet the world of science honored his Nobel stature and greenback work even more because of his unfortunate death.

In a good move, Alex had earlier invested his huge prize money and vast back pay into company stock; it rose to super value. People had stampeded to purchase Quotech investments, which helped make the Mobies rich. Those millions Zita quickly channeled into the foundation. His death as a famous scientist also prompted huge corporate donations to the Moby Foundation, eventually making it one of the largest in the world. Weeks before his death, Alex had also smartly focused the Moby Foundation goals to enhance genetic changes around the world. He designated its control be held by family members Zita, Erick, Emily, and their future dependents.

As research opened up a new world of choice for babies, Quotech's engineered greenback genes were edited into the overcrowded human populations. Those clinics in cooperative help from the Moby Foundation reached hundreds of millions worldwide, but not all nine billion people. The hope-giving already established birth control clinics were easily enlarged and smoothly added greenback traits to people's reproduction across the globe.

Most people of the world, with the exceptions of the Middle East, wanted gene changes in their children. A onetime insertion and change in their DNA would breed true in oncoming generations. These were dominant genetic changes. People were soon hooked by the ease of raising photokids.

Zita, Alex, Erick, and Emily were pioneers. They'd earlier agreed to have greenbacks. Both families had wanted a child of their own as true believers in a new way forward to ease the stress on the planet. The twins were naturals to help the cause since they had been leaders within greenback genetic work. They wanted to carry the torch of greenback technology forward. With vigor, they had the most up-to-date gene editing placed into Zita's and Emily's eggs and their husband's sperm in the Quotech clinic lab producing embryos for greenback offspring.

All this had been done prior to Alex's death. Zita was so excited about raising a child with Alex, but his sudden death put her life into turmoil. However, the family and Scott gave her solid support during those long months of sorrow, bringing them all closer together.

Three months before Zona's actual birth, Zita married Scott who stood by her in the big venture of raising a daughter with a beautiful forest-colored back. Erick and Emily had greenback Ian three days later. Zita was lucky finding such a good mate after losing Alex. Those had been traumatic times in the Starks' and Moby lives.

Zita often thought about the progress resulting from what Alex and she had accomplished along with Erick in changing how plant gene biology was now in human populations. She was hopeful human life would slowly change for the better. So with Scott as her new mate, she continued leading the research at Quotech overseeing new and unique gene-changing projects.

But now many years passed and both family greenback offspring were eighteen years of age and headed for advanced educations. It was 2076 in a slowly changing world.

Alex had been the first Nobel Prize winner ever murdered because of his work. He had led the way in making legitimate the greenback chimps and the scary leap forward to greenback people. How brilliantly he'd earlier handled all those news releases and interviews about the potentials of engineered humans.

That was as clear in Zita's mind as if it had happened yesterday instead of back eighteen years ago. She was proud they had a daughter who was engineered to reflect their work.

She awaited Zona's message wondering how so much time had passed so quickly with Zona and Ian finishing high school. The doorbell ringing ceased her reflective daydreaming, and she raced to give a greeting to Erick.

"Good morning, sis, it's a great day."

"Why so?" she asked her brother who lived on the next block with his wife and Ian.

"Ian headed for pre-registration. Never thought I'd see the day when we both had college freshmen."

"Neither did I when we decided to have these kids."

"Still think you should've let her go to school here. LA isn't as bad as those rural places where conservatives still hate greenbacks."

"She's a girl, and we'd rather have her learning than fighting. Ian's strong enough to do both. Maybe I'm just protective."

"It'll work out, I'm sure."

"If people were more open-minded, Zona would be goin' to school close by here in LA."

"It seems to take people a long time to catch up with science. Too much defending the status quo with ignorance."

"A bit of human thinking is still back in the tropical rain forest or savannah from a hundred thousand years ago."

"Don't be so cynical. I know, it's slowly changing. You don't expect people to accept new lifestyles overnight, do you?"

"No. Nothing's fast enough when my child is involved."

"You're not regretting our decision to have photokids?"

"Heavens no! It sure made life more interesting. Are you?"

"Not on your life, but sometimes I wish it were easier. I hate havin' them hide their backs when they feel uncomfortable."

"Me too!"

"Transferring those genes into your and Emily's eggs way back then seemed a big deal. Sort of like doing nuclear transfers must have seemed advanced in the early 2000s with stem cell research. But now, look what they're doing. Wow! Those new DNA analyzers and splicers are a wonderful leap just like our old stone-aged ones were."

"Alex opened the floodgates to improving people more than curing and preventing diseases via stem cells ever did. What a good thing in the long run."

"I don't know where we'd be today if he hadn't been in our lives and opened doors for all these wild green advancements."

"What's greatest has to be that greenbacks produce greenbacks in reproduction. It's slowly changing everything."

Both of their children had been easy to raise. They never had to be fed beyond vitamins, milk, and water, and no breastfeeding as babies. There were no soiled diapers, just wet ones for a few years. Food and raiding the refrigerator had not been a problem either, except for milk and drinks. Putting them in sunlight was about it. The pluses had been offset by better lighting requirements and special clothing to allow the sun on their greenback bodies even in bed at night. Without eating, they had had few illnesses from bacteria and toxins. Yet airborne viruses and bacteria had taken a toll on then, and vaccinations had been the same as for all kids. Yet they were not the best models now being engineered and born. They were just a couple of normal kids. The biggest difference between their kids and non-greenbacks was parent time. Zona and Ian craved interaction on a high-level, making parent time increase.

When they were first born, Zona and Ian were novelties, but that soon changed as millions of people worldwide had photobabies too.

Then within a few years, both Erick and Zita won the biggest prize in molecular genetics together in the mid-2060 and invested their Nobel Prize money to help educate people in undeveloped countries.

Zita in her many Nobel speeches told the world, "There are bigger things coming now that millions of greenbacks are entering adulthood. I fear a nasty division between who can photosynthesize and those who can't."

Her brother often told her, "So much had been written about all that. Now it's going to happen and we're in the middle with our kids, and it hurts." He was not comfortable with the continued raging debates about engineered people by politicians, business interests, and the Catholic church as well as other groups.

That same day when the kids were preparing to enter colleges, Scott came in the front door. He'd worked part-time as a consultant to the LA Police Department after he retired.

"How you doing, big guy?" asked Erick who viewed the gray-haired man as a brother more than a brother-in-law.

"The usual. They really don't need me down there anymore with all those smart young bucks and ladies. But I enjoy a little of it with all the freedom I now have."

"Here is a cup of chai to get you fired up," said Zita. He had been a Trojan in taking care of himself and Zona all the long years that she had almost lived in her laboratory at giant Quotech.

For those many busy past years after Alex's murder, the Stark teams at Quotech had been in a research struggle to insert nitrogen fixation into photobaby genes. They had turned every possible stone engineering a gene metabolic system taking the 80 percent nitrogen from the lungs and blood and placing some of it into protein tissue and making bone. There were great code editing setbacks since nitrogen bends would occur in the experimental greenback chimps as it had in divers who moved upward too rapidly during ocean dives.

Many chimps were destroyed and sacrificed in that intense work, as many combinations of DNA and RNA from bacteria, blue green algae, and *Nostoc* were refined into primate enzyme systems. Eventually those genes allowed nitrogen to replace calcium in the bones of chimps and also allowed nitrogen to be fixed into cellular protein synthesis that produced all the twenty proteins in the body of the test animals. It had been a massive effort keeping Erick and Zita busy during the early growing-up years of their children.

When all the altered genes were inserted into greenback embryos and worked perfectly, it was a huge success. This quantum leap allowed the newest greenbacks to take in little organic food and survive. Their bodies now used the atmosphere for oxygen, carbon dioxide, and nitrogen to maintain and grow while carrying on photosynthesis for their energy needs from sunlight. They also released oxygen along with carbon dioxide. Then these new gene systems went into all greenbacks engineering by Quotech.

This marvel of engineering was a step up from Zona and Ian who still had to consume milk since their bones were calcium based. But now Quotech's clinics would easily see to it that the new nitrogen usage genes were inserted into any possible offspring. These offspring would be like plants taking in only the earth's natural liquids and gases. But essential trace elements were another story and were still needed by greenbacks.

These great advancements earned both Erick and Zita their Nobel Prizes. Critics contended that they won the prizes because they were part of the Moby family where the first Nobel winner had been murdered.

However, both twins were happy with their life's work. They had helped make the new generations of greenback people natural and nearly perfect for the troubled hot planet.

The twins now worked when they wished helping the Moby Foundation along with Emily who was its official director. Emily had many assistants directing work and helping greenbacks across the globe since they were far different than the regular population in their living and thinking.

19 Revenge

Years later, Zita thought back to 2067 when she had reduced her Quotech work to part-time over those last years of Zona's high school days. No longer feeling up to date in the fast-moving gene sequencing field, she had taken over the presidency of the giant Moby Foundation from a tired Emily. They both had supported the welfare of greenbacks with the best up-to-date science. Zita's board of directors were a family rubber stamp group: Erick, Emily, Scott, Zona, Ian, a total family effort.

Personally, Zita also made sure the best international investigators continued looking for Charlie and reported developments to Scott who was devoted to that massive search.

Soon it was semester break time and Zona came home from Canada. Zita and Zona talked as she prepared herself a hot lunch. Scott was away fishing.

"It's wonderful having you in the house again. We miss you a ton. Tell me how school is working out."

"These first months have been wonderful. Kids are like me interested in everything intellectually that ever happened," said Zona as she contrasted high school with her university environment. Her college friends were not interested in food like many regulars had been in high school.

"Zona, I'm so happy you found people you like."

"Well, Mom, I don't like 'em all. We have big idea clashes, but it's a quantum leap from mixed school here. Nobody belittles or makes fun of anyone being a greenback, since we all are."

"Ian has to justify or defend himself from a few jealous people at his university all the time."

"It must be a drag. I'm anxious for talks with him. This time, we can compare our situations rather than imagine being at universities."

"So you want to finish the year in Vancouver?"

"Yes, it's a worry-free heaven! When will Dad be home?"

"Any minute. He called sayin' he has a big surprise. It must be something for you, or a big fish he caught since I can't tell if he's at work or out on his boat." Scott wasn't Zona's biological father, but he might as well have been since he was the only father she had ever known face-to-face.

Soon the door flung open and Scott stood tall in his trench coat with uplifted arms and shouted at the top of his lungs, "It's a miracle! We've waited forever for this day! Charlie's been found, and alive." He embraced his two girls with his big arms as they all jumped up and down. "Let's celebrate."

Zita was stunned, after an eighteen-year wait, to have justice on the horizon. Scott spilled out the news of how Charlie was in Sao Polo, Brazil, in custody. He knew little more than the bare details.

Within a few days, he'd waived extradition, and an FBI agent and Scott were sent to fly him back to California. Since Scott had worked the case for so many years, LAPD naturally selected him for the pickup. Scott was thrilled to at last face the murderer he'd never given up on.

Scott related more incoming details about how a retired laboratory technician from Quotech was vacationing in Brazil. He was eating in a crowded coffee shop and overheard a voice behind him. He knew it was Charlie's, but the man didn't look like him, except in stature and age. Since he knew a big reward was on Charlie's head, he moved away and watched the man from a window counter. His mannerisms and walk were like the boss he'd despised. He remembered with distaste several run-ins he had suffered. Then he tailed Charlie in the swank neighborhood to a very classy high-rise apartment building guarded by a burly doorman. With keys in hand, the man entered. Certain it was Charlie, the former Quotech worker electronically contacted

Quotech back in the States. Agents in Brazil did an investigation and made the arrest on behalf of the FBI.

"We finally did it," said Zita. "I can't believe it, and thanks so much for keeping this thing alive."

"This is a great homecoming present for you, Zona. Justice for your biological father, finally."

Zona quickly replied, "I'm lucky having great dads."

The next day, a happy Scott headed for Brazil along with an FBI agent. Once they landed and rested a day, police took them to a local jail. Charlie sat, thin and wrinkled, in his dank unpainted cell of musty-smelling stagnant air. Walls around him were covered with graffiti and the names of the less fortunate who had passed before him, none probably as rich as he.

Charlie greeted Scott like a long-lost friend, shaking his hand and actually giving him a hug. Scott was surprised how jolly Charlie was when turned over to them in handcuffs. They rushed him to the airport cuffed to the agent and soon onto an airliner USA bound. Seated between the two officers, Charlie said, "Well, guess the jig is really up now. I've had nearly twenty years more than I thought I would have before you got me."

"It's been a long chase," said the FBI agent who went on to explain how he was found.

"Damned lab techs! I always hated those robots. He would have gotten a bigger reward from me than by turning me in. Stupid as always." Charlie had not lost his arrogance.

"The guy never liked you anyway, Charlie," said Scott.

"What has that got to do with money?"

"Nothing, but he was more interested in seeing you nailed. He does get a big reward."

"Just told you, he's still stupid." Charlie in his old age hadn't lost his attitude toward underlings who did the routine exacting dirty work in laboratories for the PhD principal investigators.

"I'm old and in poor health. My wife is long gone, died in Chile. So there isn't a lot you can do to hurt me. That extradition agreement doesn't allow the death penalty either."

"Guess you'll just live out your days in a little cell," said Scott, wondering why Charlie was so calm about his situation.

"I'll go soon with all the health problems I have. I've had a stressful life for sixty-eight, running labs, and hiding in six countries. I don't have to fight a thing."

"You do look damn old. Where did you get the plastic surgery?"

"Francone International thought as one of the world's most wanted, I wouldn't last long with my ugly mug. Even had hair implanted. This hair and new mug have done me well. Even my wife didn't know me when we met again in Indonesia. I set it up right under your noses. Under a false name, she jumped a cruise ship there. Gave us many years together."

"How did you live?" asked Scott, surprised at how openly Charlie talked.

"After the plastic surgery and time in The Vatican, they sent me as a Catholic missionary to Indonesia with a group of 'em. Can you feature this atheist, a missionary? But the Catholics who had controlled Francone before selling it to the Muslims owed me and got me out of Europe. Once out, I used my memorized Swiss bank account numbers, living the rich life in Brunei, Perth, Australia, and Chile. With my kind of money, getting proper paperwork was a breeze. They'd set me up with several great identities in France before I became a religious man in Rome." He chuckled. "I always had a fallback and plan B."

"Why didn't you stay put? We had no idea where you were." Scott noticed the agent on the other side of Charlie had fallen asleep.

"It's that feeling that maybe someone might be closing in on me and it's time to move on, I guess. To be honest, I never felt totally safe anywhere.

"Chile was great until my wife died there. Then, I hooked up with Kate. You remember her don't you since you couldn't find her? Great agent who had a good cover spying on the company; she was working for Francone too! They had her move in on Erick to get close to Zita and Alex—eventual targets. Kate and I never knew that murder was in the plans until that desert shooting. I was ordered to help her, but I never knew where they had sent her.

"After Kate was buried, I was nervous and moved to Argentina for three years. Great place! What steaks and wild women when you were as rich as I was. Then on to Brazil where I got old, sick, and stayed too damn long, I guess."

Scott thought he might as well ask Charlie the big question since he spoke so openly and wasn't concerned about his future. "Why did you kill Alex?"

"I never wanted to. They ordered it. It was him or me, they told me. That outfit didn't mess around, and I knew there was no double-crossing them and living."

"Why'd you do it at Quotech with all that tight security?"

"Well, I'd never done anything like that before and figured to make it look like a spy had gotten him to hand over secret notes. That's why I trashed his office after shooting him in the legs, arms, shoulders, and feet before killing him in the head. Made it look like torture to get secrets."

Scott gasped at the undetached description Charlie gave as if Alex was nothing to this world. Scott had seen hundreds of criminals who had lost their humanity, and the man in the seat beside him fit the bill.

"Weren't you afraid of being heard?"

"No, I used that silencer they provided me, and I did it at night when he was working late. The only hitch was that damn lab tech working overtime and coming out of the walk-in Revco Freezer seeing me leaving with the gun. I would have gotten him too except he ducked inside and locked himself in the freezer and I couldn't get to him. If he hadn't been there, and he wasn't supposed to be, it would have been a perfect crime."

"Didn't you feel bad about Alex?"

"Sure, a bit then, but not now. His wife was pregnant, but he was the main target of those opposed to human greenback work. Alex was the big symbol, Nobel Prize and all. So I had to flee immediately: they flew me to France under their zigzag escape plan, leaving my wife and everything behind without even a goodbye. Had no choice."

"How come you got into this spying?"

"Naïve, they paid off all my big debts, set up a trust fund for my wife, and gave me a Swiss bank account to which they added big bucks each year. All I had to do was pass on our research results. Wouldn't you?"

Scott ignored the question and asked, "Are there any records between you and the Francone and The Vatican?"

"You must be kidding? It was long ago, all verbal, and with people I never saw twice nor knew by name. The gun location and contingent escape plans were over my communicator, never in writing. Contacts happened but never within the security grid at Quotech. I wasn't there alone and never knew it. Those bank accounts were the big thing, but they are secret under Swiss law and were probably set up by Francone and church agents too."

"Any regrets?"

"Of course, I didn't think it would lead me to murder. It was research stealing until those oil rich Muslims got control of Francone. Then it suddenly turned political, religious, and nasty. Had I known it would go that way when I first started, I'd never gotten involved. But it was the money all the way. But from it I've had more money than I could spend all my adult life. How about you, Scott?"

"So it was for the money, and was it worth it?"

"What else is there for a guy like me but to live big? I have had nothing but the best for thirty years?"

"What about Kate?"

"She ended up like Alex after she stole from me when she didn't need to, and she took too many chances that could have fingered me. I buried her in the desert of Chile long ago where nobody will ever find her bones. Guess I always knew I had to get rid of her; she could turn me in. But it was a good two years with her after my wife's death."

"How did you know where to find her?"

"We'd agreed if things ever went bad to meet on a cathedral's steps at high noon in Santiago on odd years during a specific festival. We did, and it went from there after agents from Francone had killed her ex-husband, Hans, for double-crossing them.

"Kate had been on the run for years, fearing for her life after those Africans blotched the Alex and Zita shootings. You people never got her because I tipped her off and, later in Chile, helped her get a new face."

"How will you handle all this when we land?"

"Plead guilty to everything. Go to prison and die there from this pancreatic cancer in three to six months. That's what my doctors say."

"You'll have to face Erick and my wife, Zita."

"You know, Scott, all that stuff I helped do for those evil people abroad for all that money didn't stop what Alex had opened with his research leading to photopeople. Just look at all the new greens worldwide, and see how I missed the boat in bettering humans." He stopped abruptly and turned to the window, saying, "I don't want to talk anymore."

Charlie fell asleep between his two captors. When he awoke, he said, "I've decided my plan when we land. You can tell Zita and everyone else that I won't talk to anyone. You can just pass on what I've told you. I'll do a formal confession, but won't talk to those I've hurt. My life is over, and I've nothing to say to anyone beyond the authorities." Scott tried to talk the tired old man into changing his mind to give people closure. But to no avail as he fell back asleep.

The media made a big splash of Charlie's capture, relating it to the Nobel Prize murder. Charlie disappointed the media and avoided trial by confessing. He never talked to the press. He was given three life sentences. The link to Francone was never clearly established enough to arrest anyone in France for ordering Alex's death. It was only Charlie's words, which were not enough from a murderer to arrest anyone. And Charlie didn't have a single name of anyone involved. He did have bank account numbers, and the FBI was keeping that aspect of the case open.

Later that spring when Zona had finished her first year of college and was at home, her mother told her, "It's time to move on. At least we know what happened, and Charlie died in prison. He and that company didn't totally get away with it."

"I hate how anti-greenbacks have now made Charlie some hero," added Scott. He was concerned about a widening division between factions across the globe. Many had carried signs with his photograph, saying, "Genetic changes will put us all in hell."

Zona said, "It cranks me off because that little rat gave a month-long interview in prison to have his life as a fugitive told in some book, and he wouldn't even talk to us, Mom."

"He was just plain evil, Zona," said Scott.

"Zona, we have to let it go. And yes, he was slime. When the book gets published, maybe we'll learn more," said Zita. "Let's have a great summer long vacation traveling and forget all this stuff. We all can't hang on to this all the time."

"I'll try, Mom."

"So will I."

The three of them enjoyed that wonderful summer visiting national parks around the country. They returned to polluted California, and Zona went off to college for her sophomore year.

During the next three years, public unrest increased between the haves and have-nots. Greenbacks were having an easier life than the regulars in so many ways, causing a deep resentment about the lack of greenback work productivity. Their lower consumptive lifestyles caused a slowdown in the economy across the board. It led to a huge recession with no end in sight, altering the nation in hundreds of areas of former production, especially agriculture. The old political system was still in control and uncomfortable with the changes they faced as the upcoming generation was not as capitalistic as in the past. Making money declined as a first priority among the greenbacks. That sparked vast debates and even violent acts across the country.

Unrest in the face of change was worldwide, but on the good side, families were having fewer offspring, and most of those greenbacks. Slowly there was change coming in human populations.

It was a time of stress in the changing of humankind with clinics across the world helping engineer smaller families, and many greenbacks were themselves producing new greenback babies since the trait bred true in the second generation and no clinics were involved. This sent a fear in the politics controlled by non-greenbacks' governments who saw their power waning. A handwriting was on the wall before them as new humans were changing their lifestyles since they were not having to work for food nor raise as much. This produced a change in human thinking as never before.

The struggle continued for three more years until Zona was a graduating senior. About that time, there was a rabid political upwelling, unrest, and major effort to curtail greenbacks for the good of the country. It was a long political and media debate battle, but big business money still had the upper hand and strongly influenced the outcome and political action in the congress and the executive branch, keeping the old guard in place.

20 Disaster Time

That summer of 2092 after Zona graduated, she took a scholarship job in Alaska and worked to help save arctic wilderness from foreign mining by China.

Then home in LA one morning that same summer, Zita watched as America's president suddenly come on the media with a decree for greenback protection.

He said, "We are facing a crisis in this nation involving our young people who are increasingly in danger. In order to prevent more violence and protect these young greenback citizens, I am declaring a national emergency and establishing martial law immediately.

"For their own safety and well-being, all greenback citizens of high school and higher education ages are required to report within forty-eight hours to detainment centers as directed by the Department of Homeland Security. Their lives are in immediate danger. Reporting instruction and details are now being posted on the media. I have activated and ordered all fifty State National Guard Units to be immediately activated to protect, move, and guard greenbacks to assure their safety and well-being."

Horrified, Zita, Erick, Scott, Emily and the rest of greenback parents across the nation were stunned by the drastic action. Upon hearing the nasty detainment orders, and then working through the Moby Foundation, Zita protested the detention of her own daughter, her nephew, Ian, and all other greenbacks in America. She could not talk to her daughter since all communication devices were confiscated by Homeland Security.

A deeply worried Zita quickly told the news media, "The true measure of our democracy is how we treat our minorities. Their civil rights are of the utmost importance and being violated. These rights are as important as their safety. What kind of a nation are we when we detain our young greenback people?"

However, the hand-wringing president and his Nazi-like attorney general had already acted. They wanted to solidify votes from the discontented and vocal conservatives before the upcoming elections. The right-wing politicians wanted limits placed on the explosion of young greenbacks across the country whose numbers had risen like a tidal wave among younger parents. More greenbacks were becoming voters with each passing day while "regulars" were slowly passing away every day and their voting numbers were in a slow decline.

Greenbacks were the top choice of young parents who easily obtained the traits through Quotech and other gene and embryo manipulation clinics across the country and around the world. The reality of designed people vastly increasing their numbers was a future problem. Public officials had always been elected by regulars, not the flood of young greenbacks who were now surging into voting ages. Entrenched politicians feared the new thinking of these young voters who didn't support old ideas. Now action was nearing to change things to stop the trend.

"Scott, how do we fight this thing with Zona headed for some awful camp we can't know about?" asked Zita when Scott returned home. He had been on a fishing trip off Long Beach where he caught some fish in the bay that was slowly becoming less polluted with national restrictions now in place.

Once she explained the situation, he said, "Let's take it to the courts fast with other groups who advocate for greenbacks. It has to be a color violation of constitutional rights just like being black couldn't be used to enslave and control people in the past."

"That can take too long."

"Get our foundation's best lawyers, and get on it, yesterday."

"I'll also go directly to the media in a big way. The foundation can do that as part of their work right now."

The situation had arisen from earlier attacks on greenbacks by regulars. It had increased at alarming rates across the country during the past eighteen months, including some riots, lynching, beatings, and even night burnings of private green schools. Underlying all the violent acts were subtle daily taunting of young greenbacks, similar to those silently and passively endured by young blacks earlier in Southern schools.

Such civil unrest and attacks had been seized upon as a reason for greenback detention and protection by the government. Zita, Scott, Emily, and Erick saw it all as policy overreach from the weak administration. Many, including Scott, suspected radical conservatives were funding the dastardly attacks on greenbacks in covert ways across the nation to force government restrictive actions.

There were bitter and immediate outcries with hostile debates across America following the detention of millions of young citizens because they were different and were being attacked. But the president and his supporters insisted it was all an effort to protect them.

At public protests and rallies, greenback supporters shouted, "Go after the attackers and violators! Don't punish the victims!" It rose to a bitter firestorm pitting neighbors against each other and, in some cases, even splitting families.

Finally, after all the chaos, and the president declaring martial law with night curfews, outrage settled down as alarming details of the detention surfaced. All female and male greenbacks were placed in separate camps to avoid any reproduction. Camps were overcrowded, and state athletic stadiums were soon filled with the lonesome young with their meager backpacks of scanty belongings.

A huge march on Washington took place with the numbers of protesters greater than anything in the past. The president and his party did not change the detentions, but those detained were finally allowed to contact their homes one time.

A rumor came out that the government soon intended to require all young greenback males to undergo vasectomies in order to be immediately released and sent home. This prompted a national outrage, but no denial came from the White House.

Then the unbelievable happened. Zita sadly remembered rushing into their library where Scott was reading and yelling, "Scott! It's awful! Zona is on that cruise ship of young female greenbacks. It just sank in Alaska's inland passageway in route to female detention camps in Hawaii." Zita sobbed.

"Good grief! My god in heaven, we have to get in touch with the authorities to help find her."

Totally stunned, Scott and Zita watched events unfold describing how four apparent fishing boats were passing the giant liner in the water-filled former glacial valley. The old cruise ship had been pressed into duty to transport detainees to a sunny warm climate so they could live naturally, safely, and easily in sunny liberal Hawaii for less government funding. In the deep fjord, two boats zipped to the hull of the liner, one foreword and one aft, and attached themselves to the hulls with magnets. Other boats picked up the two crews. They raced away for the Alaskan forested shore and then by remote control set off huge explosives in the attached boats, quickly sending the ship into 800 feet of frigid water in two minutes.

Zita cried when a report came. "There were few survivors because the blasts ripped large parts of the ship open to the fjord's icy waters. There had been little time to even launch lifeboats. Apparently, there are few survivors."

A shocked pair sat in disbelief and shaken to their core wondering if Zona was gone. Early rescue efforts found only a handful of survivors, sending Alex and Zita into anger, more tears, and disbelief.

Losing 4,500 young people in the icy waters south of Skagway left the nation dumbstruck. It was akin to 9/11, only with young greenback females dying. A major investigation was immediately launched, as the nation held its breath in fear of other attacks. The media immediately attacked the president since he had set in motion the confinement of greenbacks that led to their transport out of Alaska.

Alex and Zita had quickly hired a helicopter company to help search the shores of the heavily forested islands adjacent to the sinking area. For a week, they searched the area by air before finally giving up. The government had halted rescue efforts after finding only a dozen female greenbacks alive.

The crime was traced to eight Arabic men from a cabin in Haines, Alaska. The trail had been a difficult one that eventually ended when the FBI followed money from a Washington DC conservative think tank called "Americans for Natural Reproduction" to the bombers and captured them all during a midnight gun battle.

The United States Supreme Court immediately took up the case of greenback detentions the Moby Foundation and other groups had brought forward in conjunction with human rights organizations. The high court quickly took the case and ruled the detentions were unconstitutional. All greenbacks were released the following day under directions and protection of the National Guard and US Marshals that included Ian who was in Africa far from any big city.

There was no immediate effort to retrieve the bodies from the sunken wreckage deep in the cold-water fjord. And a service was planned for Zona for the next month by her stunned family.

Bills of impeachment were introduced in the house in Washington. The president fired his attorney general, blaming him for bad advice about greenbacks, but it wasn't enough. The debate was long and furious in the legislatures over greenback rights. The sides, older established conservatives against younger liberals, were as unbending as in the great debates over slavery before the Civil War in the 1860s. The hearings dominated the nation's media, allowing the average citizen to ponder the issue more deeply than ever before. It was a heated debate with tempers flaring in the nation's capital.

Then amazingly after two weeks, word came that a fishing boat had found Zona alive on a rugged forested island adjacent to the sinking area. She was soon joined by an elated Alex and Zita at Sitka, Alaska. In a Moby Foundation jet, they soon headed back home with their grateful daughter. Along the way, Zona told details of her ordeal.

"Remember all those swimming lessons you forced me to take for that high school swim team, Dad? Well, they really saved my life in that cold water just like that icy practice pool. And along with my survival classes for my Alaska work, they really helped me too. I was alone and up topside in that cold wind looking for whales when the blasts went off shaking the ship. Before I could even find a locker of life jackets, water was coming on the deck, and I knew this was really bad. Good thing I was on the side of the ship closest to a shore, but still a long, long distance. And I kept on my wool shirt and light jacket when I hit that cold water along with some others.

"It was a long swim, but I made it to the trees on the shore. They were tangled and clear down to the water's edge, and I was icy cold. Took off and rung out my clothes and tried to move in that tangled forest. When I looked back, there was no longer a ship, and no one else was in the water swimming. Really chilled, I kept moving but wasn't drying in that damp woods. In a small opening, I found an elk kill with scattered bones, a skull, and the untouched old hide. It still had the hair on it. So I wrapped the dirty stiff thing around me and sat on a log for a long time getting half warm as my body heat made the hide sag to cover me a lot. Hung my clothes one at a time out to dry on branches. That dead elk may have saved my life despite all that nasty hair coming off on me. It was icky.

"There were all kinds of big tracks of bear and wolves in the few snow drifts where I was. That scared the dickens out of me as I planned on what to do next. I needed shelter and sunlight plus a place where someone could see me for rescue. That seemed impossible in those dense trees with sunlight coming down from straight up, and of course, I loaded up on the rays keeping my back to it and keepin' my hide around in front or on the ground. It was scary."

Alex and Zita smiled at each other knowing their detail-oriented daughter was headed for a blow by blow of being lost in a wilderness trying to save herself. They sat back and listened.

"I was wary of wild animals, half dry, and now could hear aircraft and helicopters overhead. With the hide still on me, I fought to reach a spot to signal my position, but the shoreline was so dense there was no opening, and I didn't want to go back into that icy water. Finally, I just gave up and tried to find shelter of some kind. Luckily, there was a rocky mound in the trees with a tight opening where I could squeeze inside. I covered the top with branches and broke off tree-needled boughs for the floor. It soon got darker, and I shivered that night away in my little safe space. The next morning, I could hear aircraft again, but there was something outside. I was terrified when hearing it sniffing. Then a bear face suddenly appeared in front of me. It was huge, but could only reach a foot or so between the rocks as it showed its teeth and grunted at me. Then it thrust its paw inside trying to reach me, but was just a foot short. That was the scariest moment of my life. Finally, it gave up and went away. Took me a long time to get over that and go any distance from my tiny cave. But I did prowl along the tangled shore for an opening for the rescue planes to spot me. Nothing worked, and soon the planes went away. I was afraid of getting too far from my den in case of a bear or mountain lion, and I took some fist-sized sharp rocks into my den to whack at any intruders. The scary part was having to lie on my belly to get a sunlight charge in the midday openings from straight up. Yet helpless I did, and I had plenty of water from snow to keep me going. So there I was for day after day for a week with animals roaming by and no hope of rescue from the sky. Once I saw a cruise ship pass way out in the fjord, but they could never see me because of the trees.

"Then I found me a tough branch with a big knot on it like an Indian war club to carry as my weapon. Probably useless, but gave me confidence to move away from my den. I then went to the far side of the island only to find the same shoreline and the ocean of the same salt water. I would never be spotted from there since ships would be way out. I went back to my camp afraid that winter would come and kill me with its cold. I decided to take my hide and club and travel up the shoreline, hoping to find something, and thinking I could spend my nights up a tree beyond bear reach. So off I went north fighting my way along the shore a few meters inland. That went well, except spending the night up a tree was the pits being wrapped in my old hide. And once a big raven followed me half a day. I kept thinking of him as a winged descendant of the dinosaurs that he really was. I talked to him until he left me when I climbed my night tree. But mind you, I always found places to recharge between the trees, pausing my travel at midday.

"A week of that really didn't help much and I felt doomed, but I was not going to give up scanning the shore and hoping for something as I fought all that underbrush. I told myself I didn't need food, only people and rescue. But I feared being food for some wild animal as my club, skin, and I wandered along. How I hated my long nights up in pine tree branches.

"I was never going to give up, but was getting discouraged and thought I was kidding myself thinking of finding anything like people or a safe place. Then one struggling day, I saw a huge rock big as a room rising up out of the trees and into the water a bit along the shore. I fought my way to it and climbed atop its rounded surface, giving me my first view of the open channel of the fjord.

"I crafted a forked stick with sharp rocks to hold my elk skin making a flag as I waited for something besides the seals, whales, eagles, and waves to pass by. Oh, how I feared a bear getting me on that big rock. But it gave me hope, exposure to better charging sunlight, and a great view of my isolation. I did find a nearby tree as my awful night nesting place.

"Two days later, I was astounded when a fishing boat came by and saw me waving my skin flag. The captain pulled in close and knew I must be from the sinking, and his sailors took me aboard, treating me wonderfully in their warm cabin. I'll never forget those wonderful guys, and soon they got me on a bigger passing ship back to Sitka. I have all their names to send them something. What a miracle, and I'm never giving up this smelly elk skin in this big bag at my feet. It saved me."

Scott and Zita both knew her sharp wits and wilderness job training in Alaska had made a big difference or she would not be with them as they winged on home in the Moby jet.

21 Social Flux

Z ona had saved herself but had no way of helping anyone else in the ship disaster. She was one of the few survivors from the sinking and was hounded by the press to tell her story, which she did in stunning detail. Her story dominated the worldwide media for several days showing how she survived thanks to her intelligence and her greenback. In her many interviews, she always pined sadly over the lost crew and all the other thousands of young greenbacks women. She gripped the hearts of Americans when fighting to hold back her tears over the loss of so many young American greenback females.

Ian had luckily been in deep Africa helping isolated native people improve their lives through small solar technology. He had avoided the detention situation over those long weeks that led up to such a ship's disaster.

Because of her experience, poise, and strong presentations on nationwide media, Zita was asked to testify at the senate impeachment hearings for the sitting president. She agreed as long as Zona could join her and give testimony too. The next morning, world major media had them on screens across America and the world.

Seated with Zona at her side before the Senate Judicial Committee and representing the Moby Foundation, Zita gave her opening testimony. "I've spent my life on this issue, lost my husband, Alex Moby, a Nobel Prize Laureate over it to a murderer working for an international company and other groups opposed to greenbacks. I have had my own greenback daughter, Zona, detained in a camp and then put on that ship. As you know, she is one of the few lucky survivors of that horrid sinking in Alaska.

"I stress to you that being the mother of this greenback is little different than parenting any child. It takes love and patience. They have all the feelings, needs, and brains the rest of us do. It's imperative we treat greenbacks as equals as we have historically done very reluctantly for Native Americans, blacks, and others in our sad history. Consider, Senators, one day greenbacks will be the majority and we non-photosynthesizers will be the minority. How will we all want to be treated as the sudden minority?"

The questioning was long and harsh from some of the conservatives. They claimed that greenbacks were a threat because they did not follow the traditions of true hardworking Americans. Some senators likened them to the hippies of the historic 1960s. However, Zita was helped by friendly questioning from greenback-supporting senators as well. But she held her own during three grueling hours. Finally, Zona was called to testify before the divided committee.

In her opening statement, Zona said, "Senators, I want you to know how it feels to be a greenback in this society and how unfair it is to be treated as a second-class citizen. But first, I'd like to say that all of us fear change, especially the prejudiced. They are caught in a huge revolution, and a positive revolution for the improvement of human kind and our planet. Many special interests, the prejudiced, and all of us oppose a sudden change. We humans don't like going from what is to what can be. This can however be a peaceful greenback revolution if we only open our minds to the future. There have always been changes, and they will continue if we are to save our damaged earth. It behooves us to make the most of the potential of our differing kinds of people. I am proud to be one of the first two American greenbacks."

Suddenly she stood up, removed her jacket, pulled her bright blond hair to the front, and turned her brilliant greenback to the committee. "This is the future of our nation and the human race. It saved my life after the sinking. There was no food on the shore, and I survived for two weeks from sunlight alone rather than having starved to death." Then she said, after a pause, "This is not about me. I want you to know this; the majority of the people you represent want children. Most now want this greenback I've shown you. It works in so many ways, and this greenback will save the planet and our human race.

"And by the way, my greenback is the early model, not nearly as good as the new one people get today with CRISPR CAS 9 and PRINE DNA editing in embryos. I still have to drink milk since my bones are not nitrogen based like the new ones are now, something my mother and uncle helped develop. They won Nobel Awards for that advancement, which makes me so proud. Who besides this greenback female can stand before you who has had both parents Nobel Prize winners? This greenback trend will make a better changed world." A hush hung over the hearing chamber.

"We greens are the future!"

Then, Zona went on to enumerate specifically how some young regulars and conservatives marginalized greenbacks. It was a type of bullying that most everyone understood, and the kind of thing that takes place out of sight of teachers, professors, and parents. Then she was scoffed at by the hardliners on the committee who doubted any real good would come from her unproductive kind. All they could see was damage to jobs, the economy, and the nation's morals. God hadn't intended for human genes to be tinkered with in radical ways to produce any more the likes of her. But senators who supported greenbacks came to her rescue and balanced the hearing. Zona clearly showed that she had a quick mind and could defend her views with anyone, including senators.

Once on the plane for home, Zona unloaded to her mother. "I have mixed feelings about congressional hearings. We have been heard and had strong support, but did we change the minds of many senators?"

"I think we gave them, and the people who watched, something to think about. The population is the only force that can influence this revolution with their votes. We did some good, although it may not show up for some time. People need to think deeply on this big change in their lives. It is slow and takes time."

"Mom, I sure hope you're right that people will do something about this injustice."

"Just remember that people are better than we often give them credit for, including politicians."

"Well after that, I'm going to put my head back and sleep on all this and hope for the best."

"Zona, most of us hope for the best, expect the worst, and often get the impossible. So hang in there in this fight."

The worldwide press instantly made Zona and Zita heroines again since both had been harmed in the greenback cause along with those young Alaskan ship females. Many American citizens still rallied to underdogs in any tug-of-war. Many were more sympathetic with greenbacks since the Alaskan tragedy and studied the issue more closely. However, the country was still divided. Zona soon headed to MIT for her doctorate studies.

Within months, a congressional house of representatives finally impeached the sitting president. He resigned rather than face a senate vote. When the vice president took over, he quickly switched his views, used executive orders that opened key pro-greenback rights in America, and supported them across the globe. This incensed the conservatives, who were only a few votes away from control in the house and senate in Washington DC. Many elected officials supporting greenbacks heard death threats. Programs to help greenbacks were filibustered in the senate, bringing gridlock to reforms. Overall the conservatives were slowly losing ground and power in the fight for open minds, but they were determined not to give an inch in defending their way of life. Some wanted all greenbacks not to marry, and a few wanted a chip placed in all greenbacks to identify them electronically when they wore full clothing. This idea was met with public outrage as when Americans were reminded how Jews had been worn yellow stars and were tattooed for identification during the World War 2 Holocaust in Germany and across Europe.

In the middle of all the turmoil, the new president was ineffective, and little was accomplished except bickering and infighting until the next elections four years later.

Then once home from finishing her graduate school, Zona said, "Mom, I don't see how we stood this past four years with wishy-washy presidents and do-nothing congresses. They passed those restrictive laws limiting us greenbacks, then turned right around and repealed them. Then restricted the clinics and allowed only natural conception to slow down the revolution. Thank heavens, the courts reversed that one too. I'm so glad to be graduated with time now to get fully involved in this fight."

"Well, Doctor Zona, the trend's in the right direction with greenbacks increasing rapidly worldwide. I think more people are seeing the value in this change instead of blindly reacting. The power base is shifting according to thinkers in the Moby Foundation. Be patient."

"Be patient, my left hind leg! Now that I'm a PhD and on your board of directors, I want to do more."

"So do I. But we are now again slowly outproducing them with thousands of Quotech and other clinics back in full operation. I was worried when they'd closed them, since greenbacks are less motivated worldwide to have big families."

"Do I need to have kids to help this revolution?"

"No! I'm ready to turn all this over to you young people. Being a senior citizen isn't really so bad. Just wish Scott were here to enjoy it with me. Bless his soul. I'd like to be taking care of him now and not fighting these issues."

"Ian and I are ready for the way forward. And I sure miss Dad too."

"He was wonderful and steady all the way."

Zona said, "I remember studying how reform's slow. I want it now for the good of everything on earth. Wow, there sure is a lot to be done in the Muslim and Catholic worlds. When will they ever change their dogmas?"

"Not 'til God provides a revelation!"

"They'll ruin the planet before then, Mom!"

"I fear so. But those religious revelations have a way of coming when things get terribly bad. Remember Mormon history and polygamy?"

"Sure do. And that church now supports greenbacks instead of huge regular families."

For the next several years, mother and daughter kept busy with foundation work and witnessed a rolling silent revolution. With a majority of newborn American being greenbacks, times slowly changed. When the greenback population was young and growing, critics had not been too vicious. They were unique kids. But once they became adults, could vote, and had far different voting values, the old guard came to fear them, their ideas, and their different behavior.

Zita, Erick, and Emily slowly turned the Moby Foundation's leadership over to Zona and Ian. With new energy and a zest for ideas and directions, they ran with it concentrating on changing internal domestic trends and helping improve environments worldwide.

At a meeting, Ian told the Moby board, "Here in America, except for expanding dairy farming, our crop raising and rural incomes are heading in reverse. It is less of a problem than in the third world since fewer that .5 percent of Americans now farm in the rural USA.

"Roaring full steam ahead are big plants making varied drinking liquids, vitamins, and clothing products for the world. Cotton farming is doing wonderfully well, as is hemp growing.

"We maturing greenbacks also seem to have reduced concerns about money and retirement. Fewer are signing up for pension plans for their old age. Most spend their funds on the arts, for travel, and to enjoy life while they live it. They have reduced fears about diseases of old age that regulars face, most of which have resulted from smoking, eating plant and animal meats, and exposing themselves to myriads of microorganisms instead of our sunlight.

"Moreover, laws now allowing euthanasia are in place in the majority of nations, an alternative to nursing homes and the confined suffering of the elderly. In the past, most had been kept alive beyond reason and their desire to live. Under new laws, they can today choose to live on or not, easily signing papers to legally leave life anytime they wish. As a result, the populations of the very elderly are now in steep decline, further reducing food demands and unneeded medical care."

Erick looked at Zita and whispered, "We sure didn't have these choices in our heyday."

"Are you trying to tell me something I should do?"

"Hell no! You're healthy as a spring chicken in the Black Hills." They both chuckled to themselves and turned their attention back to Ian reporting to the foundation's board.

"Since pension funds have declined due to nonworking greenbacks, they are declining for regulars too. There is not enough new public funding to be viable in many places. Many world governments now try to step in to make the funds work financially for regulars. Laws have been passed in America here to outlaw banks from passing inherited wealth on to the next generation too, making 90 percent of earned wealth returned to governments when people pass. That has kept many state governments going. Is this enough for you to give consideration to before the next meeting? And can we do much about what we see before us in some of these tough situations?"

Erick spoke up saying, "Our foundation work is worldwide since we helped to start these changes on earth and all the ramifications. I think we should set up worldwide think tank commissions in major areas with the best minds and experts to show us a way forward to work through these problems to help save humans and the earth. It's too much for this board or you and Zona to handle."

Emily, a stickler for details, put in, "I want these think tank experts highly paid and isolated to work out some of the best solutions. It's our obligation to do this right and with the best minds possible on some island somewhere in isolation to have adequate time for reaching creative answers to these problem areas Ian has pinpointed. We need to be ready for the long-term future on this overheating earth. It was 116 degrees in Denver yesterday, and it's winter."

"I think we all can agree this is the best way forward, but we must also continue our present worldwide work saving the earth via greenback support and engineering through complicated world governments," added Zita.

The future course was set as great minds were soon probing how to face the upcoming world changes. None of the solutions would be easy, but Moby leaders wanted the best ideas to be ready as time passed on slowly. Improving an earth with the greenback revolution was making good progress in many places.

The Stark family watched as changes continued, causing resentment in the older American generation of regulars who dubbed the newcomer tide of greenbacks "lazy," "unproductive," "immoral," and "without ambitions." New ways of thinking were coming from the green young, not from the people who had created and nursed the old system to benefit themselves. Change was often opposed and could be sometimes peaceful and sometimes violent. Greenbacks were easy to blame for all the ills befalling non-greenbacks worldwide.

It was akin to the European settlers taking over the Great Plains of Native Americans and wiping out the bison and bringing a new way of life without any bison meat and products. The winds of change sounded good at times, but it was difficult to change the old ways of any humans. However, a few governments in northern Europe required all births to be greenback humans to retain the standard of living and repair the ravaged world environments as their populations declined. This trend was working in only some places.

Numerous attempts by state legislative bodies to halt the inserting of new DNA codes in gene sequences had failed in America over the long haul. High courts and the US Congress had finally upheld the right to make these changes despite many assaults by those strongly opposed. Early on, it had been outlawed in the Middle East for reproductive purposes. Yet the fight was never ending even when greenbacks neared majority around the globe.

In all this change, California held Zona since her mother and family were there. It was her home base as she and Ian worked and traveled around the world to help foundation causes with experts.

Zona, a mirror image of her mother, beautifully tall and lanky with flowing hair and a mind like a steel trap. She had followed a different path than her mother, not so much because she was a greenback but because she liked outdoor nature more than laboratory work. Yet she was a scientist in her own right having environmental science for her PhD. She also supported wildlife cooperative projects around the world. Now she lived in Zita's home and spent a lot of time close to her aging mother. They spent hours pondering the changes and life in a befriended daughter-mother relationship.

"Look at how different your world is than mine was at your age," said Zita, watching her daughter soaking up the sun's rays on a patio as she poured over scientific journals. She, like all greenbacks, kept her back to the sun hours each day. A thin blouse adhered to the edges of her forest green skin around her back to expose it to the photons that stimulated her glucose production in millions of tiny back plastids.

"Well, sitting in the sun all the time is a natural habit, but we're getting more rays and clearer days now that air pollution is waning a bit. Remember when I was a kid and had to stay in my bedroom under the grow lights and couldn't get enough clear rays outside."

"Sure do."

"It got better with banks of lights, so I now get my rays at night sleeping."

"Look how we are changing homes now. Even offices and factories with sliding doors face the sun. Everything's open to the sun in architecture. Think of the new apartments with one side balconies to allow recharging."

"I like what they have done with cars, buses, trains, and ships too. In new housing, they've reduced the size of kitchens and eating areas."

"Most everything's being geared to new greenbacks. Many regulars resent anything new being designed that way."

"Yes, but what other way is there to go?"

"Solar energy has really taken over since we beam it down from those collectors on space stations. Advanced batteries and superconductors made that storage of energy a reality. That network of collectors up there is huge, helping in reducing greenhouse gases. You and Erick sure had a big role in helping that work. But glad we can't see them cluttering up outer space. And someday they won't be needed as the pollution keeps decreasing worldwide."

"Big changes since Alex set some things in motion. I think your generation spends its time reading, talking, and watching media. Much more than when I was your age."

"Of course, your people spent hours sitting around and eating all kinds of fancy foods. We just drink a little and spend time in the sun talking, thinking, or doing other things in art and music and a ton of mental activities."

"Overall it's less time with little kitchen cleaning up to do." Zita laughed, thinking it was time for her lunch.

"One thing for sure, Mom, I think the greatest thing you and Alex ever did was to make me a greenback. I love what I am, and thank you a million times. I only regret the trauma it's put you both through. But things are better now than when I was a teenager."

"Nothing was worse than those teenaged years. Thank heavens you're past when kids were trying to find themselves by abusing others verbally."

"Speaking of the awful, I have never understood all that nasty stuff, or what happened with Scott and Erick."

Neither Zona or her mother understood fully how Scott was lost three years before. That event still haunted them both. Sport fishing had been a wonderful hobby he'd loved. Zita usually went along as a companion on his thirty-five-foot boat. They often cruised far off Los Angeles's coast. Scott would fish while she operated the boat or read or just daydreamed watching her fine man enjoy his hobby. They had done so for years, getting away into the cool Pacific Ocean breeze. Plastic masses were now being removed by navy ships that earlier had spent much of their time in ports awaiting wars or disasters. They now spent more time at sea sweeping up ocean trash pulling collecting arrays behind them.

Scott's demise came when he was with his old LAPD buddies on a fishing trip. Apparently, they were five miles out enjoying a fine run of fish when a dense fog unexpectedly closed in on them. With his navigation equipment, Scott guided the big boat for shore when a navy ship suddenly rammed them in the dense fog, sending them straight to the bottom. The Coast Guard recovered parts of the boat, but the bodies were never located. Why Scott's boat didn't detect the oncoming ship with its sensors was a mystery. His loss was nearly a deathblow to Zita. Thankfully, Zona was on hand to help her mother through her loss of her second husband.

Then on top of that came the next awful blow the very next year; Erick had suddenly died of a massive stroke. This huge loss to the family seemed to have sapped their spirits as they grieved for months. Finally, the wounded family moved ahead as Erick and Scott would have wanted. Zita feared she would never get totally over the loss of her dear twin brother and Scott.

But Emily and Zita still had Zona and Ian to lean on emotionally. The bright offspring rose to the occasion and helped their mothers move ahead by spending time with them. Now the kids were totally overseeing the foundation's commissions, working forward to find answers for a changing future. From behind they were coached by their wise mothers who still had sound insights they needed.

In the next full decade up to 2094, Ian stepped up the huge Middle East and Africa projects to help non-greenback people in countries with few resources, high death rates, and awful living conditions in high temperatures. He spearheaded development, manufacture, and distribution of small devices that combined small solar energy panels to give some night lighting and use stored battery power to sterilize drinking and cooking water on a family scale. The impact was amazing—reduced air pollution, diminished water-borne diseases, and allowed lighting for night study by students. It eliminated the wood and animal manure used in hut cooking, allowing the manure to fertilize crops and improve soils. It also kept women from having to walk miles to gather wood to burn in cooking.

Also giving them a better life was a six-month free birth control pill for both men and women. This reduced family size along with them not needing a traditional big family of the ancient past when the poor hoped someone in a host of newborn kids would survive long enough to help care for them in old age.

These combined devices resulted in more food and water to go around in smaller families now requiring less. There was a slow change in how these forgotten people lived and accepted technological help. With smaller families, they needed fewer cattle, farmed less land, used less food, and overall the environment changed for the better. Forests regeneration and more vegetation was resulting from fewer people. People were learning to accept a differing life.

Of course, the big plan would eventually lead to people worldwide accepting greenback offspring who might forever in the future save them and their environment.

For years, Ian helped lead worldwide improvement work fully knowing that someday people in such poor and isolated places would obtain their energy via their own greenbacks.

22 Conflicted Future

By her eighties in 2096, Zita had developed a deeply sensitive viewpoint and came to regret the loss of experimental animals. Many had been sacrificed in the development and changes done to chimps and apes to forge photopeople improvements. Many primates had been sacrificed around the world in her own Nobel efforts. She turned the enormous Moby Foundation in the direction of funding primate restoration programs in Africa. With this Moby money help, wild great apes were making a slow comeback, which greatly pleased her.

This funding along with greenback thinking put less pressure on primate-forested habitats, reducing jungle table meat. Primates were also being accepted as near equals by greenbacks since more people knew about the gene passages between them and ancient humans millions of years ago. In forested home countries in Africa, primates were now being treated as sacred animals.

As she enjoyed being eighty, Zita still secretly pined over the loss of the two men in her life and never saw herself as the great scientist she clearly was. But as she aged, Zona and Ian became stronger, running the futuristic approaches in the sciences. Zita was still an official emeritus president of the Moby Foundation, but it was more of a figurehead role than one of directing the research efforts in supporting numerous causes. A new generation was taking over the greenback revolution.

Zona and Ian organized a new series of Moby Foundation greenback lectures in major cities around the country. In them, Zita gave thrilling accounts and insights about how history and research had unfolded. It was done in tandem with Zona who followed her lecturing about being an early greenback pioneer and a rare survivor in Alaska's wilderness.

Such lectures were highly popular, the crowds were huge, and it didn't put too much pressure on Zita. Throngs of people, both regulars and greenbacks, attended the events coast to coast, wanting to see the lady scientist who had been such a key player in leading the greenback revolution. Zita especially enjoyed meeting those who attended wildlife fundraising receptions following the lectures. As mother and daughter, they gave these tandem lectures each spring and fall across the country as a Moby team.

There were often protesters at these events, either regulars who didn't appreciate how people like Zita had altered human genetics, or people with religious objections. These sign-carrying groups were on the outside of the field houses or stadiums but seldom came in contact with Zona or Zita who understood their feelings but rejected their ideas. Both women had helping guards as they went into the fourth year of the lecture tours in the mid-2090s.

Following one lecture at the University of Iowa, the wine, cheese, and drink reception was filled with people eager to see a famous Nobel lady. They were mostly young greenbacks, their parents, or grandparents who had crowded the field house on the campus for the lecture program. The reception line was moving along slowly. Zona always stood to Zita's left, greeting the people first to talk, ask them to hurry along, and take some of the pressure off her mother. If Zita was first, the line always was much slower with people talking to her forever and giving big hugs.

Zona greeted an aged man with a dark sun-browned face who mumbled at her, shook her hand weakly, and moved on to her mother. His left arm was in a blue cast. The man seemed to stumble forward toward Zita. Then to her horror, Zona saw the man had pulled a long dark blade from the wrist end of the cast and was lunging at her mother.

"You dirty bitch!" he yelled at the top of his lungs. "You did it to all of us!"

His thrusts went lightning fast twice into the unsuspecting Zita's chest. The man's weight knocked her onto the floor, and he reeled back for another attack. But Zona and others pounced on the man. Quickly he was subdued and disarmed although he kept shouting wildly, "I got her! I got her!"

Zita was down with blood coming from her chest and mouth. Zona shouted, "Call for help! A doctor! Please!"

Before Zona could detect a pulse, a nearby duty medical team was helping. Zita was still and didn't utter a sound as emergency procedures were done. Soon Zita was hauled away on a stretcher with Zona at her side and medical people surrounding her were inserting life-saving tubes and injections. Emergency people whisked her to the awaiting vehicle. Lights flashed and split the humid Iowa night. As the medical people did chest compressions and mouth-to-mouth, air faintly exited out of a seemingly lifeless chest.

Soon Zona sat in disbelief in the emergency room in her flood of tears wondering how this could ever have happened with all the security in place. She assumed the assassin had been taken away by security. But why would anyone want to kill an elderly legend lady in her eighties?

Once inside the emergency room at the university hospital, doctors did everything they knew including heart stimulations. Zona paced the hallway outside hoping for a miracle from medicine and technology.

Zona sat down and put her head in her hands and sobbed. How could this have happened? Her only parent she had left was terribly wounded. She sobbed openly until a surgeon emerged hours later and assured her Zita had a good chance of recovering, but she would be in the ICU for a long spell. After she saw her mother in the recovery room, attached to a dozen tubes leading to units with flashing readouts, bodyguards whisked Zona away to her hotel. She then thought, *Little good these security people ever do when someone really wants to kill in an unexpected manner.*

By the next morning, Zona had pulled herself together enough to ask to watch the police interview of the assassin in the county jail. There she sat on the opposite side of a glass only feet away from her mother's assailant. Detective Williams conducted the interrogation across the table from an apparently harmless-appearing elderly man in his seventies.

"I'm Detective Williams, and I'm here to interview you concerning the crime you will be charged with. I understand that you have been advised of your rights, and you know that you don't have to speak a word to me, Mr. Lambert, unless you wish to."

"I have nothin' to hide, I'm Clyde," replied the ordinary-looking gray-haired man in a rumpled brown suit. "And I don't want no damned lawyer neither."

"I understand, and you do understand that this interview is being recorded and media-taped?"

"Yeah, whatever. I just don't give a damn."

"Tell me about yourself, where you're from, and what you do."

"I'm just an old farmer from Marango, Iowa, west of here. Nothin' special 'bout me. Farmed all my life—corn, soybeans, and fed cattle on farms that has been in my family for over a hundred years. Wife died a year ago, and I live alone. Kids and grandkids all gone South. Gettin' too damned old to farm and nobody else to do it anymore. Damned shame!"

"How come you came to this lecture?"

"Saw a flyer on it from my local Farm Bureau knocking her as a farming enemy. And by grab, everyone knows that Moby woman did all that stuff in green genetics. Seen her on TV loads of times. It only cost fifty bucks to see her at that wildlife reception, and that got me a thinkin'.

"At first, I just wanted to give 'er a piece of my mind. But the more I thought 'bout it, the more it stirred me up, and I got madder 'en hell."

"What stirred you?"

"All that crap she done puttin' chimp and plant stuff into we humans. Mind you, I have no problem with animal and plant genetics making crops and critters better. But, goddamnit, when she and her people started messin' with humans, that's where I draw the line! I've been a good Catholic all my life and the Lord doesn't want that stuff. It's right there in the Bible asayin' human life is sacred and not to be tampered with."

"So you bought a ticket, made a donation for the reception, and came here?"

"Yeah, after I decided there was nothin' left to live for with my wife gone an' all. Found one of those plastic sugar beet cuttin' blades in my shop and knew it could get past the metal detectors in that old arm cast I had a few years back. Slipped right in too. Slick as a whistle."

"Why did you want to do it?"

"To get even for all the evil her kind's done us regulars with her crazy science experiments from Africa and all. Didn't know if I'd try to kill 'er. But after sittin' through all that stuff she said about doin' people so much good, and the wise-assed stuff that freak, greenie daughter of hers spouted out, I got really mad. Decided to either punch 'em or use my blade. Somebody had to do sometin' to show the world that what they've done is plumb wrong."

"Are you on a mission from God, then?"

"Hell no! But maybe a bit. Mostly for we farmers and our families, I guess."

Zona's attention was riveted on this ordinary man.

"How did Mrs. Moby actually harm you enough to want to kill her?"

"As I came down that long line gettin' closer and closer, I kept thinkin' how she ruined farmin' and all my family had ever done. By the time I got right up to her daughter, my blood was boilin'. It was my one chance to show the world how she'd done us growers wrong. I'd never ever hurt anyone before. Haven't even had a traffic ticket even in my old age. But there I was, and I bypassed the daughter and flew off the handle. It was like stickin' a pig. The daughter would have got it next if they hadn't all jumped on me."

"So you admit attacking Mrs. Moby."

"Sure do. Not proud of it now, but it should make people look at the harm all this greenback stuff's doin'. It was slow at first. Now it's out of control."

"The harm you think she was doing was your reason for hurting her?"

"You bet! Nowadays with such a bunch of people not eating as much meat, crops and cattle aren't worth raisin' for a profit. And the farms that my family's eight generations put their hearts and souls into aren't worth farmin' now. My boys didn't want to take over something that has no future as corn is going down and down. And mind you, my farms are all paid for, and my boys still couldn't make it work. My land is now worth nothin'. To top it off, my boys went and had my grandkids made greenbacks too. The whole kit and caboodle went and moved way south where there's more sun and less winter than Iowa. It's not just me, it's nearly all the farmers I know going broke unless they are dairy people. We can't compete when so many people don't eat meat anymore, and the darned science people make plant stuff taste like meat today. That great farmland has been our lives, we loved it, and we wanted to pass it on to our kids so they could have a good life like we'd had."

"You blame Mrs. Moby for all this?"

"Hell yes! Her and that dead husband of hers and all those people who worked doin' stuff to wreck us. My boys leaving with all those little greenback kids broke my wife's heart. She just died of a broken heart last winter, leaving me all alone sittin' on all my worthless ground. These damn genetic people wrecked our business, cost us our kids and grandkids, and ruined all we ever stood for, and they all left us behind. So they sure as hell deserve to be done in as I see it. Maybe this will make people come to their senses and realize that a few greenies are OK, but we don't want so many kids to be like that. The change is too fast an' messin' up all our lives."

"Do you think killing this lady would change things?"

"Maybe not. But people may stop and think about how good the past was. These greenies won't ever know what a good roastin' ear tastes like. Or will they ever have a big T-boned beefsteak? And, by jing, they won't ever have that love of ownin' land, workin' it, and watchin' crops grow. That life's sacred, and the new people will never know it. That's all part of why I did it."

"Anything else you want to say about all this?"

Zona watched in amazement as Clyde Lambert said, "Not a hell of a lot. This is only the tip of the iceberg. All kinds of people are havin' their lives changed and ruined. Don't think people besides farmers are going to take this changin' lyin' down forever."

Seven weeks later, they were back in California, and Zita was making a slow recovery. Now Zona, Ian, and Emily were again able to function rationally. Yet at times Zona found herself sitting in a daze thinking about the opposition to the Greenback Movement.

Having heard and seen the aged farmer Clyde Lambert relate his reasoning for stopping the movement caused her to think more deeply about the future and changes that were needed. Her mother's stabbing right before her eyes made it personal as never before. Now an uncertainty nagged her about how some regulars saw the future and reacted to it.

With a clear head, Zona soon suggested the chairperson of the Moby Foundation's Think Tank Futures Commission consider a huge new effort. He might take an isolated retreat with his entire think tank and spend weeks looking into the future and concentrating on what impacts the greenback revolution would have and how it might change people, both regulars and greenbacks, in the next two hundred years. She wanted funding to bring in any experts and futurists who could help with the task. One group could be pro and the other con with equal resources to forecast the future for the revolution. No cost might be spared in bringing in the world's best minds to work with each group of experts. The pro and con groups might have no contact with each other.

She suggested reports titled "Two Hundred Years Ahead." She hoped for the best thinking and solid speculations as to how different the earth would be heading into a future. They might consider a world dominated by the thinking and actions of greenbacks as the majority or minority. She wanted specific alternatives and detailed plans. In fact, she and Ian both wanted directions for the future.

She and Ian now personally had greater insight about the concerns of the minority caught in the rapidly declining regular populations and their futures.

Moby think tank groups soon headed for island retreats in the Pacific Ocean; Zona retreated to her office and cancelled all appointments to ponder the future. She wanted to record her own thoughts to compare with what the two sets of think tank experts might conclude and recommend.

She began the list with farming and wrote rapidly as her mind jumped randomly into other futuristic issues. Farming would probably have an inverse relationship with greenback expansion since food consumption would decrease worldwide. Exceptions would be dairy farming and crops producing flavors for drinks, medicines, and clothing fibers, and crops that produced vitamins would probably be grown as a priority. Greenbacks would keep horses to ride and sheep for wool, but hogs and range and feeder cattle would not be needed as much as in the past. No longer would there be concentrated feeding in the huge feedlots. People would not be as tied to the land as much for its food production, and marginal lands would be left for nature to slowly reclaim. Natural plant growth and trees would reclaim farmlands and wild animals could experience vast population increases, especially in the high latitudes, as greenback people migrated to the more constant sunny equator regions of the earth. CO_2 release would be reduced by all these changes. Rivers would have greater flows through the lands that were formerly farmed, and water tables would rise as irrigation steeply declined. Aquifers would gradually be restored. Water impoundments would be abandoned as crop raising declined, and fish were not eaten as much, allowing the waters to teem again with finned animals. Less farming would reduce the quantity of chemicals and fertilizers that polluted waterways, lakes, and oceans. Zona realized that the social implications were enormous just for the land alone.

Then she listed the big issues of population growth, air, travel, work, manufacturing, wildlife, homes, energy, war, religion, diseases, aging, sports, arts, ethics, morals, sex, drugs, retirements, government, leisure, and endangered species. On and on her list went, exasperating her with the worldwide implications.

Then totally frustrated, Zona decided to let her Moby Foundation's commission experts deal with the ramifications of this huge ongoing greenback human revolution. It was far too complicated for her one mind alone to tackle with some personal list. She decided not to be in the middle of all this worldwide change now, but could act in the future.

But she knew in her heart that photopeople would have to try to restore a balance with the earth in which people would be less dominant, less destructive, and more natural creatures. Could this be done with such different peoples and beliefs around the globe?

Zona surmised that she would probably live with a changing future for the next forty years unless those opposed to the coming of photopeople succeeded in taking her life at some point or a nuclear war happened.

She sat back in her office chair, feeling that empty loneliness in the pit of her stomach, knowing such dank feelings visit every scientist whose big work probed and changed the future. Even as an early photoperson with changed genes, she could not help how she had loved her mixed family as well as her natural but degraded planet. She was deeply worried about the future of life for them and all other organisms on an altered earth. How she wanted the Moby think tanks to give her and Ian the right directions for the sake of helping humans and all living things on earth. In her mind, it probably was hope for the best, expect the worst, and maybe get the impossible.

Finally, she went home concluding it was now time to let go of her work and take that long-planned vacation to New Zealand with her now-recovered mother, aunt, and brother to see one of the many intact national models for a changing world. It was now the mid-2090s, and the greenback revolution was expanding rapidly.

Later at New Zealand's stunningly beautiful Milford Sound on that delightful trip and over Zita's lamb chop and drink meal, Their recovered but aging leader told Zona, Ian, and Emily, "Sometimes I wonder if what this family has brought forth will really dominate and help change our world long term. But I still think greenbacks are our best hope for this damaged earth and future of us humans."

ABOUT THE AUTHOR

P aul W. Richard grew up loving Colorado mountain rivers and outdoor ranch life, leading him to an eventual professorship in biological science at the University of Northern Colorado. He had happily taught junior high, high school, and university students for thirty years. He also conducted scientific research in both the Arctic and Antarctica on polar expeditions. As a retired full professor emeritus of biological science, he lives and writes in Greeley, Colorado.

PAUL W. RICHARD